EARLY EARTH WITHOUT BILLIONS OF YEARS

A Young Earth Precambrian anthology (YEPA)

CONTENTS

ABSTRACT

This anthology brings together eight papers on Precambrian geology, presenting a perspective that does not rely on a deep-time framework. The papers provide a Young Earth Biblical view of geological history.

The first three articles are related to early Creation Week and the initial stages of Noah's Flood. These include the Precambrian geology of the North American continent, evidence for the rapid formation of economically important banded iron formations, and evidence for extensive transcontinental water flows.

The subsequent articles focus particularly on Noah's Flood. They discuss the fragmentation of the supercontinent as fountains of the deep burst forth, initiating the global Flood. The consequent erosion and early Flood stages are then described. An explanation of the so-called Neoproterozoic Oxygenation Event is provided, followed by evidence for the judgment on all mankind (except those saved in the Ark) in the remaining two articles.

Highlights are listed at the beginning of each article, and supplementary material is provided after the conclusion of the articles.

AUTHORS

Harry Dickens (pseudonym) is the principal author of the papers in this anthology and its organiser. He has more than 35 years' experience in petroleum and mineral exploration. He has worked in industry, government, and university institutions, and currently works as a geologist for a geological survey. He has delivered presentations and conducted fieldwork in Asia, Australia, North America, and the UK. He has qualifications in geology, geophysics, and gemmology. With a biblical worldview in mind, he has written on rapid petroleum formation, the effects of Noah's Flood (fountains, chemistry, erosion, and deposition), and Precambrian geology (including banded iron formations).

Aaron Hutchison (co-author of original papers III. C1,C2., D., and E2.)
Aaron is an associate professor of chemistry at Cedarville University. He has a B.A. in chemistry from Cedarville College (as it was then) and a Ph.D. from the University of Kentucky, where he specialized in environmental chemistry. He is interested in the geochemistry of the Flood, especially the transport and ultimate fate of toxic elements during the Flood year.

Andrew Snelling (co-author of original paper III. E1.)
Andrew has a Ph.D. in geology from the University of Sydney, Australia. Andrew worked for six years in the exploration and mining industries in Australia, variously as a field, mine, and research geologist for three different companies. He has worked for the Creation Science Foundation of Australia, the Institute for Creation Research

in the US, and currently with Answers in Genesis US. Dr. Snelling is highly respected in the Creationist community for his research, writing, and speaking on topics such as the Flood, fossils, the Grand Canyon, and the radioactive dating of rocks.

I. INTRODUCTION

Precambrian rocks do not need long ages to form. Many Precambrian geological processes do not require deep time. Such processes described in this anthology include basic chemical reactions, the origin of granite, banded iron formation, base metal sulfides, pegmatites, sedimentation, erosion, diamictites, petroleum, glauconite pellets, volcanic carbon dioxide, cap carbonates, and calcium carbonate precipitation.

You cannot observe deep time, and so it is a faith position based on extrapolation from isotopic ratios and current radiometric decay rates. The presence of four dominant radiometric "age" peaks globally—on each individual continent, in all major tectonic settings, and in modern sediments—implies the episodic nature of crustal processes. Secular researchers appear to have no clear answer as to why there are these four particular Precambrian "age" peak dates.

Interpretation of the four radiometric date clusters, and thus thermal-tectonic events, was used to infer correlation with the biblical record of the first three Days of Creation Week and of early Noah's Flood. Episodes of accelerated radioactive decay may have provided the heat source for thermal-tectonic events, which drove cataclysmic geological processes around the globe. Decay acceleration would also give the appearance of enormous age, since radiometric "clocks" would have ticked faster.

The anthology's topics include Precambrian geology of a continent, rapid formation of banded iron formation, transcontinental sediment transport, evidence for Flood fountains, Neoproterozoic oxygen, and the wiping out of land vertebrates in the judgment of Noah's Flood. These topics are all described within a Biblical event framework.

"Many of the pioneers in the development of the science of geology worked within a biblical framework. They saw in the geological record a testimony to the truth of Genesis regarding Creation and the Flood. But in the late eighteenth and early nineteenth centuries, several false assumptions began to control geological thought. Uniformitarian methodological naturalism divorced geology from the Bible and excluded God's mighty acts of creation and judgment from history. This rejection of Scripture's testimony to geologically significant events in history was conscious and intentional, and driven by anti-biblical worldviews (for example, deism and atheism)" (Mortenson 2007).

The papers in the anthology are important since they provide evidence consistent with a literal Bible framework for Precambrian geology. The currently prevailing paradigm of deep time is inconsistent with a plain reading of Scripture (6-day Creation and global Flood of Noah).

II. EARLY CREATION WEEK AND EARLY FLOOD

A. PRECAMBRIAN GEOLOGY OF NORTH AMERICA

Source: Dickens, H. 2018. North American Precambrian geology–A proposed young earth biblical model. In *Proceedings of the Eighth International Conference on Creationism*, ed. J.H. Whitmore, pp. 389–403. Pittsburgh, Pennsylvania: Creation Science Fellowship.

<table><tr><td>

HIGHLIGHTS

- Episodes of accelerated radioactive decay may have provided the heat source for thermal-tectonic events, which drove cataclysmic geological processes around the globe. Decay acceleration would also give the appearance of enormous age, since radiometric "clocks" would have ticked faster.

- However, the original radiometric "age" for the Earth (ca 4.6 Ga) is based on meteorites, and may actually be an artefact of isotopic ratios from the beginning of Creation.

In either case, subsequent heating events would have reset the "ages" to lower values.

</td></tr></table>

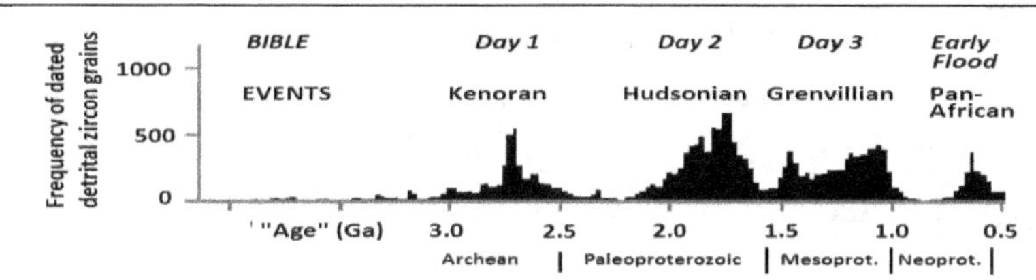

Age frequency distribution of detrital zircon U-Pb radiometric "ages" from North America, with corresponding significant thermal-tectonic Events and proposed correlation with the Biblical record. Secular researchers appear to have no clear answer as to why there are these four particular Precambrian "age" peak dates.

The presence of four dominant radiometric "age" peaks globally on each individual continent, in all major tectonic settings, and in modern sediments implies the episodic nature of crustal processes. These four global peaks:

- correspond to North America's Kenoran, Hudsonian, Grenvillian and Pan-African thermal-tectonic events,

- are respectively considered related to Archean, Paleoproterozoic, Mesoproterozoic and Neoproterozoic geology,

- in turn may be correlated with the biblical record of Creation Week's Day One, Day Two, Day Three and the early Noahic Flood.

I consider that God instigated heating events that provided the immense energy required for cataclysmic continent-scale geological processes during early Creation Week and in initiating Noah's Flood. I believe that Archean to Mesoproterozoic basement provinces formed as continental crust grew in the early Creation Week. This formed a supercontinent which, by Day Three, was thick enough to appear above the water. During the early Flood, massive tectonism, as well as immense continental erosion and enormous water flows, delivered detritus to form the Neoproterozoic sedimentary cover.

I consider that water played a significant role in all the thermal-tectonic events. Day One, Day Two, and the Noahic Flood involved a global ocean. Initial upward vertical movement of hydrothermal water is believed to have occurred during Day Two and in the early Noahic Flood. Supposed "glacials" in the Paleoproterozoic and Neoproterozoic are considered to have formed as mass flow deposits associated with downslope water movement during Day Two and early Noahic Flood times, respectively. In addition, the banded iron formations of the Archean, Paleoproterozoic, and Neoproterozoic are believed to have formed hydrothermally in association with volcanic activity.

Numerous examples are mentioned where uniformitarianism does not apply in the Precambrian. These include clusters of radiometric "ages"; lithologies with restricted ages (such as komatiite, banded iron formation, megacrystic anorthosites, ophiolites, and blueschists); tectonic styles (such as permobile Archean versus linear Proterozoic belts, intracontinental deformation versus later plate tectonics, and mountain building); and effects of fluid flow (such as massive river systems, mass flows, and the 'Great Unconformity').

Many geological processes are known to not require deep time. The paper here refers to processes such as those relating to granite, banded iron formation, sedimentation, base metal sulfides, and calcium carbonate precipitation.

ABSTRACT

Precambrian geology, especially of the crystalline basement rocks, is complex. Consequently, understanding what appears to be its long and involved history is a challenge. This paper not only aims to help address this challenge but also to interpret this history within a Young Earth biblical model. An overview of North America's Precambrian province geology is provided, and a geological history model for the whole continent is developed that aims to be consistent with both mapped regional geology and the Biblical record.

Correlation of Precambrian geological history with the sequence of acts chronicled in the Bible is based on interpreting key subjects such as mapped stratigraphy, the relative order of radiometric "ages," the role of water, and regional heating events. Interpretation of radiometric date clusters, and thus thermal-tectonic events, was used to infer correlation with the Biblical record. It is proposed that God instigated heating events and that, with the heat of each event, radiometric "ages" were systematically reset to lower values. These "ages," or isotopic ratios, provide information on the history of crystallization and cooling of rocks.

On the basis of these date clusters, the principal thermal-tectonic events in North America are as follows:

1. Kenoran (late Archean) – associated with simultaneous cooling and convective heat dissipation of earlier hotter crust within individual Archean provinces, and the beginning of stable cratons.

2. Hudsonian (late Paleoproterozoic) – associated with internal deformation and further metamorphism of Archean provinces, as well as metasomatism.

3. Grenvillian (late Mesoproterozoic) – associated with huge thickening of continental crust and high mountain building.

4. Pan-African (late Neoproterozoic) – associated with massive rifting on the Cordilleran and Appalachian margins, as well as immense continental erosion and enormous water flows.

Biblical descriptions of Day One (initial global ocean and hovering over the waters), Day Two (the waters above and below), Day Three (dry land appears), and the early Noahic Flood (fountains bursting forth and rain) were respectively correlated with North America's Archean, Paleoproterozoic, Mesoproterozoic, and Neoproterozoic geology (including Kenoran, Hudsonian, Grenvillian, and Pan-African thermal-tectonic events). Some specific locations of pre-Flood geography were inferred in relation to today's Precambrian areas.

KEY WORDS

Creation days, Flood, thermal-tectonic event, North America, Precambrian provinces, Archean, Paleoproterozoic, Mesoproterozoic, Neoproterozoic.

INTRODUCTION

An earlier paper (Dickens and Snelling 2008) reviewed Precambrian geology on a global scale but did not refer to individual mapped Precambrian provinces, together with their temporal and spatial relationships. To address this, the North American continent was chosen as a case study. It is a well-studied region of the Earth and provides among the most complete geological, geophysical, and isotopic data sets of any continent (Whitmeyer and Karlstrom 2007). The geology of successive Archean to Mesoproterozoic basement provinces, as well as the overlying Neoproterozoic sedimentary cover, is outlined.

Due to the relative paucity of suitable fossils in Precambrian successions, and particularly their absence in crystalline basement rocks (including granite), radiometric dating is routinely used to indicate the "age" of Precambrian rocks. I consider that these "ages" are useful in a relative rather than absolute time sense. Resetting of "ages" due to heating events has global significance. Heating events are related in this paper not only to regional geology but also to the biblical record.

METHODS

A search of scripture identified key verses considered to be relevant to geological history, along with their possible time sequence. This paper adopts a Young Earth biblical perspective of scripture: a literal 24-hour six-day framework for Creation Week and the global Noahic Flood some centuries later. Dickens and Snelling 2008 provided a useful starting point for the concept and approach of this paper.

Through a search of the geological literature, I became aware of various aspects of North American regional geology and associated interpretations of geological history. A generalized geological map (Fig. 1) provides necessary basic data for the proposed geological history model, as it shows major geological provinces, their principal rock types, and relative ages. In this paper, I use the terms Archean, Paleoproterozoic, Mesoproterozoic, and Neoproterozoic not as deep-time "Eons" or "Eras" but as mappable stratigraphic units having characteristic features. Relevant Bible verses, mapped regional stratigraphy and radiometric dates provided key data for the proposed time sequence model.

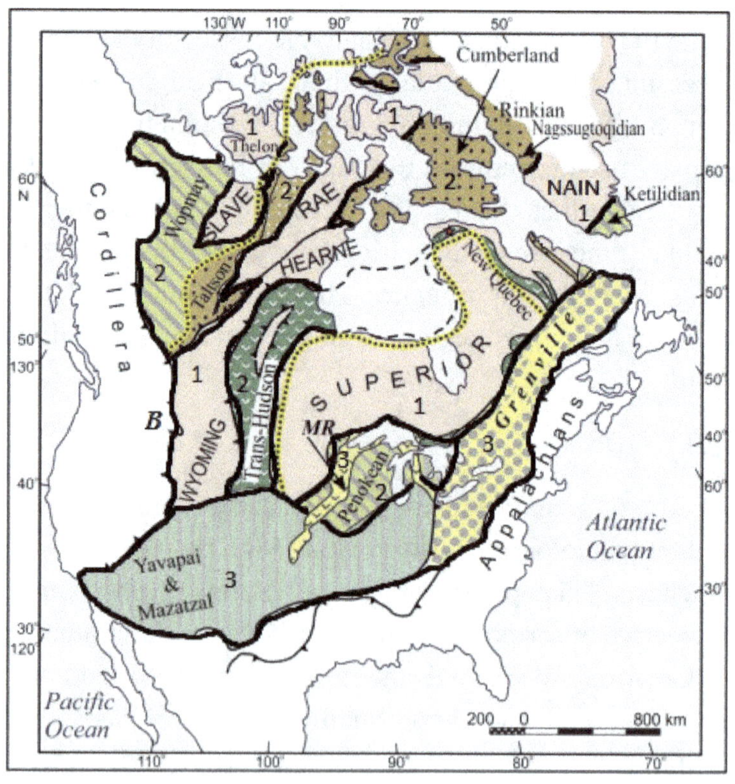

Figure 1. Generalized map showing North America and Greenland's major Precambrian provinces (with platform cover removed) and their principal rock types (after Mints, 2015). MR = Midcontinent Rift. B = approximate location of Belt-Purcell Basin. In this paper's proposed model, it is inferred that Archean to Mesoproterozoic geology formed during early Creation Week, and specifically that the 1, 2, and 3 numbering in this figure's legend respectively refers to formation of provinces in Creation Days One, Two, and Three.

REGIONAL GEOLOGY

1. Radiometric "age" dates and heating events

Zircon is commonly found as a trace constituent of most granitoid rocks. Zircons are resilient and contain high concentrations of important trace elements, including radiogenic isotope systems of geochronological importance, namely U-Pb and Th-Pb (Hawkesworth et al. 2010). A profound episodicity exists in the Precambrian geological record (O'Neill et al. 2013). Both igneous and detrital zircon populations show that major age peaks are global in extent (Condie and Aster 2010; Condie et al. 2017) (Fig. 2). The deformation age distribution of greenstone belts (most abundant at 2.70, 1.85, 1.05, and 0.60 Ga) is broadly similar to the age distribution of Precambrian granites and detrital zircons (Bradley 2011). Due to its hardness, durability, and chemical inertness, zircon is a common constituent in detrital form in most sedimentary deposits (Fedo et al. 2003). Detrital zircon grains can be used for sedimentary sequence provenance studies (Rainbird et al. 2012).

On the basis of clusters of radiometric dates (U-Pb, K-Ar, Rb-Sr) that occur in well-defined areas (provinces), the three principal thermal-tectonic events in the Canadian Shield have been named the Kenoran, Hudsonian, and Grenvillian (King 1976; Stockwell 1964) (Fig. 2). Reworking of earlier provinces (and overprinting of earlier events) is indicated on the Tectonic Map of North America (King 1976). Regional patterns of radiometric ages are correlatable with field relationships mapped on a province scale (Fig. 1).

2. Archean provinces geology

The Earth's radiometrically oldest continental crust is exposed in Archean cratons (Zientek and Orris 2005). Archean provinces display intense deformation over their entire area and show no stable areas at all. In contrast, for most terranes other than the Archean, crustal deformation is restricted to narrow belts (Frazier and Schwimmer 1987). Archean metamorphism is distinctively a low-pressure/high-temperature variety (Anhaeusser 1975). North America's Archean provinces include the Superior, Wyoming, Slave, Rae, Hearne, and Nain provinces (Fig. 1). The Superior Province is the world's largest Archean province. These provinces essentially consist of high metamorphic grade granulite-gneiss terranes and low-grade granite-greenstone terranes. The Archean contains the oldest rocks, including the Acasta Gneiss Complex in the westernmost Slave Province (Iizuka et al. 2007). Only Archean megacrystic anorthosites have a highly calcic composition (Ashwal 2010). Sedimentary rocks and pillow lavas occur in greenstone belts such as the Isua greenstone belt of southwestern Greenland (Sharkov and Bogatikov 2010).

Early Archean gneisses mainly consist of hydrous tonalite, trondhjemite, and granodiorite (TTG) (Hamilton 2003). Greenstone belts are large and complexly deformed belts that consist of thick and deeply infolded sequences of mainly mafic volcanics and associated sediments. Commonly, granitic and gneissic rocks surround and locally intrude the greenstone belts. Greenstone belt sequences have been subjected to relatively low-grade metamorphism and contain komatiite (a high-magnesium basalt) which has a high melting point and is characteristic of the Archean.

Archean greenstone belts commonly contain banded iron formations (BIFs) and are called Algoma-type after a location in Canada. These deposits are mined in the Superior Province's Abitibi greenstone belt and are rich in magnetite (Taner and Chemam 2015). Banded iron formations (BIFs) consist of bands of iron oxide and chert.

Archean sedimentation in the Canadian Shield was dominated by the resedimented (turbidite) facies association of submarine fans—greywacke, mudstone-siltstone, and conglomerate. Archean sedimentary rocks consist largely of greywacke—an immature sandstone containing abundant mafic minerals like hornblende and biotite (Dickens and Snelling 2008).

Archean stromatolites are found in sedimentary carbonate rocks, almost always associated with extensive volcanic sequences (Hofmann 2000). Millimeter-scale layers of fine ash at regular intervals attest to periodic explosive volcanic eruptions during the deposition of microbial mats in the Back River volcanic complex of the Slave Province (Lambert 2011). Stromatolites are more abundant in Paleoproterozoic and Mesoproterozoic sediments (Hofmann 1998) along with extensive carbonates (Lucas and St-Onge 1998). North American carbonates and quartz arenites are much less well developed in Archean strata (Okajangas 1985).

Archean greenstone belts have economically significant gold and other metal deposits (Rey et al. 2013). Most major lode gold deposits have a late Archean "age" (Cameron 1988). The Abitibi greenstone belt of the Superior Province, for example, contains world-class copper-zinc massive sulfide orebodies as well as banded iron formations (Pirajno 1992; Taner and Chemam 2015).

There is a large zircon "age" peak in the late Archean geology of North America and all continents (Bradley 2011; Condie 2018; O'Neill et al. 2013; Voice et al. 2011) (Fig. 2).

3. Northern Paleoproterozoic provinces geology

There is a remarkable change in tectonic style going from Archean granite-greenstone terrane and high-grade granulite-gneiss metamorphic terrane to the adjacent linear Proterozoic belts (Frazier and Schwimmer 1987). Proterozoic tectonic style was indeed different from the permobile style of the Archean, but it also differed from that of the Phanerozoic in that intracontinental deformation and igneous activity were much more extensive than they have been since (Frazier and Schwimmer 1987).

North America's Paleoproterozoic provinces (Fig. 1) largely consist of two types (Mints 2007):

- Low metamorphic grade sedimentary-volcanic belts (greenschist to low-temperature amphibolite facies metamorphism) and

- Granulite-gneiss belts (with a predominance of high-temperature amphibolite to ultrahigh-temperature granulite facies).

Northern Paleoproterozoic provinces include the low metamorphic grade Trans-Hudson, New Quebec, Penokean,

Wopmay, and Ketilidian belts, together with the high metamorphic grade Talston-Thelon belt, as well as the Cumberland, Rinkian, and Nagssugtoqidian provinces (Fig. 1).

The Trans-Hudson Province is North America's largest and best -exposed Paleoproterozoic belt (Zhao et al. 2002). This belt has Archean provinces on both sides. Deep seismic reflection lines (Nelson et al. 1993) indicate that the Trans-Hudson province has a complex structure that dips to the west in the west and to the east in the east. The North American Central Plains (NACP) conductivity anomaly, a very large electrical conductor delineated by electromagnetic induction studies, is collinear with the Trans-Hudson province (Alabi et al. 1975). In the Trans-Hudson Province of northern Saskatchewan, uranium-thorium-hosted granitic pegmatites have an intrusive relationship to Early Paleoproterozoic metasedimentary rocks and interfolded granitoids that unconformably overlie Late Archean gneisses.

Economic sources of unconformity-related uranium occur in association with Paleoproterozoic basins such as Canada's Athabasca Basin, which contains the highest-grade and largest deposits of this type in the world (Hanly et al. 2006). Early Paleoproterozoic gold-uranium conglomerates are found at Elliot Lake and the Huronian Supergroup of Canada (Pirajno 1992). Supposedly "glacial" diamictite is found in locations such as the Huronian Supergroup (Bekker et al. 2005). Paleoproterozoic basins, such as the Athabasca and Thelon of northern Canada, contain detrital zircons of similar "age" to the Trans-Hudson Province (Rainbird et al.

2012). Paleoproterozoic sediments of Arctic Canada contain sedimentary structures indicative of incised valleys and sheet-braided rivers (Ielpi and Rainbird 2016b).

Worldwide, by far the most important type of banded iron formations are located in relatively undeformed Paleoproterozoic sedimentary basins that have unconformable contacts on granite-greenstone terrains (Lascelles 2013). These Superior-type deposits are large in dimensions (more than 100 meters in thickness and over 100 km in lateral extent) (Evans et al. 2013). Superior-type BIFs contain most of the world's hematite-goethite ore deposits (Douglas 1970). The Marquette Lake deposit is an example of a Superior-type deposit in the Penokean Province (Schmidt 1980).

Sediment-hosted copper deposits first appear in the Paleoproterozoic. Precambrian chemical sediments are said to have changed from mainly sulphide facies before 1.85 Ga to predominantly oxide facies (Slack and Cannon 2009). Metamorphic microdiamonds have been found to contain high concentrations of nitrogen within Paleoproterozoic magmatic rocks at Nunavut, Canada (Cartigny et al. 2004).

There is a large zircon "age" peak in the late Paleoproterozoic geology of North America and all continents (Bradley 2011; Condie 2018; O'Neill et al. 2013; Voice et al. 2011) (Fig. 2).

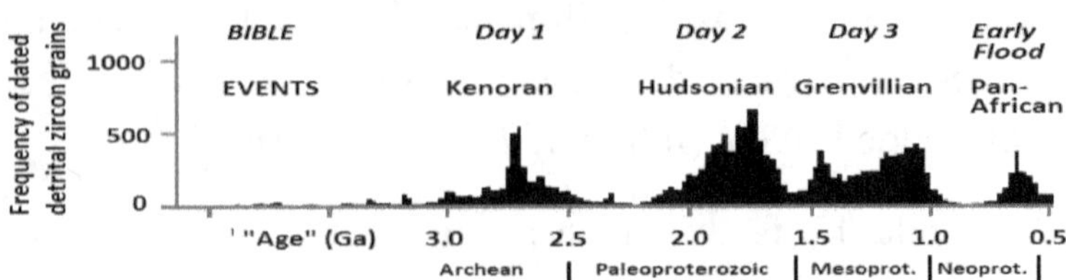

Figure 2. Age frequency distribution of detrital zircon U-Pb radiometric "ages" from North America, with corresponding significant thermal-tectonic Events and proposed correlation with the Biblical record. (figure modified from Voice et al., 2011).

4. Southeastern Proterozoic provinces geology

In striking contrast to most of North America's older Proterozoic provinces, the lithosphere of southeastern North America has an overall northeast-southwest regional trend. This includes the Late Paleoproterozoic Yavapai and Mazatzal provinces, as well as the Mesoproterozoic Grenville Province (Fig. 1). These northeast-trending provinces are characterised by voluminous granitoid plutonism (Mints 2015; Whitmeyer and Karlstrom 2007). The principal Mesoproterozoic province of North America is the Grenville Province. In addition, there are significant Mesoproterozoic rift basins. These include the Midcontinent Rift Basin (also known as the Keweenawan Rift), which is largely basaltic, and the Belt-Purcell Basin, which is mainly sedimentary (Fig. 1).

The Grenville Province is characterized by extremely high grades of metamorphism (amphibolite and granulite facies) in both basement terranes and supracrustal rocks of the Grenville Supergroup. Rock types are ensialic, with

20

quartzofeldspathic gneisses and metasediments, including marble (Davidson 1998). Regions with similar isotopic signatures and geochemistry have been found in other parts of the world, including Western Australia, and have been correlated with the Grenville Province (Van Kraendonk and Kirkland 2013).

The Midcontinent Rift Basin contains thick Mesoproterozoic basalt lavas (15 to 20 km) and an overlying Neoproterozoic terrigenous sedimentary sequence (Allen et al. 2015; Hoffman, 1989) and has been extrapolated southwestward beneath Phanerozoic cover on the basis of gravity and magnetic anomalies (Davidson 1998). The basalts are tholeiitic and host world-class copper deposits (Presnell 2004).

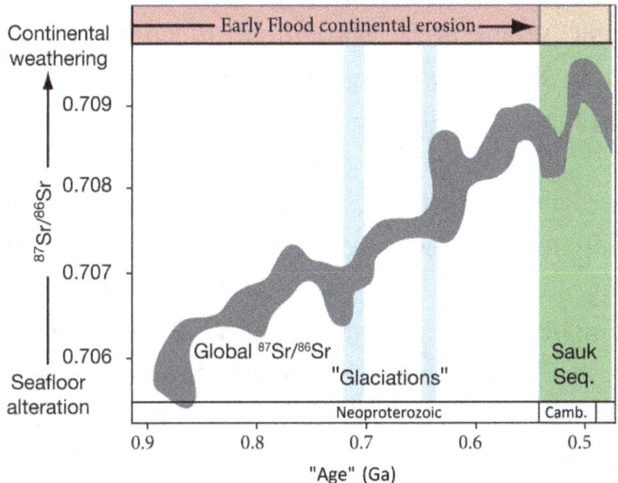

Figure 3. Summary of major geochemical and sedimentary patterns derived from Neoproterozoic to Cambrian strata (modified from Peters and Gaines 2012). 1) The observed increase in Neoproterozoic strontium isotope ratios $^{87}Sr/^{86}Sr$

can be explained by accelerated rates of erosion due to the impact of the early Flood's enormous rain on the supercontinent and to associated Pan-African Event tectonism., and 2) The subsequent decline in $^{87}Sr/^{86}Sr$ ratio in post-Cambrian strata may be due to the globe being totally covered with ocean so that the Flood's rain no longer directly impacted the land.

The Belt-Purcell Basin is found on the western margin of North America but is considered here along with the southeastern Proterozoic provinces because it has a similar "age". It outcrops over an area of about 200,000 km^2 (Lydon 2007). This sedimentary basin is enormously thick, ranging from about 6 km in thickness along its eastern margin to a probable maximum of 20 km in the center of the Belt Basin (King 1976). Rock types include clastics, carbonates, and volcanics (Lydon 2007). Throughout much of their extent, these rocks have been subjected only to lower grades of metamorphism and still retain their primary sedimentary structures (Frazier and Schwimmer 1987). Belt-Purcell rocks are overlain across a slight unconformity by the Neoproterozoic Windermere Group – a westward-thickening group of mainly detrital sediments up to 6 km thick (Frazier and Schwimmer 1987). The Belt-Purcell Basin hosts the world-class Sullivan sedimentary-exhalative (SEDEX) stratiform lead-zinc deposit (Presnell 2004).

Grenville-age detrital zircon comprises a significant proportion of most sedimentary successions in western and southeastern North America (Rainbird et al. 2012). In western North America, this includes northwest Canada

(Rainbird and Young 2009) and the central Cordillera of California and Nevada (Fedo et al. 2003).

There is a large zircon "age" peak in the late Mesoproterozoic geology of North America and all continents (Bradley 2011; Condie 2018; O'Neill et al. 2013; Voice et al. 2011) (Fig. 2).

5. Neoproterozoic sedimentary cover geology

Neoproterozoic sedimentary cover is found in areas such as the Appalachians, and the Cordillera (Fig. 1), as well as cratonic sequences (Frazier and Schwimmer 1987; Schermerhorn 1974). There is a significant $^{87}Sr/^{86}Sr$ ratio increase in Neoproterozoic successions in North America of "age" between 0.9 Ga and 0.5 Ga (Peters and Gaines 2012) (Fig. 3). The Neoproterozoic to Lower Paleozoic geology of North America is characterized by thick sedimentary successions in rift basins and extensional margin sedimentary wedges (Miall 2008). In the Grand Canyon, the 'Great Unconformity' is the contact between underlying either Paleoproterozoic crystalline basement or tilted Neoproterozoic Chuar Group sediments, and overlying Paleozoic layered sediments. This unconformity is traceable across North America (Peters and Gaines 2012; Timmons et al. 1999).

Lower Neoproterozoic sequences in North America contain braided-type well-sorted sheet sandstones. These sequences contain Grenville-age detrital zircons in regions such as northwestern Canada, southeastern North America, and overlying basaltic rocks in the Midcontinent Rift Basin (Krabbendam et al. 2017; Rainbird et al. 1997). In contrast, mid-Neoproterozoic deposits are mainly poorly sorted immature clastic sediments with lesser volcanic rocks and are characterized by deposits commonly interpreted to be "glacial" (Hoffman 1989). The geochemistry of Neoproterozoic cap carbonates, which overlie "glacials", carries a strong hydrothermal signal (Young 2013). The Rapitan Group of the lower Windermere Supergroup in Canada consists of mixtite, siltstone, shale, sandstone (including arkosic sandstone), volcanic ash, and tuff, as well as banded iron formation (Baldwin et al. 2012; Frazier and Schwimmer 1987).

High-pressure metamorphic/orogenic belts are restricted to rocks of "age" < 0.6 Ga (Brown 2007). It has been claimed that there are no ophiolites or blueschists in rocks older than Neoproterozoic (Hamilton 2011).

There is a large zircon "age" peak in the late Neoproterozoic geology of North America and all continents (Bradley 2011; Condie 2018; O'Neill et al. 2013; Voice et al. 2011) (Fig. 2).

DISCUSSION

1. Radiometric "age" dates and heating events

There are regional patterns in radiometric dates that can be systematically related to different Precambrian geological provinces (Fig. 1). A relative time sequence of geological formations can be deduced from Precambrian rocks using observable measurable data such as field relationships and isotopic ratios. However, the interpretation of the absolute age of formations is debatable, based on uniformitarian assumptions on matters such as process rates. Granitoid rocks are key targets for radiometric dating as they commonly contain zircon. Deep-time is not necessary for the generation of granitic magmas and their subsequent intrusion, crystallization, and cooling. Crystallization and cooling would be facilitated by hydrothermal convective circulation (Snelling 2008). The growth of large crystals from magmas within hours has now been experimentally determined (London 1992).

Zircon ages do not usually correspond to peak metamorphism but instead provide information on the history of cooling from high temperatures, including the timing and rates of exhumation of the deep hot roots (foundations) of mountain chains (Harley et al. 2007). "Age" peaks are associated with major tectonic and magmatic events, including inferred addition of new continental crust, orogeny (mountain building), voluminous high-temperature volcanism, massive mantle depletion, and mineralization (O'Neill et al. 2013). The continental crust has been said to be the archive of the "deep-time" geological history of the Earth (Hawkesworth et al. 2010; Roberts and Spencer 2015).

For a fire is kindled by my anger, and it burns to the depths of Sheol, devours the earth and its increase, and sets on fire the foundations of the mountains (Deuteronomy 32:22 ESV).

God is said to have set on fire the foundations of the mountains. Whether this particular verse is literal or poetic, God is certainly capable of literally setting on fire the foundations of the mountains. Mineral assemblages, consistent with this, provide evidence of ultrahigh-temperature metamorphism (900^0C-1100^0C) during mountain building (Harley et al. 2007). In addition, the day of the Lord described in 2 Peter 3 has repeated references to the effect of heat.

Four heating events (Kenoran, Hudsonian, Grenvillian and Pan-African) (Fig. 2) are believed to be key to the creation of Precambrian stratigraphy in North America. I propose that God supernaturally instigated heating episodes (thermal-tectonic events) which drove cataclysmic geological processes around the globe. That is, I propose that the geological work that took place on Day One, Day Two, and the earlier part of Day Three was the result of divine actions involving three global heating episodes. Each heating event would have reset the "ages" to lower values. Thus, Precambrian crystalline basement rocks, with their radiogenic "age" clusters, are considered to be geoscientific evidence of the Creator's actions in early Creation Week. In addition, Noah's Flood is considered to have been initiated by God, causing the mantle to heat in a fourth global heating episode, and so drive out water to the Earth's surface. The subsequent rain eroded the land, the resulting detritus was entrained in flowing water, and sedimentary cover sequences were then deposited over the crystalline basement.

For by him [Jesus] all things were created, in heaven and on earth, visible and invisible, whether thrones or dominions or rulers or authorities—all things were created through him and for him. And he is before all things, and in him all things hold together. (Colossians 1:16-17 ESV).

"All" includes atoms. Therefore, Jesus (by whom the universe was created) could also allow atoms to transform or transmute for both creative purposes (such as the growth of continental crust in the early Creation Week) and destructive purposes (such as flooding the whole Earth in Noah's time). It is (Fig. 1).

It has been estimated that the early Earth had a greater quantity of radionuclides, resulting in greater amounts of interior heat and that radiogenic heat production declined at a geometric rate throughout the Archean so that lithosphere thickness probably increased with time as the actual amount of heat decreased (Frazier and Schwimmer 1987). Higher temperature conditions are indicated by the presence of komatiite in Archean provinces. An overall cooling Earth would have influenced the depths and, hence, the geochemical signatures at which melt generation takes place, as well as the rheology of the crust and lithosphere, which in turn would have influenced tectonic processes. In addition, the lithosphere is believed to have thickened and crustal reworking increased, resulting in higher erosion fluxes and changes in ocean chemistry (Hawkesworth et al. 2016).

It is suggested that heating events drove cataclysmic geologic processes during the early part of the Creation Week Days One to Three, fashioning the land to be inhabited (Isaiah 45:18) while avoiding damage to life created on Days Five and Six. This fits the model proposed, with radioisotope ages indicating relative order and rocks being rapidly 'aged' during the early Creation week through the Archean-Mesoproterozoic (Dickens and Snelling 2008).

2. Archean provinces' history

A. Watery early world

The earth was without form and void, and darkness was over the face of the deep. And the Spirit of God was hovering over the face of the waters. (Genesis 1:2 ESV).

For they deliberately overlook this fact, that the heavens existed long ago, and the earth was formed out of water and through water by the word of God (2 Peter 3:5 ESV).

The Earth's continental crust appears to be unique compared with crusts on other planets and satellites in the solar system, as a result of the Earth's abundant free water (Taylor and McLennan 1995). "Water is essential for the formation of granites, and granite, in turn, is essential for the formation of stable continents. The Earth is the only planet with granite and continents because it is the only planet with abundant water." (Campbell and Taylor 1983). It has been claimed that for the major part of the Earth's fluid history, fluid transport was mostly one way, from the outer core to the surface, and that the rifting of continents during orogenic events delivered mantle water to the surface (Santosh et al. 2010).

Before Day Three, there is no mention of land, but there is mention of the "deep" or ocean, so one can infer that there was a global ocean that, from space, appeared to be without topographic relief and empty (Dickens and Snelling 2008). The description of water on Day One (in the beginning) is proposed to relate to the role of water in the Archean. The Spirit of God hovering upon the waters (Genesis 1:2b) may imply shaking or vibrating, with convection cells operating in the waters and in the hot crustal rocks below. There may have been submarine volcanic mountains and turbidite facies associated with submarine fans, but no shelf deposits (Dickens and Snelling 2008). The Archean is said to have had a permobile tectonic regime with no stable areas (Burke et al. 1976). This is believed to relate to the idea of convective dissipation of heat generated in the early Earth (Burke et al. 1976).

It has been inferred that water was important for early Archean granitoid (tonalite-trondhjemite-granodiorite) (TTG) petrology, with hydrous basaltic melts as parental liquids, undergoing extensive fractional crystallization (Hamilton 2003; Kleinhanns et al. 2003). Indeed, there is evidence for granitoid formation processes in the presence of liquid water oceans on the early Earth (Iizuka et al. 2007). The high water content of parental melts may explain the highly calcic composition only found in megacrystic anorthosites of the Archean (Ashwal 2010). The occurrence of sedimentary rocks and pillow lavas (products of submarine eruption) in the Isua greenstone belt of southwestern Greenland indicates that water basins existed in the early Archean (Sharkov and Bogatikov 2010). Archean-banded iron formations (BIFs) have been interpreted as formed in deep water below the wave base (Pirajno 1992). The minimal development of Archean carbonates and quartz arenites in North America implies a lack of stable shelf areas (Okajangas 1985). From the observation that most Archean continental flood basalts were emplaced on flooded continents, a theory was proposed for the hypsometry of the early Earth, showing that most

Archean continental crust was flooded and the Earth was largely a water world. (Rey et al. 2013).

B. Tectonism

Most models for generating new continental crust involve differentiation of basalt by fractional crystallization to higher silica compositions (Hawkesworth et al. 2010). In other words, the melting of mafic rock may produce a surface crust composed mainly of less dense, more buoyant rocks of granitoid composition. Crust formation is related to heat generation (stern et al. 2007). Thus, there are believed to be links between granite magmatism, high-grade metamorphic events, and crustal growth (Hawkesworth et al. 2010). The formation, rise, and emplacement of granitoids via dikes may only take days, so millions of years are not necessary (Snelling 2008).

The paleomagnetic record indicates that the Precambrian continental crust was essentially intact from the Archean to the Neoproterozoic (Piper 2015). Mints (2018) has written an alternative to the model of supercontinent cycles. This involves the growth of an Archean to Neoproterozoic supercontinent during and as a result of, high-temperature events accompanied by granulite-facies metamorphism.

For most terranes other than the Archean, crustal deformation is restricted to narrow belts (Frazier and Schwimmer 1987). In contrast, Archean terranes have intense deformation over their entire area. This indicates that rigid lithospheric plates, at least as known today, may not have existed in the early Earth and that modern-style plate tectonic processes may not have been involved. Archean tectonism may have been dominantly intracontinental deformation as the hotter crust would have been far too weak and mobile to behave as rigid plates (Hamilton 2003, Hamilton 2007). Thus, with high heat flow, the Kenoran Event would have had tectonism and magmatism but not necessarily orogeny since the hotter crust may have been too weak to support high mountains. The Archean may only have had subdued topography (< ca. 2000 m) (Rey et al. 2013).

It has been claimed that bedrock mapping and associated geochronology of the Superior Province provides evidence that microcontinental fragments and juvenile oceanic terranes were amalgamated into a composite Superior superterrane in a series of orogenic events at ca. 2.7 Ga (Percival et al. 2004). However, an alternative interpretation to the amalgamation idea, based on the paleomagnetic record, is that the Precambrian continental crust was essentially intact from the Archean to the Neoproterozoic (Piper 2015). This interpretation is more consistent with the idea of the progressive growth of only one supercontinent from Day One to the first part of Day Three. There is no indication of numerous supercontinent cycles in the Bible.

The Kenoran Event, or so-called "orogeny," was defined on the basis of ca. 2.5 Ga K-Ar ages from provinces including the Superior, Slave, and Nain Provinces (Stockwell 1964). The Kenoran Event is associated with simultaneous tectonism in North American Archean provinces. The Kenoran Event has been described as the last important period of widespread folding, metamorphism, and intrusion in the Canadian Shield, with the Superior Province chosen as the type region (Stockwell et al. 1970). The late Archean age peak represents coincidental cooling within individual provinces (Percival 2004) and the beginning of stable cratons (Frazier and Schwimmer 1987). This is the first global pulse of crustal generation as reflected by the large late Archean zircon "age" peak (Condie 2018) (Fig. 2).

C. Foundations of the Earth

And I have put my words in your mouth and covered you in the shadow of my hand, establishing the heavens and laying the foundations of the earth, and saying to Zion, 'You are my people.' (Isaiah 51:16 ESV)

Where were you when I laid the foundation of the earth? Tell me if you have understanding. (Job 38:4b ESV)

Archean cratons may have cold mantle roots (Hoffman 1990) that extend twice as deep (to about 200 km) as the lithosphere beneath younger continental crust and thermally mature ocean basins. Evidence favoring this includes the correlation of these cratons with areas of high shear-wave velocities, low surface heat flow and high lithospheric flexural rigidities (Dickens and Snelling 2008). Mantle roots of Archean cratons may be considered as the foundations of the Earth's crust. Most major lode gold deposits formed in the late Archean, corresponding to the principal time of crustal thickening and stabilization, and were associated with the formation of granulite, the anhydrous, refractory base for the crust (Cameron 1988).

D. Hydrothermal activity

"Archean greenstone belts are richly endowed with gold and other metals deposits. On flooded continents, an infinite fluid reservoir was available to feed crustal-scale hydrothermal circulations promoting the formation of craton-wide metal deposits in the interior of continents, far away from their margins." (Rey et al. 2013). The world-class copper-zinc massive sulfide orebodies of the Abitibi greenstone belt of the Superior Province are considered to have formed as chemical precipitates from submarine hydrothermal volcanic vents (Pirajno 1992). Gold deposits of Archean greenstone belts are also said to have a hydrothermal origin (Pirajno 1992).

The origin of a typical Algoma-type banded iron formation (BIF) in the Abitibi greenstone belt is said to be closely related to regionally extensive submarine hydrothermal activity associated with the emplacement of volcanic and related subvolcanic rocks. (Taner and Chemam 2015). Earlier models of BIF formation referred to the slow deposition of annual micro-laminations over millions of years (for example, Garrels 1987). However, episodic and rapid deposition of turbidity and density currents may have only lasted a few hours to days! (Dickens 2017a; Lascelles 2013). Modern interpretations consider BIFs as deep-sea sediments with iron and silica sourced from reactions between circulating seawater and hot mafic to ultramafic rocks as hydrothermal systems vented onto the sea floor. Hot acidic hydrothermal fluids would immediately precipitate colloidal particles of iron hydroxide and iron silicates on quenching by cold neutral seawater (Lascelles 2013).

Banded iron formations (BIFs) are concentrated in the later Archean and Paleoproterozoic regions (Groves et al. 2005), with a few small occurrences in the Neoproterozoic (Reddy and Evans 2009).

.. worship him who made heaven and earth, the sea and the springs of water. (Revelation 14:7b ESV).

.. when he established the fountains of the deep. (Proverbs 8:28b ESV)

Springs and fountains may have included sites in the vicinity of hydrothermal areas where stromatolitic structures formed. The Bible's first mention of the creation of lifeforms is that of seed-bearing land plants on Day Three (Genesis 1:11-12). The Bible does not give a comprehensive listing of lifeforms created. Thus cyanobacteria in the form of stromatolites may have been present even on Day One. Fully functioning stromatolites and even stromatolite reefs may have been created by God before Day Three, along with the carbonate sediments on the floor of the pre-flood global ocean (Purdom and Snelling 2013; Wise 2003). Death referred to in the Bible applies to "nephesh" organisms. and since stromatolites are not "nephesh" organisms, they could have died during Creation Week and not violated God's "very good" creation.

In summary, it is proposed that Day One processes be correlated with the development of Archean provinces along with North America's Kenoran Event (Fig. 2).

3. Northern Paleoproterozoic provinces history

A. Movement of waters

And God said, "Let there be an expanse in the midst of the waters, and let it separate the waters from the waters." And God made the expanse and separated the waters that were under the expanse from the waters that were above the expanse. And it was so. And God called the expanse Heaven. And there was evening, and there was morning, the second day. (Genesis 1:6-8 ESV).

The Hebrew word râqî yaʿ (עִיְקָרַ) is translated as the expanse (ESV) or firmament (KJV) and has Strong's Concordance number H7549, which indicates that this apparently represents the visible arch of the sky. This Hebrew word is also used on Day Five of Creation Week where "birds fly above the earth across the expanse of the heavens." (Genesis 1:20 ESV). The same word is also used on Day Four of Creation Week with "lights in the expanse of the heavens to separate the day from the night". Thus, there is a sense of vertical separation of water. It has been claimed that for the major part of the Earth's fluid history, fluid transport was mostly upwards, from the outer core to the surface, and that the rifting of continents during orogenic episodes delivered mantle water upwards (Santosh et al. 2010). I believe that such a process is consistent with the operation of major episodes of proposed fluid flow on Day Two and with Noahic Flood fountains, which can be inferred from some common features of Paleoproterozoic and Neoproterozoic geology.

Provenance analysis using zircon grains has been used to infer that big river systems transported Paleoproterozoic sediments shed from the Trans-Hudson Province to northern Canada (basins such as the Athabasca and Thelon). (Rainbird et al. 2012). These Paleoproterozoic sediments may have resulted from erosion as continental crust thickened during the Hudsonian Event on Day Two (Dickens 2017b). In addition, sheet-braided rivers and incised paleovalleys have been inferred from Paleoproterozoic sediments of Arctic Canada (Ielpi and Rainbird 2016b). I suggest that such deposits also resulted from a great tectonic movement (Hudsonian Event) during Day Two.

B. Paleoproterozoic tectonism

Various North American Archean provinces have commonly been interpreted as "welded together" by Paleoproterozoic belts (Hoffman 1989; Hoffman 1998; Presnell 2004). In a global review, North American Archean provinces have been said to have sutured along 1.9–1.8 Ga orogens, including the Trans-Hudson, Penokean, Wopmay, and Nagssugtoqidian (Fig. 1) (Zhao et al. 2002). However, an alternative view is that as Proterozoic provinces developed, they underwent deformation and thickening but without the major fragmentation, widespread dispersion, and collision of continents typical of the post-Permian (Engel and Kelm 1972; Hamilton 2011). Proterozoic magnetostratigraphy provides evidence that the Hudsonian Event is associated with internal deformation and further metamorphism of Archean provinces rather than with dismemberment and continental drift (Irving et al. 1976). This is consistent with the idea of the progressive formation of only one Precambrian supercontinent (Mints 2018; Piper 2015) by Day Three.

The Trans-Hudson Province is believed to have involved internal rifting rather than a collision between two Archean continental blocks (Mints 2015). It is suggested that the region of the North American Central Plains (NACP) conductivity anomaly (the Trans-Hudson province) was a site where hydrothermal fluids burst out, consistent with the vertical separation of waters on Day Two. Rock sampling has provided evidence that the migration of sulfides during tectonism is responsible for the anomaly (Jones et al. 2005). Subsequent recovery provided compressional thickening (Hamilton 2007).

Apparently, ensialic Paleoproterozoic belts were involved in large-scale reworking (remobilization and further metamorphism) of the Archean basement (Frazier and Schwimmer 1987). Vertical tectonic motions have been inferred (Anhaeusser 1975). On Day Two, submarine mountains may have formed with North America's Hudsonian Event, prior to the emergence of land on Day Three. The claimed rise in atmospheric oxygen in the Paleoproterozoic (called the "Great Oxygenation Event") has been related to tectonism (Lee et al. 2016; Och and Shields-Zhou 2012).

C. Some common features of Paleoproterozoic and Neoproterozoic geology

1. Lithologies

A review of tectonic settings of late Neoproterozoic "glaciogenic" rocks and Paleoproterozoic (Huronian) "glaciogenic" rocks, found a preponderance of settings interpreted as rift related (Eyles 2008). The geochemistry of Neoproterozoic cap carbonates carries a strong hydrothermal signal, and Paleoproterozoic (Huronian) carbonates have been interpreted to have formed in a hydrothermally influenced, restricted rift setting (Young 2013). "Glacials" of Early and Late Proterozoic successions are closely associated with sedimentary rocks formed in warm climates (Young 2013). Warm, not cold, weathering conditions have been interpreted from the occurrence of minerals such as kaolinite and diaspore in parts of the Huronian Supergroup (Nesbitt and Young 1982). These features described for Paleoproterozoic and Neoproterozoic strata may be related to the effects of the movement of hydrothermal fluids in a rifting environment during Day Two and the early Flood, respectively. The Paleoproterozoic "glacial-epoch," exemplified by the Huronian Supergroup of Ontario, Canada, and strata in the U.S., is associated with rifting (Eyles 2008).

Transfer of carbon dioxide to the ocean during rifting may have enabled rapid precipitation of calcium carbonate in warm surface waters. This could have caused the precipitation of cap carbonate rocks over Neoproterozoic mixtites which are observed globally (Shields 2005) and observed in North America's Paleoproterozoic (Bekker et al. 2005). I interpret both the Paleoproterozoic and Neoproterozoic mixtites as mass flow deposits rather than "glacials".

"Or who shut in the sea with doors when it burst out from the womb" (Job 38:8 ESV)

A pouring out of volcanics and associated hydrothermally-formed banded iron formations in the Paleoproterozoic and Neoproterozoic (Barley et al. 1999; Pirajno 1992) is inferred to have occurred catastrophically on Day Two and in early Flood, respectively. The main iron oxide mineral in Superior-type and Rapitan-type BIF is hematite (Fe_2O_3) and this may have appeared blood-colored (Dickens and Snelling 2008).

2. Atmosphere growth

...when he made firm the skies above ... (Proverbs 8:28a ESV)

It has been claimed that there were rises in atmospheric oxygen in both the Paleoproterozoic and Neoproterozoic and that these were related to tectonism (Lee et al. 2016; Och and ShieldsZhou 2012) and magmatism (Ciborowski and Kerr 2016). These inferred episodes of increased atmospheric oxygen are called in the secular literature the "Great Oxygenation Event" (GOE) and the "Neoproterozoic Oxygenation Event" (NOE), respectively. It is suggested that God used the GOE on Day Two to prepare the Earth's atmosphere for life on Earth.

The "Great Oxygenation Event" has been indicated by sulfur isotopes and base metal sulfide deposits. Sediment-hosted copper deposits first appear in the Paleoproterozoic, and their formation is ascribed to the reaction of oxidized copper-bearing solutions with sulfide-containing solutions at the site of deposition (Farquhar et al. 2010). Oxygenation associated with volcanism has been described (Gaillard et al. 2011; Lyons et al. 2006; Macouin et al 2015). Metamorphic micro-diamonds containing high nitrogen concentrations within Paleoproterozoic magmatic rocks at Nunavut, Canada (Cartigny et al. 2004) may be evidence for volcanic degassing also enriching the Earth's atmosphere with nitrogen.

3. Radioactive mineral deposits and fluid flow

Uranium deposits related to sodium metasomatism have been described for both the Paleoproterozoic and the Pan-African Event, with thermal events able to circulate large volumes of fluids at high temperatures (550°-350°C) to produce metasomatism along crustal-scale structures (several tens to hundreds of kilometers) (Cuney 2010). Sodic metasomatism has been described from the Huronian Supergroup in particular (Fedo et al. 1997). Economic sources of unconformity-related uranium are associated with Paleoproterozoic basins such as Canada's Athabasca Basin (Hanly et al. 2006). Such unconformity on Archean basement rocks (Hanly et al. 2006) is consistent with this paper's model framework — expected erosional action of Day Two water movement on rocks formed on Day One. Early Paleoproterozoic gold-uranium conglomerates of Canada (Pirajno 1992), are inferred to have resulted from great tectonic upheavals of Day Two.

The intrusion of radioactive pegmatites in the Trans-Hudson Province of northern Saskatchewan is described as being associated with high-temperature hydrous melts during peak and late-metamorphic events and deformation-induced rapid melting of the Hudsonian Event (McKeogh et al. 2013; Stockwell 1964). Volatile saturation and metasomatic interaction with host rocks during ascent and emplacement of pegmatite is indicated by field relationships, mineralogical and textural evidence (McKeogh et al. 2013). Steep pegmatite structures in fractures would have enabled rapid heat loss and crystallization of the pegmatite (McKeogh et al. 2013; Snelling 2008). It is proposed that Day Two fluid flow processes be correlated with the development of northern Paleoproterozoic provinces along with North America's Hudsonian Event (Fig. 2).

4. Southeastern Proterozoic provinces' history

A. Huge crustal growth and high mountain building

And God said, "Let the waters under the heavens be gathered together into one place, and let the dry land appear." And it was so. God called the dry land Earth, and the waters that were gathered together he called Seas. And God saw that it was good (Genesis 1:9-10 ESV).

The northeast-trending Yavapai, Matzatzal, and Grenville provinces are considered to represent episodes of huge continental (granitoid) growth and crustal thickening as part of a great accretionary orogen (Condie et al. 2009; Spencer et al. 2015; Van Kranendonk and Kirkland 2013). The Grenvillian Event has been described as an orogeny, with the Grenville Province as the type region (Stockwell et al. 1970). The Grenvillian Event was preceded by, and was partly contemporaneous with, extensive rift systems that developed following the Elsonian Event (Fig. 2), which was a phase of dominantly granitoid intrusion (Frazier and Schwimmer 1987; Irving et al. 1976). The western Nain Province of northeast Canada is the type region for the Elsonian Event (Stockwell et al. 1970). Unlike the much larger region of the

Grenville Province, the Nain Province was unaffected by later metamorphism (Ashwal 2010) (Fig. 2). During the Grenvillian Event, northwest directed contraction at the southern margin of North America was accompanied by intracratonic extension and voluminous mafic magmatism including the Midcontinent Rift (Whitmeyer and Karlstrom 2007).

The Grenvillian Event has been described as "Perhaps the greatest orogenic event in Earth's history…" (Rainbird et al. 2012). Huge crustal thickening and mountain building are inferred. The peak in geochemical and isotopic signatures, identified in North America, Western Australia, and global data sets, indicates that the Grenvillian Event represents a unique episode in Earth's history. Indeed, paleogeographic reconstructions and tectonic analysis reveal that the Grenville orogen was perhaps the longest and widest in Earth history, spanning a quarter of the globe, or a distance of approximately 20,000 km long and as wide as 800 km, including a core zone several hundred kilometers wide (Van Kranendonk and Kirkland 2013).

B. Pre-Flood seas, land, and associated mineralisation

The Belt-Purcell Basin is of Mesoproterozoic age, similar to the Grenville Province. It is considered to be filled by marine and fluviatile sediments (Lydon 2007). This may be consistent with formation in a pre-flood sea created on Day Three. The most favourable environment for forming SEDEX deposits, such as that at Sullivan, is believed to be intracratonic rifts filled by marine sediments, with the deposits spatially associated with synsedimentary faults. (Lydon 2007). Thus, such ore deposits are considered to have formed associated with tectonism as the preFlood seas gathered on Day Three. Interaction with anoxic, cool, reduced deep seafloor sediments and more alkaline seawater enabled rapid precipitation of base metal sulfides on the pre-Flood seafloor (Dickens and Snelling 2015).

And the waters prevailed so mightily on the earth that all the high mountains under the whole heaven were covered. (Genesis 7:19 ESV).

Antediluvian high mountains may have been located at the site of Proterozoic belts adjacent to Archean provinces. The rocks of today's Grenville Province may represent the Flood-eroded roots (Dickens 2017b, Rainbird et al. 2012) of some pre-Flood high mountains (Genesis 7:19) formed on Day Three. The late Paleoproterozoic and Mesoproterozoic are considered to represent a time of growth and huge thickening of continental crust to form high mountains and, emergent land of a supercontinent. This is prior to the latter part of Day Three when seed-yielding plant life was created.

The voluminous granitoid plutonism of overall northeast-trending late Paleoproterozoic provinces (Yavapai and Mazatzal provinces) (Mints 2007; Whitmeyer and Karlstrom 2007) may be associated with an initial thickening of crust. This, then, is considered to have led to the emergence of land on Day Three, associated with the mountain-building of the Grenvillian Event. It is proposed that the formation of late Paleoproterozoic and Mesoproterozoic provinces of the southeast of the North American craton, along with North America's Grenvillian Event (Fig. 2), be correlated with processes in the earlier part of Day Three.

5. Neoproterozoic sedimentary cover history

A. Supercontinent breakup

by his knowledge, the deeps broke open... (Proverbs 3:20a ESV)

In the six hundredth year of Noah's life, in the second month, on the seventeenth day of the month, on that day all the fountains of the great deep burst forth, and the windows of the heavens were opened. (Genesis 7:11 ESV)

'Deeps were divided' and 'springs of the great deep burst forth' imply the rifting and fracturing of the Earth's crust. This is inferred to correlate with the Neoproterozoic breakup of a supercontinent (Dickens and Snelling 2008). The Pan-African Event is associated with the massive Neoproterozoic breakup of a supercontinent, including the Cordilleran and Appalachian margins of North America. In this article the Pan-African Event is inferred to have initiated with the breaking open of the fountains of the great deep.

It has been postulated that episodic rifting events at the margins of North America between 0.8 and about 0.6 Ga record the fragmentation of a Neoproterozoic supercontinent (Bond et al. 1984; Hoffman 1989). This is consistent with the initial breaking open of the crust with the bursting forth of the fountains of the great deep on a specific day, followed by further extension and then ocean formation. Subsidence histories of passive margins are a key indicator of worldwide continental extension and then ocean formation beginning at 0.6 Ga, and this has been described as the dismemberment of the supercontinent "by the most important single continental breakup event in geological history shortly before the dawn of the Cambrian." (Bond et al. 1984; Piper 2009). During the Pan-African Event, continental rifting cut across all earlier tectonic grain initiated Cordilleran sedimentation and gave birth to the EoPacific between North America and Asia (Carey 1976).

B. Enormous water flows and continental erosion

and rain fell upon the earth forty days and forty nights. (Genesis 7: 12 ESV).

and that by means of these the world that then existed was deluged with water and perished (2 Peter 3:6 ESV)

"and they were unaware until the flood came and swept them all away, so will be the coming of the Son of Man." (Matthew 24:39 ESV).

he who removes mountains, and they know it not, when he overturns them in his anger (Job 9:5 ESV)

Worldwide simultaneous (commencing on the same day) erupting of springs or fountains (including the eruption of volcanic material) was followed by global rainfall. Much of the water for the Noahic Flood may have come from various depths within the Earth. The mantle may be a major water source (Bergeron 1997). The Earth's mantle transition zone, between 410 to 660 km, could be a major repository for water due to the ability of the higher-pressure polymorphs of olivine-wadsleyite and ringwoodite to host up to ~2.5wt. % H_2O (Pearson et al. 2014).

An anti-creationist geologist said "Sedimentation in the past has often been very rapid indeed and very spasmodic. This may be called the Phenomenon of the Catastrophic Nature of the Stratigraphical Record." (Ager 1973). In North America, braided-type sheet sandstones are found in lower Neoproterozoic sequences whereas poorly sorted "glacial" deposits are found in mid-Neoproterozoic sequences. This is considered consistent with subaerial sheet flow when the Flood rain began and later mass flows on slopes as the marine transgression of the Flood progressed, respectively.

Zircon grains of Grenvillian age were recovered from lower Neoproterozoic sedimentary basins in northwestern Canada, more than 3000 km away from the nearest probable source in the Grenville Province on the other side of the continent. In addition, paleocurrents derived from cross-bedding in thick fluvial deposits in these basins indicate regionally consistent west-northwesterly transport (Rainbird 2008; Rainbird et al. 2012). The presence of mature quartz-arenite sandstone bodies and braided river systems in lower Neoproterozoic successions (Rainbird et al. 2012) is consistent with extremely high energy and relatively short duration (days and weeks) for global early Flood geological processes. Braided rather than meandering river systems are characteristic of Precambrian successions (Eriksson et al. 2013).

This is all evidence of enormous water flow systems as part of a gigantic erosional episode due to the Flood's tectonic activity and the impact of prolonged and geographically extensive rain on the land (Dickens 2017b). The Grenville Province is inferred to contain the roots of a deeply eroded pre-Flood high mountain chain (Dickens 2017b).

The stupendous rain of Noah's Flood would have caused immense continental erosion and would have led to the deposition of Neoproterozoic sediments (Dickens 2016; Dickens and Snelling 2015), including mass flow deposits. The major ^{87}Sr/^{86}Sr isotope ratio increase between 0.9 Ga and 0.5 Ga (Fig. 3) is consistent with the erosion of highly radiogenic continental crust (Dickens 2016; Dickens 2017b; Dickens and Snelling 2015; Meert and Powell 2001; Peters and Gaines 2012) during the Pan-African Event (Derry et al. 1994). Neoproterozoic mixtites have been interpreted as mass flows rather than as "glacials" (Schermerhorn 1974). The pre-Flood earth's surface was destroyed (Genesis 6:13) in the sense of being totally wiped away (eroded). Pre-Flood people were swept away (Matthew 24:39) in the immense water flows. The subsequent decline in the ^{87}Sr/^{86}Sr ratio in post-Cambrian strata may then be due to the presence of a globe-covering ocean so that the rain no longer directly impacted the land.

The 'Great Unconformity' (first named for its occurrence in the Grand Canyon, but traceable across North America) provides evidence for the erosion of continental crust as Flood rain impacted the land. Locations where Paleozoic sediments lie directly on the basement are considered to be where there was basement erosion only and not deposition of detritus eroded off the land (Dickens 2017b). While the Flood rain was eroding the land (and depositing the Chuar Group sediments), the sea elsewhere continued to rise. The land was then progressively covered by water leading to a global ocean (depositing Paleozoic sediments in the process).

In the Grand Canyon area, the Mesoproterozoic Unkar Group and associated mafic magmatism appear to record the presence of a basin within the continent that formed in response to northwest contraction and northeast extension related to the Grenvillian Event to the south. The overlying Neoproterozoic Chuar Group deposition indicates renewed continental rifting in an east-west sense, probably related to the early stages of supercontinent breakup (Timmons et al. 1999). I infer that along with the emergence of land on Day Three, a basin formed into which the Unkar Group was deposited. The Chuar Group formed later from detritus derived from the early Flood's erosion of the land (Dickens 2017b).

C. Mass flows

Mid-Neoproterozoic mixtites of the North American Cordillera have been interpreted as submarine mass flow deposits during Noah's Flood (Sigler and Wingerden 1998; Snelling 2009; Wingerden 2003). The Kingston Peak Formation in California is an example, with debris flows and catastrophic coarse clastic deposits having been interpreted (Sigler and Wingerden 1998). The final basin-forming episode of Proterozoic rocks involved a series of rift basins that once more preserve evidence of multiple "glaciations" and contain banded iron formations (Yeo 1981). The Rapitan-type iron formation of northwest Canada is associated with Mid-Neoproterozoic mixtites (so-called "glacial" sediments), debris flow deposits, turbidites and widespread continental flood basalts (Cox et al. 2016). Iron isotope values are consistent with oxidation of ferruginous waters during marine transgression and rift-related hydrothermal activity associated with the breakup of a supercontinent is inferred (Cox et al. 2016).

Accommodation space for many mixtites may have been provided by rifting. (Young 2013). Geochemical data indicates that Neoproterozoic iron formations result from mixing between a hydrothermal and detrital component, while rare earth element data indicates substantial interaction with seawater (Cox et al. 2013). The Rapitan's iron formation has been described as an "apparent sudden reappearance of iron formation after a ca. 1 billion year hiatus in the sedimentary record" (Cox et al. 2016). I infer that the Flood's fountains, which rifted the crust open, provided the hydrothermal component (Dickens and Snelling 2015) and that erosion of land caused by the Flood's rain (Dickens 2016) supplied the detrital component, including mass flow deposits (Dickens 2017a).

D. Subduction and plate tectonics

Have you ... walked in the recesses of the deep? (Job 38:16b ESV).

A trench marks the position at which a subducting slab begins to descend beneath another lithospheric slab (Stern 2002). High-pressure metamorphic/orogenic belts are restricted to rocks of "age" < 0.6 Ga, and it has been concluded that this indicates cold subduction along convergent margins (plate tectonics) (Brown 2007). It has been claimed that there are no proven Archean, Paleoproterozoic, Mesoproterozoic ophiolites or blueschists (Hamilton 2011). Correlation of paleomagnetic poles also provides evidence for the integrity of Precambrian continental crust between Archean and Neoproterozoic times (Piper 2015). Only by very late Neoproterozoic or early Paleozoic time do significant indicators of subduction (and thus "true" plate tectonics) appear, including complete ophiolites and high-pressure, low-temperature metamorphism (Stern 2005). Thus, modern-style plate tectonics may not have existed in the Archean to Mesoproterozoic. This is consistent with the idea of the growth of only one supercontinent by Day Three.

It is proposed that early Noah's Flood be correlated with the development of Neoproterozoic geology and the Pan-African Event. Processes involved are considered to include supercontinent breakup, enormous water flows, continental erosion, mass flows, and subduction.

CONCLUSIONS

I consider that God instigated heating events which provided the immense energy required for cataclysmic continent-scale geological processes during early Creation Week and in initiating Noah's Flood. I believe that Archean to Mesoproterozoic basement provinces formed as continental crust grew in the early Creation Week. This formed a supercontinent which by Day Three was thick enough to appear above the water. During the early Flood, massive tectonism, as well as immense continental erosion and enormous water flows, delivered detritus to form the Neoproterozoic sedimentary cover.

North America's Kenoran, Hudsonian, Grenvillian, and Pan-African thermal-tectonic events are respectively related to the Archean, Paleoproterozoic, Mesoproterozoic, and Neoproterozoic provinces' geology, along with the biblical record of Day One, Day Two, Day Three, and the early Noahic Flood.

I consider that water played a significant role in all the thermal-tectonic events. Day One, Day Two and the Noahic Flood have a global ocean. Initial upward vertical movement of hydrothermal water is believed to have occurred on Day Two and in the early Noahic Flood. Supposed "glacials" in the Paleoproterozoic and Neoproterozoic are then considered to have formed as mass flow deposits associated with downslope water movement on Day Two and early Noahic Flood times respectively. In addition, the banded iron formations of the Archean, Paleoproterozoic and Neoproterozoic are believed to have formed hydrothermally in association with volcanic activity.

Numerous examples have been mentioned where uniformitarianism does not apply in the Precambrian. These include clusters of radiometric "ages", lithologies with restricted ages (such as komatiite, banded iron formation, megacrystic anorthosites, ophiolites, and blueschists), tectonic style (such as permobile Archean versus linear Proterozoic belts, intracontinental deformation versus later plate tectonics, and mountain building) and effects of fluid flow (such as massive river systems, mass flows, and the 'Great Unconformity'). Many geological processes are known to not require deep time. This paper has referred to processes such as those relating to granite, banded iron formation, sedimentation, base metal sulfides and calcium carbonate precipitation.

The Flood drastically altered the world's topography. Nevertheless, inferences have been made regarding some specific locations of the pre-Flood world's geography in relation to today's North American Precambrian rocks:

Pre-Flood land	supercontinent, including North America
High mountains	eroded mountain roots in the Grenville Province
A pre-Flood sea	in the vicinity of the Belt-Purcell Basin
Fountains of the great deep	adjacent to western and eastern continental margins

This paper is intended to encourage further work to improve and refine our understanding of geological and geochemical processes in Precambrian provinces within a young Earth biblical framework. A possible application for further investigation is to examine the relevance of continental-scale Phanerozoic tectonic episodes and detrital zircon provenance studies to models of the Flood and post-Flood times.

SUPPLEMENTARY MATERIAL
Accelerated radioactive decay – evidence of young Helium diffusion age of zircons

There is powerful evidence that at least one episode of greatly accelerated radioactive decay has occurred.
When uranium decays to lead, a by-product is the formation of helium, a very light, inert gas that readily diffuses from rock. In 1982, Robert Gentry found

remarkably high retentions of nuclear-decay-generated helium (He) in zircon crystals recovered from a borehole in Precambrian granitic rock at Fenton Hill, New Mexico. The zircons were mainly within biotite.

In 2001 the RATE group (Radio activity and the Age of The Earth) contracted a world-class laboratory on helium diffusion from minerals to measure the rate of helium diffusion out of the zircons. The measured rates emphatically confirmed a numerical prediction RATE made based on the reported retentions and young age.

"Combining rates and retentions gave a He diffusion age of 6000±2000 (1σ) years. This contradicted the uniformitarian age of 1.5 billion years based on nuclear decay products in the same zircons. This data strongly supported the hypothesis of episodes of highly accelerated nuclear decay occurring thousands of years ago. Such accelerations shrink the radioisotopic "billions of years" down to the 6000-year timescale of the Bible." (Humphreys 2005).

RATE's 6,000-year helium age of the earth supported by Argon diffusion data

Analysis of argon retention data was made from the same borehole that provided the RATE group with helium retention data. The deepest part (4.56 km) of the borehole was hot enough to cause more than a 20% loss of radioactivity-generated argon-40 from feldspar in the granitic basement rock, conventionally dated to be 1.5 Ga old. Data and equations from the 1986 article show that at the present temperature (313°C) at that depth, it would take only 5,100 (+3,800/- 2,100) years for the feldspar to lose that much argon. This supports the 6,000 (± 2,000) year helium diffusion age that RATE found for zircons in the same borehole (Humphreys 2011).

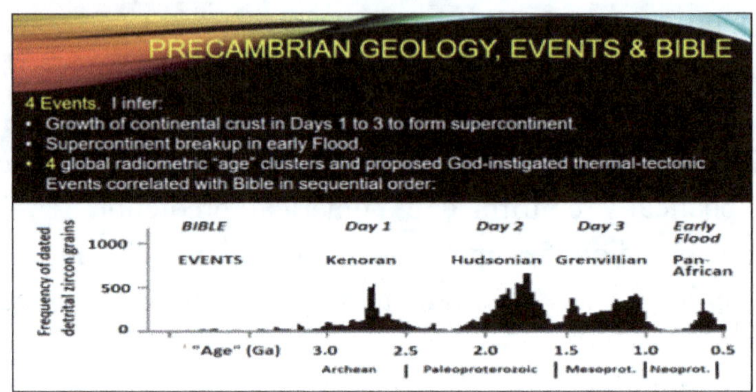

1. Archean – oldest rocks & granitoid continental crust forms underwater – Day One.

2. Paleoproterozoic rifting, hydrothermal metasomatism, oxygenation, and mass flows – consistent with Day Two water movement.

3. Mesoproterozoic evidence of huge thickening of continental crust, consistent with appearance of land to appear above water on Day Three.

4. Rifting, erosion of land by Flood's rain, enormous water flows – evidence of Neoproterozoic sedimentary cover.
   Corollary is that underlying Archean to Mesoproterozoic basement rocks can be correlated with early Creation Week.

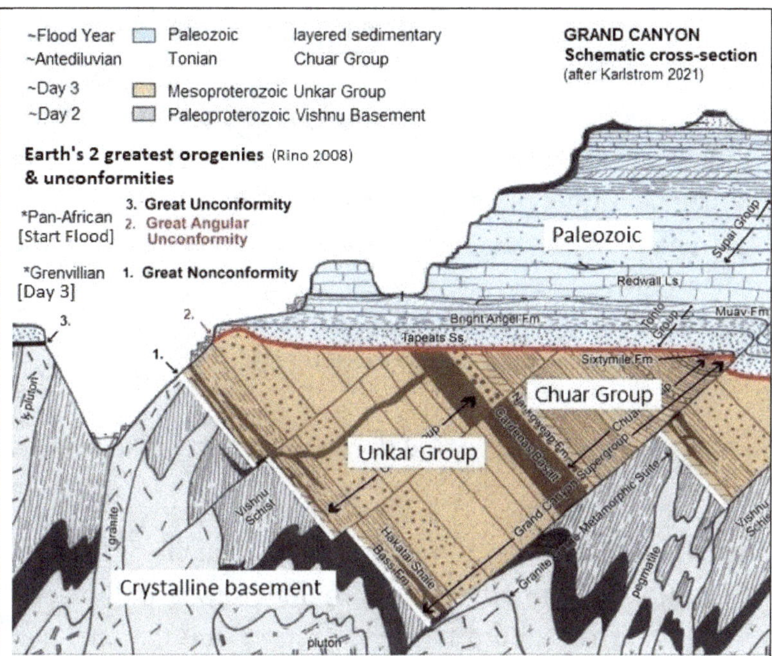

Schematic section with a proposed correlation of Grand Canyon strata with the Bible

Earliest Earth not hellish

"Hadean Eon" is an informal division of Precambrian occurring between about 4.6 billion and about 4.0 billion years ago radiometric time. The name of the interval is a reference to Hades, a Greek translation of the Hebrew word for hell. In the absence of direct evidence of Hadean rocks, scientists came up with the idea of a very hot (magma ocean) early Earth (Hadean) arising out of the belief in the nebular hypothesis (whereby a swirling cloud of hot dust and gas accreted to form the planets and moons of our solar system).

The world's oldest minerals are believed to have been found at Jack Hills, Western Australia. These ancient zircons in metasediments indicate liquid water was present in the early Earth. Analysis suggested that the early Earth, instead of being a boiling ocean of magma, was cool enough to have water.

https://earthobservatory.nasa.gov/features/Zircon

Day One: … *the face of the deep. …the face of the waters.* (Genesis 1:2)

The Earth was formed *to be inhabited* (Isaiah 45:18).
In addition, there are some retrograde orbits in the solar system. This doesn't make sense in the nebular hypothesis. For example, Jupiter has a band of outer moons which go around the opposite way (retrograde orbits) to its inner moons (prograde orbits). I think the Creator has a sense of humour! (-;

B. BANDED IRON FORMATIONS FORMED FAST

Source: Dickens, H. 2017. Banded Iron Formations Formed Rapidly. *Journal of Creation* 31 (2): 14–16. Invited paper.

HIGHLIGHTS

Non-uniformitarian occurrence of BIFs: although BIFs are widespread geographically in Precambrian provinces, they have a limited occurrence in time, being principally found in Archean and Paleoproterozoic 'age' provinces, with some smaller occurrences in Neoproterozoic 'age' provinces. BIFs are absent from Mesoproterozoic 'age' provinces.

Earlier models of BIF formation invoked the slow deposition of annual micro-laminations (chemical varves) over millions of years. However, modern evidence indicates that BIFs formed rapidly in deep water by catastrophic precipitation from volcanic and associated silica-rich and iron-rich hydrothermal fluids. Laboratory studies show that colloidal solutions rapidly precipitate into regular and ordered bands.

This Young Earth model correlates BIFs with the Bible's two occasions of globe-covering ocean—early Precambrian BIFs forming in the early Creation Week and late Precambrian BIFs forming in the initial phase of Noah's Flood.

Early Creation Week

- Earth had its first global ocean (the deep) on Days 1 & 2, before the gathering of waters and appearance of land on Day 3.

- It is inferred that the earlier Precambrian iron formations (Algoma and Superior-types) formed early in the Creation Week by catastrophic pouring out of volcanic and associated banded iron formations.

- In Genesis 1:2, the Earth would have appeared from space like a relatively smooth, formless, watery ball, without obvious features or landmarks such as mountains protruding above the water.

Initial Noah's Flood

- The second and only other global ocean was during the peak of Noah's Flood.

- Rapitan-type iron formations are interbedded with Neoproterozoic mixtites (detrital) and these mixtites are considered to represent mass flows (not glacials) early in Noah's Flood.

- Geochemical data indicate that Neoproterozoic iron formations resulted from mixing between a hydrothermal and detrital component, while rare earth element data indicate substantial interaction with seawater.

  - Hydrothermal component provided by Flood's fountains, that rifted open the supercontinent.

> - Detrital component provided by erosion of land caused by the Flood's rain.
>
> BIFs are clear-cut examples of non-uniformitarianism in the Earth's history:
>
> - Modern analogues are unknown.
>
> - BIFs are restricted in time to the Archean, Paleoproterozoic and Neoproterozoic.

Features of BIFs

A banded iron formation (BIF) is a sedimentary rock characterized by alternating bands of iron oxide and chert. Individual bands may vary in thickness from less than a millimetre to metres, and the overall succession of bands may be hundreds of metres thick. The principal iron minerals are the iron oxides hematite and magnetite (Zientek and Orris 2005). BIFs have a chemical composition unlike any sedimentary material being deposited in significant quantities on the modern Earth (Trendall 1990).

BIFs are economically important since over 95% of iron resources of the world occur in BIFs (Gross 1996). They are the principal source of iron for the global steel industry. BIFs have been found on all continents except Antarctica (Zientek and Orris 2005). Giant (100,000 billion tons or more) BIFs are located in South Africa, Australia, Brazil, Russia and Canada. Smaller but still significant BIFs are found in many other places including in the USA, India, Ukraine, and China (Fig. 1) (Bekker et al. 2010).

Although BIFs are widespread geographically in Precambrian provinces, they have a limited occurrence in time. They are principally found in Archean and Paleoproterozoic 'age' provinces (Groves et al. 2005), with a few smaller occurrences in Neoproterozoic 'age' provinces (Reddy and Evans 2009). BIFs are absent from Mesoproterozoic 'age' provinces (Fig. 2) (Klein 2005).

The Algoma, Superior, and Rapitan types are the three main types of BIFs and are named after locations in Canada (Stockwell et al. 1970). Algoma-type BIFs are chiefly found in volcano-sedimentary sequences of Archean greenstone belts. These BIFs are stratigraphically linked to or interlayered with submarine-emplaced volcanic rocks in greenstone belts and, in some cases, with volcanogenic massive sulfide (VMS) deposits (Bekker et al. 2010). Typical Algoma-type iron formations rarely extend for more than 10 km along strike and are less than 50 m thick. Algoma-type and Superior-type iron formations are similar in mineralogy (Bekker et al. 2010).

Superior-type deposits are by far the most economically important type of BIFs globally and are situated in relatively undeformed continental margin sedimentary basins around unconformable contacts on granite-greenstone terrains around the Archean/Proterozoic boundary (Lascelles 2013). These BIFs are large in size (over 100 km in lateral extent and more than 100 m in thickness) (Evans et al. 2013). (Trendall 1990). The Paleoproterozoic Hamersley Basin in Western Australia contains one of the world's largest areas of BIFs. The basin itself outcrops over an area of about 100,000 km^2. The chemical and lateral stratigraphic continuity of these BIFs on a variety of scales is quite extraordinary. Microbands (approximately 1 mm thick) can be traced for hundreds of kilometres. In addition, the broad alternation and concordance of BIFs with other sedimentary rocks (mainly shale and carbonate) and volcanics (including dolerite and rhyolite) can be easily recognised over the whole area of the outcrop (Trendall 1990).

Rapitan-type iron formations are interbedded with what is commonly interpreted in the mainstream literature as Neoproterozoic 'glacials' (Klein 2005). These iron formations are found in extensional grabens associated with the initial breakup of the Rodinia supercontinent (Baldwin et al. 2012) and are commonly found in association with mafic volcanics (Cox et al. 2013).

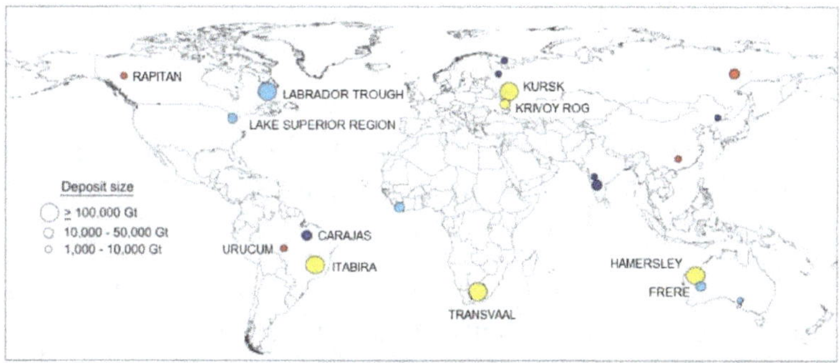

Figure 1. Global occurrence and size of large Precambrian BIFs. Gt = 109 tons or billion tons. (from Bekker et al. 2010).

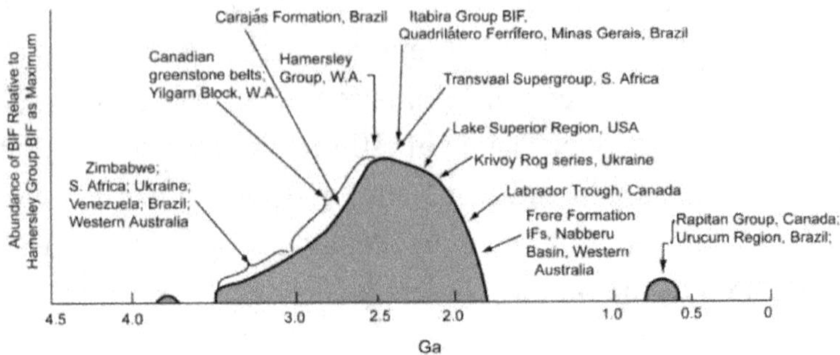

Figure 2. Schematic diagram indicating the relative volume of BIFs over time. A number of the major BIFs or major BIF regions are shown. Refer to Figure 1 for many of their locations. Estimated abundances are relative to the Hamersley Group BIF volume, which is taken as a maximum. Ga = billion years ago radiometric time. (Klein 2005).

BIF deposition

Earlier models of BIF formation invoked the slow deposition of annual micro-laminations (chemical varves) over millions of years (Garrels 1987). However, modern interpretations consider BIFs as deep-sea sediments with iron and silica sourced from reactions between circulating seawater and hot mafic to ultramafic rocks as hydrothermal systems vented onto the sea floor. Hot acidic hydrothermal fluids would *immediately* precipitate colloidal particles of iron hydroxide and iron silicates on quenching by cold neutral seawater. Episodic and rapid turbidity and density currents deposition may have lasted only a few hours to days (Lascelles 2013)! Laboratory studies show that colloidal solutions rapidly precipitate into regular and ordered bands (George and Varghese 2005).

Laboratory studies also show that the rate of chemical reactions increases exponentially with temperature (Loewenthal et al. 1993). This explains why various mineral assemblages and petroleum can form rapidly under hydrothermal conditions. High-temperature fluids can also extract and transport large quantities of silica and iron from mafic igneous rocks (Lascelles 2013).

Geochronologic studies emphasize the episodic deposition of giant early Precambrian iron formations since their formation is coeval with and genetically linked to time periods when large igneous provinces (LIPs) were emplaced (Bekker et al. 2010). Neoproterozoic BIFs are also associated with periods of intense magmatic activity (Bekker et al. 2010).

Evidence has been put forward (Barley et al. 1997) that the thickest and most extensive Paleoproterozoic BIFs in Hamersley Basin formed along with pulses of intense magmatism (including the emplacement of a large igneous province comprising more than 30,000 km^3 of volcanic rocks) driving a period of enhanced submarine hydrothermal activity. The emplacement of such an enormous volume of volcanic rocks is beyond anything happening in today's world (for example, the famous Mt St Helens on 18 May 1980 erupted only 1.2 km^3 (0.3 mi^3) of ash (USGS 1987). The description of high energy processes, such as huge and intense volcanic activity along with enhanced hydrothermal activity, is in stark contrast to the description in the same paper of the rate of BIF deposition being compared with the gentle rate of the settling of fine sedimentary particles in the modern open ocean.

A YEC framework for BIFs

The chemical makeup, common fine lamination, and the lack of detrital components in most BIFs suggest that they resulted from deposition as chemical sediments below wave base in the deeper anoxic parts of ocean basins (Klein 2005). The rare-earth element profiles of almost all BIFs, with generally pronounced positive Europium anomalies, indicate that deep ocean hydrothermal activity admixed with sea water was the source for the precipitation of the iron and silica (Klein 2005).

I was there when he set the heavens in place when he marked out the horizon on the face of the deep. (Proverbs 8:27 NIV).

Now the earth was formless and empty, darkness was over the surface of the deep, and the Spirit of God was hovering over the waters. (Genesis 1:2 NIV)

The Earth had its first global ocean (the deep) on Days 1 and 2, before the gathering of waters and appearance of land on Day 3 (Genesis 1:2–10). In Genesis 1:2, the Earth would have appeared from space like a relatively smooth, formless, watery ball, without obvious features or landmarks such as mountains protruding above the water (Dickens and Snelling 2015).

Or who shut in the sea with doors when it burst out from the womb (Job 38:8 ESV)

A common iron oxide mineral in BIFs is hematite (Fe_2O_3), which may have appeared blood-coloured as if from the womb (Dickens and Snelling 2015). I consider that the earlier Precambrian iron formations (Algoma and Superior-types) formed early in the Creation Week by catastrophic pouring out of volcanics and associated banded iron formations (Dickens and Snelling 2015).

The second and only other global ocean was during the peak of Noah's Flood (Genesis 7:19– 20). Rapitan-type iron formations are interbedded with Neoproterozoic mixtites, and these mixtites are considered to represent mass flows that occurred early in Noah's Flood (Dickens and Snelling 2015). Geochemical data indicates that Neoproterozoic iron formations result from mixing between a hydrothermal and detrital component, while rare earth element data indicates substantial interaction with seawater (Cox et al. 2013). I infer that the Flood's fountains, which rifted the crust open, would have provided the hydrothermal component (Dickens and Snelling 2015), and erosion of land caused by the Flood's rain (Dickens 2016) would have supplied the detrital component.

Conclusions

Modern evidence (Lascelles 2013) indicates that BIFs formed rapidly in deep water by catastrophic precipitation from volcanic and associated silica-rich and iron-rich hydrothermal fluids. This is consistent with my Young Earth model correlation of BIFs with the Bible's two occasions of globe-covering ocean—early Precambrian BIFs forming in the early Creation Week and late Precambrian BIFs forming in the initial phase of Noah's Flood (Dickens and Snelling 2008). BIFs are clear-cut examples of non-uniformitarianism in the Earth's history (Groves et al; 2005; Reddy and Evans 2009) modern analogues are unknown, and BIFs are restricted in time to the Archean, Paleoproterozoic, and Neoproterozoic.

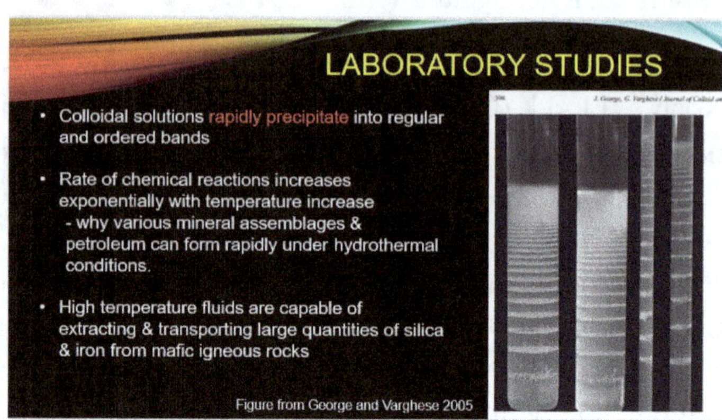

Laboratory studies illustrate rapid precipitation of banding

Neither uniformitarianism nor naturalism

Source: Dickens, H. 2017. Reply to Letter to the Editor. Regarding Banded Iron Formation. *Journal of Creation* 31(3):56-58.

BIF and Flood onset are defined by more than just radiometric age

The three types of BIF referred to in the article are described in terms of their field relationships and lithology and so can be recognized in the field independent of radiometric age dating. However, there are consistent trends, such as Rapitan BIFs being younger in age than Algoma and Superior-type BIFs.

Relative radiometric age dating is consistent with relative age indicated by field stratigraphic relationships. In many locations worldwide, Neoproterozoic sedimentary strata can be found overlying older Precambrian crystalline basements. Such geology can be correlated, respectively, with early Flood and early Creation Week.

I do not define the onset of the Flood on radiometric dates independently of other evidence. In numerous cases, the order of radiometric dates, lithologies, and chemical and other isotopic trends go together consistently.

I infer that

- The erosion of land associated with the Flood's enormous rain can be correlated with Neoproterozoic geology (including mixtites interpreted as mass flows rather than as "glacials" and that Sr isotope trends indicate continental erosion (Peters and Gaines 2012). The corollary of this is that Archean to Mesoproterozoic crystalline basement rocks can be correlated with early Creation Week.

- The pre-Flood Earth surface was destroyed (Genesis 6:13) in the sense of being totally wiped away (Matthew 24:39).

Global processes involved in early Creation Week should be considered. There is no need to lump so much geology into the Flood and not allow that some rocks may have formed during Creation Week. Similarly, rocks consistent with the early Flood erosion of land due to the rain should not be discounted.

The baby and the bathwater

I am not defining and applying specific uniformitarian geologic time "Periods" *ad hoc* to biblical history. There are patterns and order in radiometric dates that can be useful in a relative rather than absolute time sense.

Recognising literal sequences of observable, mappable rock units is not tantamount to accepting uniformitarianism and naturalism.

I consider that much valuable work has already been done in mapping lithological sequences around the globe. There is a need to keep the baby and throw out the bath water:

- The baby is the *observable*, mappable, correlatable order of stratigraphic successions with their characteristic fossils, lithologies, chemical signatures, and consistent pattern and order of isotopic ratios.

- The bathwater is the *interpreted* long ages and molecules-to-man evolution.

Order in the rock record has been put there by God during His sequence of acts recorded in Genesis. In stratigraphy, there are significant patterns that can be related to God's creative work in designing the earth as man's home. As with many scientific datasets, there may be some anomalous values. However, not using relative patterns in radiometric dates that reflect stratigraphic order may be considered "throwing the baby out with the bathwater." The stratigraphic and isotopic order in the rocks is important evidence.

Neither uniformitarianism nor naturalism

The work by Dickens and Snelling (2008) on the Precambrian was definitely not uniformitarian in terms of the rapidity of processes, including radiometric decay. A number of tectonic events (e.g., global rifting) and lithologic types (e.g., komatiites and BIFs) described and inferred environments (global oceans in early Creation

Week and early Flood) are not uniformitarian and do not occur today.

Global Precambrian rock radiometric dates show profound episodicity (episodicity is not uniformitarian!). (O'Neill et al. 2013). The deformation age distribution of greenstone belts (most abundant at 2.70, 1.85, 1.05, and 0.60 Ga) is broadly similar to the age distribution of Precambrian granites and detrital zircons (Bradley 2011). Heating events can reset radiometric dates to lower values (Harley et al. 2007; Nyquist et al. 1991). There are regional patterns in radiometric dates that can be related to different Precambrian geological provinces.

Naturalism excludes the Bible. When God created, He brought order to the universe even in atoms and continents, for God is not the author of confusion (1 Corinthians 14:33). Thus, there should be harmony between God's Word and His Creation. Despite the complexity, we should not discount the order in observable, mappable Precambrian geology and associated measurable isotopic and chemical trends. Correlating such trends and patterns with God's Word is not naturalism.

C. TRANSCONTINENTAL SEDIMENT TRANSPORT

Source: Dickens, H. 2017. Colossal Water Flows During Early Creation Week and Early Flood. *Answers Research Journal* 10:221–235.

HIGHLIGHTS

The Grenvillian and Pan-African tectonic Events have been claimed to be the largest such events in the earth's geological history, based on detrital zircon age data derived from river sands.

North America's Proterozoic geology provides evidence for enormous erosion and the formation of colossal water flow systems, even spanning the continent. It is proposed that these processes be correlated with the early Creation Week and the early Flood.

The Grenvillian thermal-tectonic Event, associated with huge Mesoproterozoic crustal thickening, is inferred to correlate with Day Three emergence of land and high mountain-building. Some synorogenic Mesoproterozoic sediments would also have formed since the emergence of land on Day Three would have fostered water flow, erosion, and transport of detritus downslope towards the sea.

It is important that the enormous erosion of land aspect of the Flood be recognized (including the Great Unconformity) and not just the marine transgression aspect of the Flood. Continental denudation, enhanced chemical weathering and changes in global ocean chemistry are indicated by numerous geochemical signatures associated with the Great Unconformity.

The Pan-African thermal-tectonic Event is consistent with an enormous erosional and depositional regime expected in the early stages of the Flood of Noah. It has been postulated that episodic rifting events at the margins of North America between 0.8 Ga and about 0.6 Ga record the fragmentation of the Neoproterozoic supercontinent. This is consistent with the initial breaking open of the crust with the bursting forth of the fountains of the great deep on a specific day, followed by rifting.

The observed increase in Neoproterozoic strontium isotope ratios $^{87}Sr/^{86}Sr$ has been explained by accelerated rates of erosion. The subsequent decline in $^{87}Sr/^{86}Sr$ ratio in post-Cambrian strata is inferred due to the presence of a globe-covering ocean so that the rain no longer directly impacted the land. The Flood's rain caused enormous erosion of the land, and at the same time, the sea level rose until, eventually, all of the earth's land was covered. It is considered that immense Neoproterozoic erosion of the land and related abrasion was not favorable for the preservation of fossils, including land vertebrate fossils. It was only once the sea transgressed the land that marine macrofossils could be formed and preserved.

Today's North American Grenville Province is considered the roots of a high mountain chain built on Day Three of Creation Week and subsequently deeply eroded during Noah's Flood.

Braided-type deposits are found in the earlier Neoproterozoic sequences, whereas "glacial" deposits are found in the mid-Neoproterozoic (Cryogenian) sequences. This is considered consistent with subaerial sheet flow when the Flood rain began, and later mass flows on slopes as the marine transgression of the Flood progressed, respectively.

Abstract

North America's Proterozoic geology provides evidence for enormous erosion and the formation of extensive water flow systems, even spanning the continent. It is proposed that these processes may be correlated with the early Creation Week and early Flood.

The emergence of land on Day Three implies the formation of a topographic gradient from land to the sea and associated water movement on land and undersea, with immense runoff from the newly emergent land. This article infers that what is now southeastern North America became a region of pre-Flood mountains.

Immediate pre-Flood topography was drastically changed by the erosional effect of the Flood's prolonged and globally extensive rain. Even high mountains were not spared. This article infers that today's Grenville, Mazatzal, and Yavapai provinces in southeastern North America represent the roots of mountains eroded in the Flood.

Keywords: Proterozoic, North America, tectonism, erosion, water flows, sedimentation, Creation Week, Flood, Grenville, zircon

Introduction

The case has been put that a number of North American Proterozoic sedimentary sequences formed when enormous water flow systems ensued as major tectonic events took place in areas to the east of the sedimentary basins (Rainbird, Cawood, and Gehrels 2012). The Grenvillian and Pan-African tectonic Events have been claimed to be the largest such events in the earth's geological history, based on detrital zircon age data derived from river sands (Rino et al. 2008). These continent-scale events may be correlated with the Bible.

Young-earth creationist (YEC) geoscience research is needed to make continent-scale sedimentary models of early Creation Week and early Flood more tangible, better identify provinces that were eroded even on a continent-scale, and infer first-order current directions resulting from such enormous water flows.

The Grenvillian Event is associated in secular literature with the Mesoproterozoic thickening of continental crust. In striking contrast to most of North America's older Proterozoic provinces, the lithosphere of southeastern North America has an overall northeast-southwest regional trend. This includes the Late Paleoproterozoic Yavapai and Mazatzal provinces, as well as the Mesoproterozoic Grenville province. It is proposed that the formation of these provinces, along with North America's Grenvillian Event, be correlated with processes in the earlier part of Day Three. The Grenvillian Event is inferred to correlate with the building of high mountains and the emergence of land on Day Three of Creation Week (Snelling 2009). It is inferred that in addition to the formation of crystalline rocks on Day Three, some synorogenic Mesoproterozoic sediments also formed since the emergence of land on Day Three would have fostered water flow, erosion, and transport of detritus downslope towards the sea.

In secular literature, the Pan-African Event is associated with the Neoproterozoic rifting of the Rodinian supercontinent, including the Cordilleran and Appalachian margins of North America. In this article, the Pan-African Event is inferred to have initiated the breaking open of the fountains of the great deep. Catastrophic plate tectonics have been used for a global Noahic Flood model of Earth history (Austin et al. 1994).

The stupendous rain of Noah's Flood would have triggered immense erosion of all the pre-Flood land and the consequent deposition of huge volumes of sediment. Grenvillian-age detrital zircons and early Neoproterozoic sandstone cross-bedding together provide evidence that mountain belts in the southeastern part of the North American continent contributed sedimentary detritus to enormous surface water flow systems that crossed to the west side of the North American continent, a distance of 3000 km (Rainbird, Cawood, and Gehrels 2012). Paleocurrents derived from cross-bedding in thick fluvial deposits in basins indicate regionally consistent west-northwesterly transport (Rainbird, Cawood, and Gehrels

2012). Along with tremendous erosion of subaerial continental landmasses, torrential rain would have caused huge submarine mass flows, especially on continental margins (Sigler and Wingerden 1998; Snelling 2009; Wingerden 2003) commonly interpreted as mid-Neoproterozoic (Cryogenian) "glacials".

In this paper, radiometric "ages" are used in a relative sense, not absolute time. Ga refers to the radiometric "age" of billions of years ago.

1. Geology Today

1.1 Precambrian crystalline basement provinces

Significant basement rock provinces and their approximate radiometric ages in North America include the southeastern Grenville (1.55–1.0 Ga), Yavapai (1.7–1.68 Ga), and Mazatzal (1.65–1.6 Ga) provinces, together with the adjacent more northern Trans-Hudson (1.9–1.8 Ga) and Superior (> 2.5 Ga) provinces (Fig. 1).

In striking contrast to most of North America's older Paleoproterozoic and Archean provinces, the lithosphere of southeastern North America has an overall northeast-southwest regional trend. This includes the Late Paleoproterozoic Yavapai and Mazatzal provinces, as well as the Mesoproterozoic Grenville Province. These northeast-trending provinces are characterized by voluminous granitoid plutonism (Mints 2015; Whitmeyer and Karlstrom 2007).

The Grenville Province is characterized by extremely high grades of metamorphism (amphibolite and granulite facies) in both basement terranes and supracrustal rocks of the Grenville Supergroup. Rock types are ensialic with quartzofeldspathic gneisses, migmatites, and metasediments, including marble (Davidson 1995; Jamieson et al. 2011). The Grenville Province commonly has moderate to high-grade metamorphic rocks outcropping at the surface today. In the type area for the Grenville Province (eastern Canada and the State of New York), most of its rocks are greatly deformed and consist of upper amphibolite to granulite facies metamorphic minerals (Gower, Kamo, and Krogh 2008).

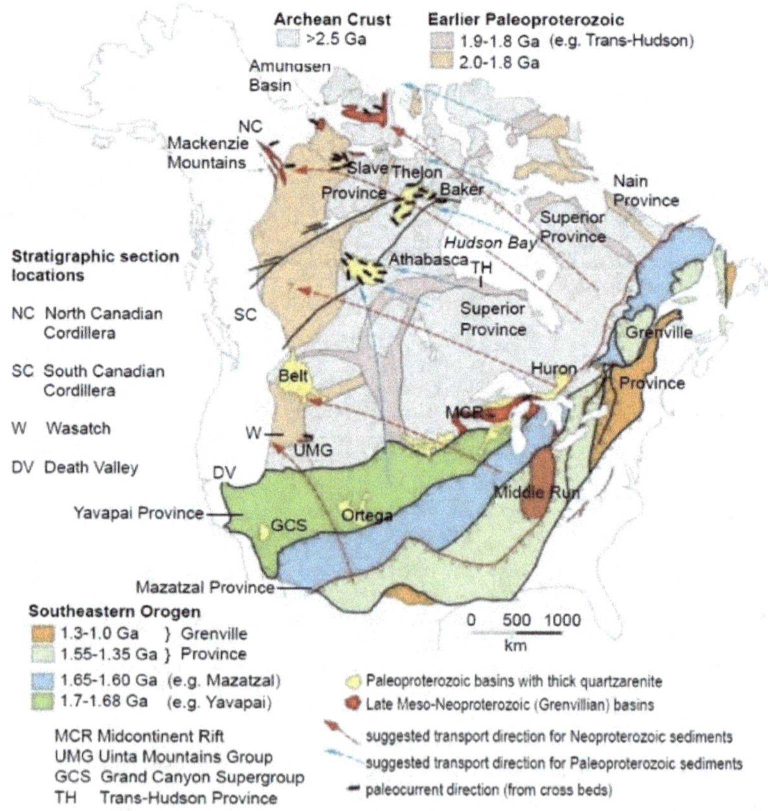

Figure 1. Precambrian geological map of North America showing location of key Proterozoic basins and southeastern orogenic provinces. The Grenville Province has been interpreted as the roots of a deeply eroded mountain chain that formed from about 1.2 to 1.0 Ga during multi-stage continental growth. The proximal part of the Grenvillian depositional system includes deposits located in the Middle Run Basin and the Midcontinent Rift.

- Dashed red arrows illustrate proposed transport directions of huge water flow systems that crossed the continent, spreading northwesterly. Basement provinces in the southeastern part of the continent are inferred to have contributed sedimentary detritus to form the thick Neoproterozoic sandstone successions preserved in basins of western North America (for example, Amundsen Basin, Mackenzie Mountains, Uinta Mountains Group [UMG], and Grand Canyon Supergroup [GCS]). Detrital zircon grains that are commonly found there yield "ages" that are characteristic of the Grenville Province, several thousand kilometers away, on the other side of the continent.

- Dashed blue arrows show the suggested transport direction of Paleoproterozoic sediments, shed from the Yapavai and Trans-Hudson provinces (shown in green and pink, respectively, on the map) to thick sandstone successions of Paleoproterozoic basins such as the Athabasca and Thelon.

- Black arrows indicate paleocurrent directions interpreted from cross-bedding in thick fluvial deposits in

Proterozoic basins in northern Canada. Regionally consistent west-northwesterly transport is indicated.

The location of stratigraphic sections on the western margin of North America (Fig. 3) is shown.

(Figure modified from Rainbird, Cawood, and Gehrels 2012)

There is a Grenvillian age peak in geochemical and isotopic signatures, identified in North America, Western Australia, and global data sets. It spans a quarter of the globe, or approximately 20,000 km long and as wide as 800 km, including a core zone several hundred kilometers wide (Van Kranendonk and Kirkland 2013).

The Trans-Hudson Province consists of low metamorphic-grade sedimentary-volcanic complexes (Mints 2007). It is the largest and best exposed Paleoproterozoic belt in North America (Zhao et al. 2002). This belt has Archean provinces on both sides.

Archean provinces include the Superior Province, the world's largest such province. These provinces essentially consist of high metamorphic-grade granulite-gneiss terranes and low-grade granite-greenstone terranes (Mints 2007) (Fig. 1).

1.2 Earlier Proterozoic sedimentary sequences

Western North America

The Mesoproterozoic Unkar Group of the southwestern United States consists of limestone, shale, quartzite, sandstone, and lavas (Timmons et al. 2001). All units within the Unkar Group contain a complex distribution of Paleoproterozoic zircons, typically between 1.8 and 1.6 Ga, with large age peaks at ca. 1.45 Ga and young populations between 1.3 and 1.2 Ga (Mulder et al. 2017). Mudstone petrology studies and interbedded sandstone detrital zircon geochronology indicate that Unkar mudstones were derived largely from the southeastern orogenic region of North America (including the Grenville Province of southwest Texas and the adjacent Yavapai-Mazatzal terranes) (Bloch et al. 2006).

The Mesoproterozoic Belt-Purcell Basin contains an 18- to 20-km-thick sedimentary succession dominated by fine-grained terrigenous facies, including marine turbidites with tholeiitic sills (Lydon 2007). The lower part of the succession contains abundant distinctive 1.6–1.5 Ga detrital zircon populations not characteristic of southeast North America. Upper Belt-Purcell strata contain ca. 1.73 Ga detrital zircon age populations that match the signature of metasedimentary rocks of the Yavapai Province to the south and southeast (Jones, Daniel, and Doe 2015).

Northern Canada

The widespread, relatively flat-lying upper parts of the Paleoproterozoic Thelon and Athabasca basin successions in northern Canada are dominated by hematite-stained quartz arenites (Palmer, Kyser, and Hiatt 2004). The middle and upper sequences of the Thelon Basin contain Archean-age detrital zircons. A 3.4 Ga zircon population cannot be correlated to the immediately surrounding basement (Palmer, Kyser, and Hiatt 2004).

The Paleoproterozoic Burnside River Formation, of the Kilohigok Basin in Arctic Canada is dominated by sandstone and overlies Archean granite-greenstone basement rocks of the Slave Province (Ielpi et al. 2015).

1.3 Neoproterozoic sedimentary sequences

Neoproterozoic sedimentary cover is found in both the western (Cordilleran) and eastern (Appalachian) margins of North America, as well as cratonic sequences (Frazier and Schwimmer 1987). These Neoproterozoic deposits are mainly immature clastic sediments with lesser volcanic rocks, and include mixtites, which are commonly interpreted to be "glacial" (Hoffman 1989).

Western North America

Northwestern Canada's Amundsen Basin and Mackenzie Mountain areas contain Grenvillian age zircons (Rainbird et al. 1997; Rainbird and Young 2009). Detrital zircon geochronology of the Amundsen Basin's Shaler Supergroup enables potential correlation with strata from the Ogilvie and Mackenzie platforms (Rainbird, Jefferson, and Young 1996; Rainbird et al. 1997). The Nelson Head Formation within the Shaler Supergroup has cross-bedded sandstone (Fig. 2).

Figure 2. Distant western end of the Grenvillian river system represented by braided-type deposits of the Shaler Supergroup, Amundsen Basin, Canada. The exposed section has a thickness of about 35 m (from Ielpi and Rainbird 2016a). The Shaler Supergroup can be correlated with other earlier Neoproterozoic sequences, such as the Little Dahl/ Fifteenmile Group of the North Canadian Cordillera (Macdonald et al. 2010) (Fig. 3).

Regional lithostratigraphic correlation of early Neoproterozoic Sequence B and Fifteen Mile Group (Fig. 3) on the northwest margin of North America includes a laterally continuous, 0.5–2 km thick, quartz arenite marker. The vast majority (85%) of the zircons in this sequence are of Mesoproterozoic age, with a high fraction clustering between 1.25–1 Ga, and this closely matches the age of synorogenic intrusions of the Grenville Province (Rainbird et al. 1997).

Grenville-age detrital zircon comprises a significant proportion of most sedimentary successions in western North America, including Neoproterozoic successions of southwestern USA (Rainbird, Cawood, and Gehrels 2012). In the southwestern United States, the Grand Canyon Supergroup, in effect, represents a "Time gap of ~1.2 Ga" in the 'Great Unconformity' between the Paleozoic (~0.5 Ga sandstone) and the Paleoproterozoic basement (including ~1.75 Ga gneiss) (Timmons, Karlstrom, and Dehler 1999). The Grand Canyon Supergroup essentially consists of the Neoproterozoic Chuar Group and the underlying Mesoproterozoic Unkar Group sedimentary sequences (Timmons et al. 2001).

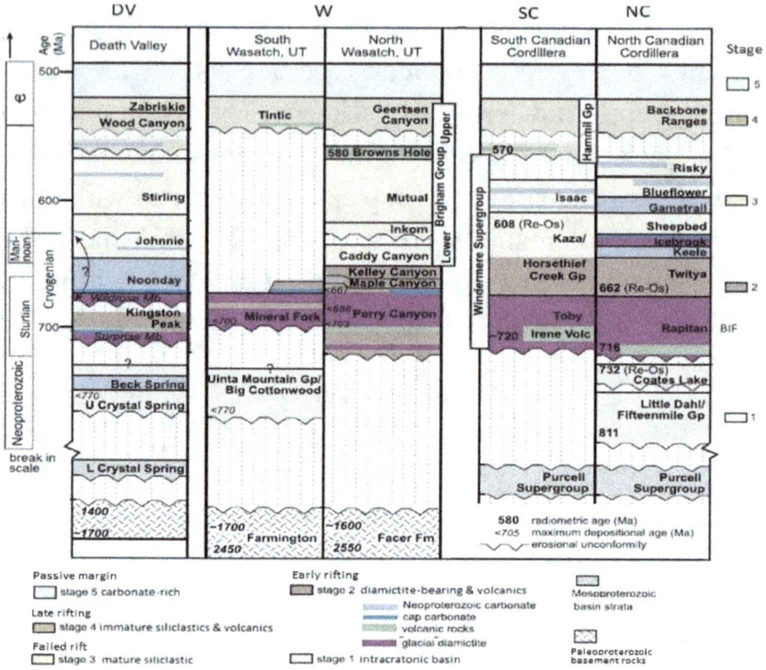

Figure 3. Reference stratigraphic sections and published age constraints for Neoproterozoic to Cambrian strata along the Cordilleran margin (see Fig. 1 locations of sections). Stratigraphic sections range from Paleoproterozoic basement rocks upwards to Cambrian carbonate-rich strata. Data is from Death Valley, Wasatch, and the Canadian Cordillera. Interpreted rifting and "glacial" episodes are indicated (Yonkee et al. 2014).

Detrital zircon geochronology of Neoproterozoic and lowermost Cambrian rocks from sedimentary basins located along the western margin of North America, now exposed mainly in the central Cordillera of California and Nevada, has yielded detrital zircons with characteristic "Grenvillian" ages (Fedo, Sircombe, and Rainbird 2003).

The correlation of Uinta Mountain (Utah), Pahrump (Death Valley), and Chuar (Grand Canyon) strata (Fig. 1) in southwestern USA is supported by similar patterns in detrital zircon ages, provenance, biostratigraphy, and, to some extent, C-isotope stratigraphy. (Dehler et al. 2017). The Kingston Peak Formation within the Pahrump Group contains mixtites that are commonly said to be "glacial" (Fig. 3).

Southeastern North America

There are several early Neoproterozoic deposits proximal to the Grenville Province, including the Middle Run Formation (Fig. 1), which contains Grenvillian detrital zircons (Krabbendam et al. 2017). The Midcontinent Rift (Fig. 1) has a very thick succession of basaltic lavas (15–20 km) and overlying early Neoproterozoic sedimentary rocks (Allen et al. 2015; Hoffman 1989; Krabbendam et al. 2017).

2. Inferred Geological History

2.1 Zircon geochronology

Zircons contain high concentrations of important trace elements, including the U-Pb radiogenic isotope system which is highly suited to high-precision U-Pb geochronology. Dates from individual zircon grains typically reflect the magmatic crystallization age (and also metamorphism) of a crystalline basement rock (Hawkesworth et al. 2010).

Because zircon is highly refractory and resilient at earth's surface, it occurs in virtually all sedimentary deposits and so provides a critical link in understanding the provenance of sediments (Fedo, Sircombe, and Rainbird 2003). Sedimentary rocks contain eroded and transported detritus derived from precursor igneous, metamorphic, and sedimentary material. The age composition of detrital zircons within such sedimentary rocks provides an indication of crystalline source rock regions and so input to sedimentary basins (Spencer and Kirkland 2016). Since zircons are by nature resistant they may undergo multiple recycling events in sedimentary deposits (Rainbird, Cawood, and Gehrels 2012).

2.2 Early Creation Week versus Early Flood

The first three days of Creation Week may be seen as a fashioning of an initial ex nihilo-created earth (Dickens and Snelling 2008).

Strontium isotope trends of the Neoproterozoic indicate enormous continental erosion (Peters and Gaines 2012) (Fig. 4). This can be correlated with the erosion of land associated with the Flood's rain (Dickens 2016). The corollary of this is that underlying Archean to Mesoproterozoic crystalline basement and sedimentary rocks can be correlated with early Creation Week. The Pre-Flood Earth's surface was destroyed (Genesis 6:13) in the sense of being totally wiped or eroded away (Matthew 24:39). It is considered that immense erosion of the land and related abrasion was not favorable for the preservation of fossils. It was only once the sea transgressed the land ("Cambrian transgression" [Matthews and Cowie 1979]) that macrofossils had a chance to be formed and preserved.

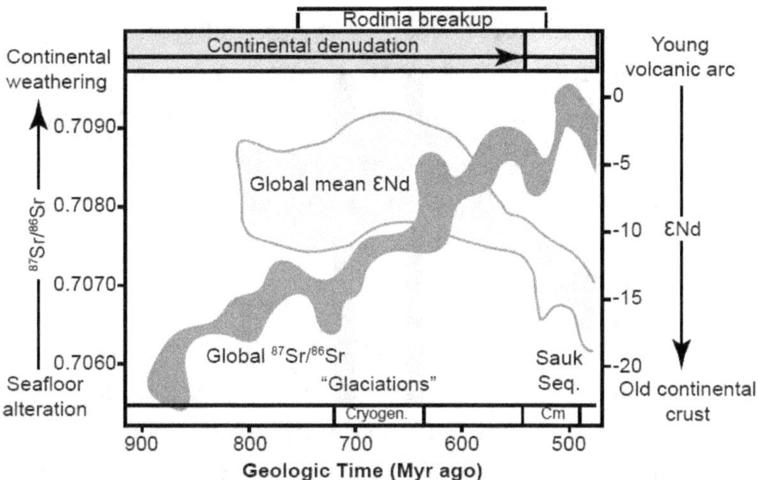

Figure 4. Summary of major geochemical and sedimentary patterns derived from Neoproterozoic to Cambrian strata (modified from Peters and Gaines 2012):

- ^{87}Sr is a radiogenic daughter isotope of ^{87}Rb and is found in silicate rocks such as granite. The abundance of radiogenic ^{87}Sr relative to "common" ^{86}Sr in a sample of sediment is related to the amount of sediment that originated from the erosion of continental crust as opposed to that originating from the ocean. The observed increase in Neoproterozoic strontium isotope ratios ^{87}Sr/^{86}Sr has been explained by accelerated rates of erosion.

- The subsequent decline in the ^{87}Sr/^{86}Sr ratio in post-Cambrian strata indicates greater oceanic influence and a time of accumulation of sediments on the continents as more of the Sauk Sequence began to be deposited, reducing the direct erosive impact of rain on landmasses.

- High rates of erosion of basin hinterlands can also explain the very negative neodymium isotope ratio $\varepsilon Nd(t)$ in the Cambrian. A more negative $\varepsilon Nd(t)$ is related to the fractionation of neodymium isotopes observed in crustal rocks compared to a standard.

- The erosion of land associated with the Flood's rain can be correlated with Neoproterozoic sequences (including mixtites interpreted as mass flows rather than as "glacials" and that Sr isotope trends indicate continental erosion). The radiometric "timespan" for the Neoproterozoic to Cambrian increase in $^{87}Sr/^{86}Sr$ ratio is approximately 0.4 Ga, but in the biblical framework, the actual time elapsed would have been of the order of weeks to months.

- A corollary is that Archean to Mesoproterozoic rocks can be correlated with early Creation Week.

- The pre-Flood land surface was destroyed (Genesis 6:13) in the sense of being totally wiped away (eroded) (Matthew 24:39).

- The subsequent decline in $^{87}Sr/^{86}Sr$ ratio in post-Cambrian strata is due to the presence of a globe-covering ocean so that the rain no longer directly impacted the land.

Braided-type deposits are found in the earlier Neoproterozoic sequences whereas "glacial" deposits are found in the mid-Neoproterozoic (Cryogenian) sequences.

2.3 Water flow episodes

Braided rather than meandering river systems have been described as characteristic of the Precambrian (Eriksson et al. 2013). The lack of channelized, meandering (low energy) river systems and the presence of mature quartz-arenite sandstone bodies (Rainbird, Cawood, and Gehrels 2012) is consistent with extremely high energy and relatively short duration (days) for global early Flood and early Creation Week geological processes. These are subaerial sheet-braided deposits, not submarine landslide (mass flow) deposits. Sheet-braided deposits mainly consist of sandstone whereas mass flow deposits consist of poorly sorted sediments. These episodes' high energy and immense erosion did not require deep time. The Flood, likely removed evidence of any pre-Flood meandering river channels.

A very different hydrologic regime compared to today's rivers is indicated for these sheet-braided deposits since they have a relatively high percentage of coarse sediments, and there is little evidence for the presence of deep channels (Rainbird, Cawood and Gehrels 2012). The sources of detritus for some modern large river systems, such as the Amazon and Mississippi, are mainly local (Iizuka et al. 2005; Mapes et al. 2004). However, the Grenvillian belt-sourced detritus may have been deposited up to thousands of kilometers away (Rainbird, Cawood, and Gehrels 2012). Although the Amazon has a high water flow, it has meanders, indicating a relatively low energy flow.

By measuring the inclination direction of crossbeds formed by migration of underwater dunes, the way ancient water flowed can be inferred (Rainbird and Young 2009). It has been inferred that a "braided river system of pan-continental proportions that may have emanated from sources along the entire 5000+ km length of the Grenville orogenic front" (Rainbird et al. 1997). The water flow may have been a laterally extensive sheet flow regime, rather than just braided river systems.

The hypotheses of "big-river" systems and the presence of a craton scale fluvial blanket in Neoproterozoic and Early Cambrian times are supported by the successful integration of sedimentological information, such as paleocurrent analysis, with U-Pb geochronology (Fedo, Sircombe, and Rainbird 2003). The configuration of sandstones in Neoproterozoic basins of northwestern Canada provides evidence for laterally extensive sheet-braided flow, indicative of high energy. Amalgamated, fluvial sheet sandstones in the stratigraphic record are often interpreted as the deposits of braided rivers (McLaurin and Steel 2007).

Not just the Flood, but Creation Week would also have had great water movements! There was a global ocean on Days One and Two, and land only emerged on Day Three. Separation of land from the sea may be consistent with sufficient continental crust growth that land emerged. This would have resulted in downslope water flow draining newly emergent land and downslope water currents in the sea.

It has been proposed that several large intracontinental sedimentary basins of late Paleoproterozoic to Mesoproterozoic age are remnants of a regional sand blanket deposited unconformably on crystalline rocks of the Canadian Shield by a series of large river systems (Rainbird, Cawood, and Gehrels 2012). The sedimentology, sequence stratigraphy and basins' fill depositional age are similar and can be correlated between thousands of kilometers apart basins. Similar westerly paleocurrent directions have been interpreted for these depocenters. These observations and those from Neoproterozoic sequences led to the suggestion that the preserved sedimentary basins were the remnants of enormous river systems that emerged when several major regional tectonic Events (such as the Hudsonian and Grenvillian) were taking place in areas to the east of the sedimentary basins (Rainbird, Cawood, and Gehrels 2012; Young 1978). Such conditions and relationships existed several times during the development of the ancient North American craton (Rainbird, Cawood, and Gehrels 2012).

2.4 Precambrian basement provinces and early Creation Week

And God said, "Let the waters under the heavens be gathered together into one place, and let the dry land appear." And it was so. God called the dry land earth, and the waters that were gathered together he called Seas. And God saw that it was good. (Genesis 1:9–10 ESV)

the one who, by his strength, established the mountains, being girded with might. (Psalm 65:6 ESV)

Southeastern crystalline basement provinces

Massive river systems have been interpreted to have formed when major mountain building (the Grenvillian thermal-tectonic Event) occurred on the eastern side of the North American continent. (Rainbird, Cawood, and Gehrels 2012). In addition, major rift and aulocogen-related basins, such as the Midcontinent Rift Basin and the Belt-Purcell Basin, were formed in the Mesoproterozoic (Pirajno 1992).

It has been claimed that as Proterozoic provinces developed, they underwent deformation and thickening but without the major fragmentation, widespread dispersion, and collision of continents typical of the post-Permian (Hamilton 2011). This is consistent with the idea of the progressive formation of only one supercontinent by Day Three, which later broke up in Noah's Flood. I propose that by Day Three, the supercontinent had thickened sufficiently for dry land to emerge and that formation of late Paleoproterozoic and Mesoproterozoic provinces of the southeast of the North American craton, along with North America's Grenvillian Event, be correlated with processes in the earlier part of Day Three.

The rocks of the Grenville Province in the southeast of the North American craton have been interpreted to represent the roots of a deeply eroded mountain chain (Rainbird, Cawood, and Gehrels 2012). I propose that the rocks of today's Grenville Province represent the eroded roots of pre-Flood high mountains (Genesis 7:19), which formed on Day Three. Many Bible translations refer to high mountains in Genesis 7:19 (ESV, NIV, NASB, TLV, YLT98). Strong's concordance has a *mountain* or *range of hills*. Within the Grenville Province, the common occurrence of high-grade (amphibolite to granulite facies) metamorphic rocks at the earth's surface today indicates the uplift and erosion of tens of kilometers of crust since the bulk of mountain building was complete (Rainbird, Cawood, and Gehrels 2012).

Thermodynamic constraints on pressure-temperature stability of metamorphic mineral assemblages of gneisses and migmatites have been used to infer tens of kilometers depth of formation (Jamieson et al. 2011; Rivers 2015). Using Grenvillian examples, metamorphic petrologist Wynn-Edwards maintained that the occurrence on all scales of folds with similar style (that is, thick hinges and thin limbs), together with coaxial refolding, were signs of extreme ductility during deformation. (Rivers 2015).

The Grenvillian tectonic Event has been described as "Perhaps the greatest orogenic (mountain-building) event in earth's history. . ." (Rainbird, Cawood, and Gehrels 2012, 584). Tectonic analysis and paleogeographic reconstructions indicate that the Grenvillian orogen was possibly the longest and widest in Earth history, extending for a quarter of the globe, or a distance of approximately 20,000 km long and as wide as 800 km, including a core zone several hundred kilometers wide (Van Kranendonk and Kirkland 2013).

The 1.2–1.1 Ga radiometric "age" peak in oxygen isotope and incompatible trace element signatures, identified in North America, Western Australia, and globally, indicate that the Grenvillian orogeny may represent a unique episode in Earth history (Van Kranendonk and Kirkland 2013). Oxygen isotopes ($\delta^{18}O$) in zircon grains and incompatible trace element (ITE) (Zr, Th) concentrations in magmatic rocks are used as proxies to test for variations in the degree of crustal recycling through geological time (Van Kranendonk and Kirkland 2013). ITEs are preferentially excluded from common rock-forming minerals during fractional crystallization due to their unsuitable size and/or charge to fit within the cation sites of crystals and are partitioned into silicate liquids during melting. Elevated concentrations of Zr and Th above crustal values in magmas reflect enhanced crustal recycling and the importance of preexisting continental crust in the orogenic cycle. Oxygen isotopes are also elevated toward heavy values with crustal recycling. The significant peak in ITEs and oxygen isotopes at 1.2–1.1 Ga (during the Grenvillian Event) is consistent with episodic crustal growth.

The mountains melt like wax before the Lord, before the Lord of all the earth. (Psalm 97:5 ESV)

The Grenville Province has been described as a large hot orogen (Rivers 2015). Geothermometry (based on metamorphic mineral assemblages) of upper amphibolite- and granulite-facies gneisses in the Grenville hinterland revealed temperatures in the range $700 \pm 50°C$ or higher, although subsequently shown to commonly underestimate peak temperature due to post-peak resetting. Enhanced radioactive decay has been considered a possible factor in such heating (Clark et al. 2011).

The Grenville Province is known for its complex ductile gneissic structure, high grade of metamorphism, and polyphase reworking, features indicative of residence in the deep crust (Rivers 2015). Field relations indicate that the crust underwent melt-enhanced ductile flow laterally for tens of kilometers (Jamieson et al. 2011) and, thus, erosion of tens of kilometers of crust. The record of this erosion was expected to be preserved in the vestiges of a pan-Rodinian drainage system that would have delivered huge volumes of detritus to adjacent basins, located across the interior of North America (Fedo, Sircombe, and Rainbird 2003).

The northeast-trending Yavapai, Matzatzal, and Grenville provinces are characterized by voluminous granitoid plutonism (Mints 2015; Whitmeyer and Karlstrom 2007) and considerable thickening of continental crust (Van Kranendonk and Kirkland 2013). It is proposed that the growth and huge crustal thickening of late Paleoproterozoic and Mesoproterozoic provinces of the southeast of the North American craton (Fig. 1), along with the Grenvillian orogeny, were processes from Day Three when land emerged for the first time. Only by very late Neoproterozoic or early Paleozoic time do significant indicators of subduction (and thus "true" plate tectonics) appear, including complete ophiolites and high-pressure, low-temperature metamorphism (Stern 2005). Thus plate tectonics may not have existed in the Archean to Mesoproterozoic. This is consistent with the idea of the growth of only one supercontinent by Day Three.

Northern Paleoproterozoic and Archean crystalline basement provinces

Based on the paleomagnetic record, an interpretation has been made that the Precambrian continental crust was essentially intact from the Archean until late Neoproterozoic rifting (Piper 2015). This interpretation may be consistent with the idea of the progressive growth of only one supercontinent from Day One to the earlier part of Day Three.

Provinces such as the Superior Province may have together formed part of one late Archean supercraton (Condie et al. 2017). The large late Archean zircon U-Pb age peak is thought to represent coincidental cooling within individual provinces (Percival 2004) and the beginning of stable cratons (Frazier and Schwimmer 1987). The Paleoproterozoic Trans-Hudson Province is believed to have involved internal rifting and reworking of the Archean crust rather than collision between two Archean continental blocks (Mints 2015).

2.5 Earlier Proterozoic sedimentation and early Creation Week

The sea is his, for he made it, and his hands formed the dry land. (Psalm 95:5 ESV)

Western Northern America

The combination of mudstone petrology and interbedded sandstone detrital zircon geochronology affords insights into the provenance, hydrodynamic effects, weathering regime, and diagenesis of the Mesoproterozoic Unkar Group. It has been concluded that Unkar mudstones were derived largely from the Grenville Province of southwest Texas and the adjacent Yavapai-Mazatzal provinces (Bloch et al. 2006). All units within the Unkar Group contain a complex distribution of Paleoproterozoic zircons. (Mulder et al. 2017) This may be a result of water flowing from mountains formed on Day Three in North America's southeastern region. Unkar Group and other Late Mesoproterozoic strata in southwestern North America have been inferred to indicate north-flowing continental-scale rivers sourced from the developing Grenville Orogen.

The Belt-Purcell Basin (Fig. 1 and Fig. 3) is considered to have been filled by marine and fluviatile sediments (Lydon 2007), and this may be consistent with formation in a Pre-Flood sea. The ca. 1.47–1.45 Ga lower Belt-Purcell strata contain abundant distinctive non-Laurentian 1.61–1.50 Ga detrital zircon populations. Exotic cratonic sources such as Australia have been inferred! However, upper Belt-Purcell strata contain strongly unimodal ca. 1.73 Ga detrital zircon age populations that match the detrital zircon signature of Paleoproterozoic metasedimentary rocks of the Yavapai Province to the south and southeast (Jones, Daniel, and Doe 2015).

Northern Canada

Provenance analysis using zircon grains has been used to infer that big water flow systems transported Paleoproterozoic sediments shed from the Yapavai and Trans-Hudson Provinces to Paleoproterozoic basins of northern Canada, such as the Athabasca and Thelon (Rainbird, Cawood, and Gehrels 2012). Such late Paleoproterozoic sediments may have resulted from erosion as continental crust thickened and land emerged on Day Three. The Thelon and Athabasca basins have been interpreted to have formed in a dominantly fluvial environment and from zircon provenance studies to include far-traveled detritus (Palmer, Kyser, and Hiatt 2004; Rainbird and Young 2009). Economic deposits of unconformity-related uranium occur in association with Paleoproterozoic basins such as the Athabasca Basin (Hanly et al. 2006). Unconformity on Archean crystalline basement rocks is consistent with inferred erosional action of Day Two water movement on Archean crystalline rocks that may have formed on Day One.

Outcrop evidence from Paleoproterozoic sediments of the Kilohigok Basin in Arctic Canada (such as the occurrence of incised paleovalleys and sand sheets with high width-to-thickness ratios) indicates deep-channeled drainage as well as sheet-braided rivers (Ielpi and Rainbird 2016b). "Glacial" deposits (and sheet-braided rivers) may have resulted from the great movements of waters during Day Two (Dickens and Snelling 2008).

2.6 Neoproterozoic sedimentation and Early Flood

by his knowledge the deeps broke open, and the clouds drop down the dew. (Proverbs 3:20 ESV)

In the six hundredth year of Noah's life, in the second month, on the seventeenth day of the month, on that day all the fountains of the great deep burst forth, and the windows of the heavens were opened. (Genesis 7:11 ESV)

Tectonism

The phrases "deeps broke open" and "fountains of the great deep burst forth" imply fragmentation of the earth's crust. I correlate this with the Neoproterozoic breaking up of the Rodinian supercontinent (Dickens and Snelling 2008). Worldwide simultaneous (commencing on the same day) erupting of fountains (including the eruption of volcanic material) was followed by global rainfall (Dickens and

Snelling 2008). Neoproterozoic rifting, volcanic, and deposition stages are inferred (Yonkee et al. 2014) (Fig. 3).

Assuming a configuration of Rodinia supercontinent like that in Fig. 5, it may be inferred that these high mountains were situated close to a site of Pan-African breakup east of the Grenville Province and thus Flood fountains which poured out rain. There are other configurations of Rodinia than that shown in Fig. 5, but one thing in common is that the eastern margin of North America is a site of breakup of Rodinia. I correlate this with when the fountains of the great deep burst forth. Intense erosion of these high mountains may have been accentuated due to their proximity to such fountains and the ensuing rain. Reconstruction of the Rodinia supercontinent was based on the recognition of Neoproterozoic rifted passive margins (Evans 2013).

Worldwide continental rifting (and subsequent ocean formation beginning at 0.6 Ga) has been inferred (Hoffman 1989). This was described as the dismemberment of Rodinia supercontinent "by the most important single continental break-up event in geological history shortly before the dawn of the Cambrian" (Bond et al. 1984; Piper 2009). The Pan-African thermal-tectonic Event is associated with this massive global rifting (Hoffman 1989). It has been postulated that episodic rifting events at the margins of North America between 0.8 and about 0.6 Ga record the fragmentation of a Neoproterozoic supercontinent (Bond, Christie-Blick, and Kominz 1984; Hoffman 1989). This is consistent with initial breaking open of the crust with the bursting forth of the fountains of the great deep on a specific day, followed by rifting, further extension, and ocean formation.

Worldwide continental rifting (and subsequent ocean formation beginning at 0.6 Ga) has been inferred (Hoffman 1989) and this has been described as the dismemberment of the Rodinia supercontinent "by the most important single continental break-up event in geological history shortly before the dawn of the Cambrian" (Bond et al. 1984; Piper 2009). The Pan-African thermal-tectonic Event is associated with this massive global rifting (Hoffman 1989). It has been postulated that episodic rifting events at the margins of North America between 0.8 and about 0.6 Ga record the fragmentation of a Neoproterozoic supercontinent (Bond, Christie-Blick, and Kominz 1984; Hoffman 1989). This is consistent with the initial breaking open of the crust with the bursting forth of the fountains of the great deep on a specific day, followed by rifting, further extension, and ocean formation.

The final basin-forming episode of Proterozoic rocks involved a series of rift basins that once more preserve evidence of multiple "glaciations" and contain banded iron formations (Yeo 1981). The Rapitan-type iron formation of northwest Canada (NC of Figs. 1 and 4) is associated with Neoproterozoic mixtites, debris flow deposits, turbidites, and widespread flood basalts (Cox et al. 2013). Iron isotope values are consistent with oxidation of ferruginous waters during marine transgression and rift-related hydrothermal activity associated with the breakup of Rodinia is inferred (Cox et al. 2013). Remarkably similar Neoproterozoic "glacials" are found on North America's west and east

Figure 5. One possible configuration of the supercontinent Rodinia. The Grenville Mountain Belt is shown in orange. Sediments have been interpreted to have been transported by an enormous system of braided rivers over a huge area of the supercontinent, as suggested by the arrows on Laurentia (the North American craton). G is the Southeastern Orogen shown in Fig. 1. (Rainbird, Cawood, and Gehrels 2012). There may be other interpreted configurations of Rodinia, but the Grenville Mountain Belt remains immediately adjacent to a region where Rodinia is inferred to have fragmented.

margins, and this has been related to supercontinent fragmentation (Young 1995). Accommodation space for many "glacials" may have been provided by rifting. (Young 2013). A rift-related tectonostratigraphic model has been proposed for most of the Neoproterozoic diamictite-bearing successions (Eyles and Januszczak 2004; Schermerhorn 1974). Whatever the primary cause of the "glaciation" may have been, there is overwhelming evidence for a link with the Pan-African tectonic events (Deynoux et al. 2006).

Rain-triggered erosion

Behold, I will destroy them with the earth. (Genesis 6:13b ESV)

and rain fell upon the earth forty days and forty nights. (Genesis 7: 12 ESV)

and they were unaware until the flood came and swept them all away, so will be the coming of the Son of Man. (Matthew 24:39 ESV)

The mountains saw you and writhed; the raging waters swept on. (Habakkuk 3:10b ESV)

he who removes mountains, and they know it not, when he overturns them in his anger. (Job 9:5 ESV)

The Flood's rain caused enormous erosion of the land, and at the same time, the sea level rose until, eventually, all of the earth's land was covered (Dickens 2016). It is important that the enormous erosion of land aspect of the Flood be recognized and not just the marine transgression aspect of the Flood. The pre-Flood surface topography was thoroughly destroyed (Genesis 6:13) by the Flood's subaerial erosion and ensuing deposition. However, Creation Week's crystalline basement would have remained though eroded. The destruction of the earth mentioned in Genesis 6:13 is not annihilation (going to nothing), but instead, it is the total transformation of the surface of the Earth, such that the Pre-Flood world was no longer recognizable.

The initial erosional phase of Noah's Flood correlates with the timing of the initial Pan-African continental breakup (~0.8 Ga [Hoffman 1989]) and with the development of Neoproterozoic geology (Dickens and Snelling 2015). It is inferred that immense continental erosion (Peters and Gaines 2012) and enormous water flow systems occurred early in the Flood due to the rain impacting subaerial land (Dickens and Snelling 2015; Dickens 2016).

In addition to massive erosion of continental landmasses, enormous torrential rain would have eventually caused huge mass flows to sweep down from higher areas into the seas, depositing immense volumes of sediments. A modern analogy is Hawaii, with giant undersea landslides and large debris fields on the seafloor (Ten Bruggencate 2001). In today's world, heavy rainfall and earthquakes set off landslides in rugged areas (Bai et al. 2013). How much more so would earthquakes have occurred with rifting episodes during the Flood Event, thus setting off gigantic submarine landslides, now recognized as Neoproterozoic mixtites on North America's western and eastern margins. Mid-Neoproterozoic (Cryogenian) mixtites, interpreted by secular scientists as occurring during "glaciations" are more likely submarine mass flow deposits (Schermerhorn 1974) formed in the rain stage of Noah's Flood due to enormous water flow on the continents (Dickens 2016).

In the modern world, local downpours of rain persisting over a limited period can cause great devastation of property and habitats, loss of life, landslides, mudflows, erosion, and swollen rivers. A recent study has concluded that the magnitude of flooding in the USA is highest in regions that experience the most extraordinary precipitation, and that precipitation is the primary driver of floods. In addition, maximum peak discharges tend to occur in basins close to the ocean with mountainous terrain (Saharia et al. 2017). The Bible describes the greatest rain event ever recorded—40 days and nights of rain falling on the whole earth (Genesis 7:12) and so the effects were vastly greater than for today's floods which are restricted to local basins.

The Neoproterozoic Sr ratio indicator trend is consistent with immense erosion of the continents (Peters and Gaines 2012) (Fig. 4). The major $^{87}Sr/^{86}Sr$ isotope ratio increase between 0.9 Ga and 0.5 Ga is consistent with erosion of highly radiogenic continental crust (Dickens 2016; Dickens and Snelling 2015; Meert and Powell 2001; Peters and Gaines 2012) during the Neoproterozoic (Fig. 4). This evidence is consistent with what would be expected from the effects of enormous rainfall on the North American continent during the early Noahic Flood. Rubidium (Rb) is common in the crust's silicate minerals. ^{87}Sr is a radiogenic daughter isotope of ^{87}Rb. Therefore the abundance of radiogenic ^{87}Sr relative to "common" ^{86}Sr in a sample of sediment is related to the amount of sediment that originated from continental crust as opposed to that originating from the ocean. Similarly, a negative $\varepsilon Nd(t)$ is related to the fractionation of neodymium isotopes observed in crustal rocks compared to a standard.

Continental denudation, enhanced chemical weathering, and changes in global ocean chemistry are indicated by numerous geochemical signatures associated with the Great Unconformity (Peters and Gaines 2012). The evidence is consistent with what would be expected from the effects of enormous rainfall and on the North American continent during the early Noahic Flood (Dickens 2016). The sharp stratigraphic contact typically separates the Precambrian crystalline basement from the quartz- and feldspar-rich marine sands of the basal Sauk Sequence (Sloss 1964). Exposure and chemical weathering of silicate minerals derived from continental basement rocks during the formation of the Great Unconformity exerted an important control on seawater chemistry and global biogeochemical cycling in several ways, including the consumption of atmospheric CO_2 and the release of a number of types of ions to the oceans (Peters and Gaines 2012).

In the Grand Canyon, the Great Unconformity is said to represent about 1.2 Ga of "missing" radiometric time since 1.75 Ga gneiss is overlain directly by 0.5 Ga sandstone. Such locations where Paleozoic sediments lie directly on the basement are considered to be where there was erosion only and not deposition of detritus eroded off of the land. The Grand Canyon Supergroup represents the "missing time" (Timmons, Karlstrom, and Dehler 1999). The Chuar Group of the Grand Canyon Supergroup may represent detritus derived from continental erosion. Subsequently the Grand

Canyon's Paleozoic sediments were deposited as the sea level rose sufficiently to cover the land of the whole earth then completely.

Western North America

The style of sedimentation would have varied in time and location as the Flood Event progressed (Fig. 3). In early Neoproterozoic basins of northwestern Canada, paleocurrent directions (Figs. 1 and 2) derived from cross-bedding in thick subaerial fluvial deposits indicate regionally consistent west-northwesterly transport. Detrital zircon grains commonly occur on the western side of the continent, which give ages characteristic of the Grenville Province, several thousand kilometers away (Rainbird, Cawood, and Gehrels 2012). Neoproterozoic sandstone cross-bedding and detrital zircons together provide evidence that mountain belts in the southeastern part of the North American continent contributed sedimentary detritus to enormous river systems that crossed the continent, spreading northwesterly and forming the thick sandstone successions preserved in Neoproterozoic sedimentary basins of northwestern Canada. Some zircons may have been transported more than 3000 km. The lateral extent of the inferred fluvial system was at least 1200 km, much broader than any fluvial system on today's earth (Rainbird et al. 2017).

Zircon grains of Grenvillian age were recovered from early Neoproterozoic sedimentary basins in northwestern Canada (including the Amundsen Basin), more than 3000 km away from the nearest probable source in the Grenville Province on the other side of the continent. In addition, paleocurrents derived from cross-bedding in thick fluvial deposits in these basins indicate regionally consistent west-northwesterly transport (Rainbird, Cawood, and Gehrels 2012). Braided rivers indicate high energy, unlike meandering rivers. This is all evidence of enormous water flow systems as part of a gigantic erosional episode. In the USA Cordillera, thousands of kilometers to the south of northwestern Canada, there are correlative strata that show similar detrital zircon patterns. Such strata include the Uinta Mountains Group and the Grand Canyon Supergroup. This provides further evidence for large-scale river systems transporting laterally extensive detritus, originating from multiple sources along the great Grenville Mountain Belt (Rainbird, Cawood, and Gehrels 2012).

The Uinta Mountain Group of west-central USA formed with the deposition of fluvial to marine, feldspathic to quartzose sandstone, conglomerate, and mudstone. Detrital zircon patterns indicate a mix of local basement sources to the north and distal sources to the southeast of North America. Subsequently, in association with rifting and volcanism, the Perry Canyon formation was deposited and included mixtites claimed to be "glacials" (Yonkee et al. 2014) (Figs. 1 and 3).

In areas such as the Grand Canyon, the Great Unconformity is the contact between overlying Paleozoic layered sediments and underlying, either Paleoproterozoic crystalline basement or tilted Grand Canyon Supergroup's Neoproterozoic Chuar Group, sediments. Locations where Paleozoic sediments lie directly on the basement are considered to be where there was erosion only and not deposition of detritus eroded off the land. The

Neoproterozoic Chuar Group has been associated with breakup of the Rodinia supercontinent, whereas the underlying Mesoproterozoic Unkar Group has been associated with the "assembly" of Rodinia (Timmons, Karlstrom, and Dehler 1999). I infer, respectively, early Flood detritus from rain's erosion of the continent and Day Three emergence of land with thickening of crust and synorogenic intracratonic basin sedimentation.

Mid-Neoproterozoic (Cryogenian) "glacials" may instead be mass flow deposits formed with enormous submarine landslides during tectonic activity as the Flood progressed. Neoproterozoic mixtites of the North American Cordillera have been interpreted as submarine mass flow deposits (Sigler and Wingerden 1998; Snelling 2009; Wingerden 2003). California's Kingston Peak Formation (Figs. 1 and 4) provides evidence for debris flows and catastrophic coarse clastic deposits in Noah's Flood rather than glaciation (Sigler and Wingerden 1998). Neoproterozoic mixtites have an intimate association with sedimentary rocks indicating warm climates (Young 2013).

In addition, the Rapitan-type banded iron formations associated with such "glacials" in the Neoproterozoic may have formed hydrothermally in deeper water and in association with volcanic activity (Pirajno 1992). A catastrophic pouring out of volcanics and associated banded iron formations in the Neoproterozoic is inferred to have occurred early in Noah's Flood (Dickens 2017a).

Southeastern North America

Evidence for significant rifting on the eastern (Appalachian) margin in southeastern North America has been identified (Frazier and Schwimmer 1987). This was more or less simultaneous with an event of worldwide continental rifting (and subsequent ocean formation beginning at 0.6 Ga) (Hoffman 1989).

The upper Keweenawan of the Midcontinent Rift (Fig. 1) has Neoproterozoic sediments proximal to and believed to be sourced from the Grenville Orogen. (Krabbendam et al. 2017). This thick detrital sediment overlies volcanic fill (Lucas and St-Onge 1998). Water flow may have diverted into the rift. Other proximal early Neoproterozoic sequences containing detritus derived from the Grenville Orogen include the Middle Run Formation (Fig. 1), the Hazel Formation and the Flinton Formation (Krabbendam et al. 2017).

Conclusion

In striking contrast to most of North America's older Proterozoic provinces, the lithosphere of southeastern North America has an overall northeast-southwest regional trend. This includes the Late Paleoproterozoic Yavapai and Mazatzal provinces, as well as the Mesoproterozoic Grenville Province. It is proposed that the formation of late Paleoproterozoic and Mesoproterozoic provinces of the southeast of the North American craton, along with North America's Grenvillian Event, be correlated with processes in the earlier part of Day Three.

The Grenvillian thermal-tectonic Event, associated with huge Mesoproterozoic crustal thickening, is inferred to correlate with the emergence of land and high mountain-building on Day Three. In addition to the formation of crystalline rocks on Day Three, some synorogenic Mesoproterozoic sediments also formed since the emergence of land on Day Three would have fostered water flow, erosion, and transport of detritus downslope towards the sea.

The Pan-African thermal-tectonic Event is consistent with an enormous erosional and depositional regime expected in the early stages of the Flood of Noah. It has been postulated that episodic rifting events at the margins of North America between 0.8 Ga and about 0.6 Ga record the fragmentation of the Neoproterozoic Rodinia. This is consistent with the initial breaking open of the crust with the bursting forth of the fountains of the great deep on a specific day, followed by rifting, volcanism, further extension, and eventually ocean formation.

The Flood's rain caused enormous erosion of the land, and at the same time, the sea level rose until eventually all the earth's land was covered. It is important to recognize the enormous erosion of land aspect of the Flood and not just the marine transgression aspect of the Flood.

North America's Grenville Province is inferred to be the roots of a deeply eroded pre-Flood mountain chain. It was situated just to the west today of a zone where fountains of the great deep later erupted and rain fell at the onset of the Flood. The intense erosion of Grenvillian high mountains may have been accentuated due to their proximity to Flood fountains and the ensuing rain and tectonism.

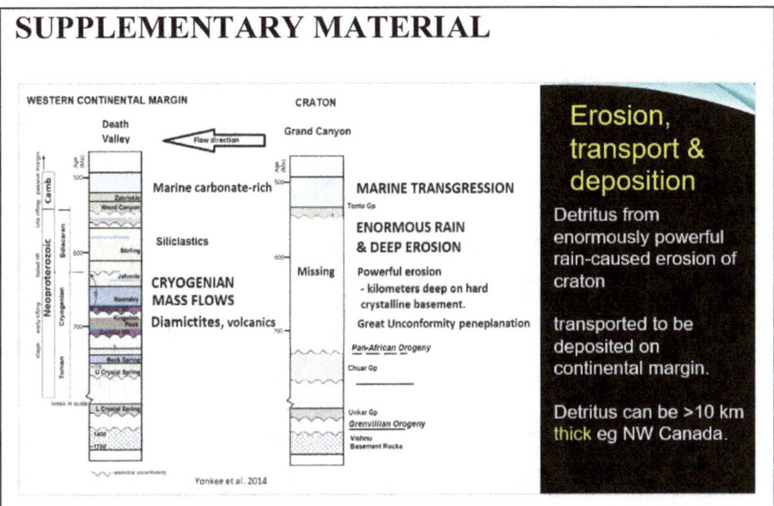

Enormous erosion and deposition (including mass flows) during the early Flood as inferred from Grand Canyon and Death Valley stratigraphy.

III. FLOOD AND AFTERMATH

A. FLOOD FOUNTAINS OF THE GREAT DEEP

Source: Dickens, H. 2018. Evidence for Flood fountains adjacent to the cratonic margin of southwestern Australia" *Journal of Creation.* 32(1):16-20.

HIGHLIGHTS

In this model of the early Noahic Flood, the vicinity of the Darling Fault is considered to be a region where continental crust fragmented and the fountains of the great deep broke open.

The Darling Fault of southwestern Australia is a major geological boundary between the Archean Yilgarn Craton in the east and the Perth Basin in the west. It can be recognised at the surface and by geophysical methods for some 1,000 km in a generally north-south direction. Up to 15 km thickness of Phanerozoic sedimentary rocks occur in the Perth Basin.

In southwestern Australia, numerous pieces of evidence taken together are consistent with the Bible's account of the Flood event initiating as "the fountains of the great deep burst forth":

- Rb-Sr and Ar-Ar isotope system traverses, petrography, and magnetotelluric data all point to a regionally extensive and major hydrothermal event in the region of the Darling Fault.

- Paleomagnetic data, mafic dykes close to the Darling Fault, a seismic traverse across the Darling Fault Zone, and intracontinental high-temperature melting suggest a model of Neoproterozoic rifting. This may be associated with the fragmentation of a supercontinent. The Rb-Sr system is very sensitive to hydrothermal fluid alteration. This enables the diffusion of Rb and Sr and the preferential loss of Rb from biotite, thus thermally resetting radiometric ages.

  Similar trends have been inferred for $^{40}Ar/^{39}Ar$ 'ages'. Younger biotite $^{40}Ar/^{39}Ar$ 'ages' from the western margin of the craton are consistent with a late Neoproterozoic tectonic event between Greater India and Australia, and paleomagnetic studies indicate that 'Greater India' was in a position adjacent to Western Australia in the late Neoproterozoic.

Numerous articles in the creation literature refer to the fountains of the great deep that burst forth in Noah's Flood. However, this paper uses isotopic, petrographic, and geophysical data as evidence for the actual location of where Flood fountains burst forth near today's Darling Fault in southwestern Australia in the context of a new proposed model of the early Flood (Dickens 2017b).

Geological setting

Key tectonic elements in southwestern Australia include the Yilgarn Craton, the Albany-Fraser Orogen, the Leeuwin Complex and the Perth Basin (Fig. 1).

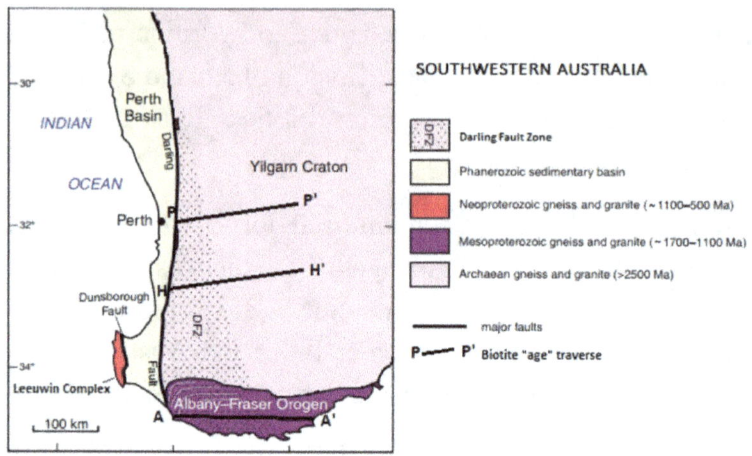

Figure 1. Map showing key tectonic elements of southwestern Australia (after Janssen et al. 2003) and approximate location of biotite 'age' traverses of Libby and De Laeter 1998, shown in figure 2.

The Archean Yilgarn Craton consists of granitoids, greenstones, and high-grade gneiss belts. It is bounded on its western margin by the Darling Fault. Along the southwestern margin of the Yilgarn Craton, an escarpment (the Darling Range) separates the extensive plateau of the craton from the coastal plain. The scarp's location closely parallels that of the Darling Fault, which separates the Precambrian rocks to the east from the Phanerozoic sediments of the Perth Basin to the west.

The Mesoproterozoic Albany-Fraser Orogen is located along the southern and southeastern margin of the Yilgarn Craton. It consists of high-grade gneisses and granitoid intrusions.

The Neoproterozoic Leeuwin Complex is situated in the far southwest of Western Australia. It is bounded to the east by the Dunsborough Fault and to the west by the Indian Ocean. The Leeuwin Complex is a small segment of the sialic crust and essentially consists of granulite metamorphic facies felsic gneisses (Wilde1999). The Leeuwin Complex is considered part of the Pinjarra Orogen, which is the name proposed for Precambrian rocks west of the Darling Fault (Myers 1990b).

The Darling Fault is a major geological boundary between the Yilgarn Craton in the east and the Perth Basin in the west. It can be recognised at the surface and by geophysical methods for some 1,000 km. Up to 15 km of Phanerozoic sedimentary rocks occur in the Perth Basin (Myers 1990b).

Rb-Sr radiometric 'ages' of biotite can be reset at temperatures well below magmatic conditions and are well suited for studying the post-emplacement history of crystalline basement rocks (Libby and De Laeter 1998). Biotite is particularly useful because of its wide distribution and well-known closure temperature (Libby and De Laeter 1998). The Rb-Sr system is very sensitive to hydrothermal fluid alteration, as this enables the diffusion of Rb and Sr, and the preferential loss of Rb from biotite (Lu et al. 2015).

Isotopic and petrographic data

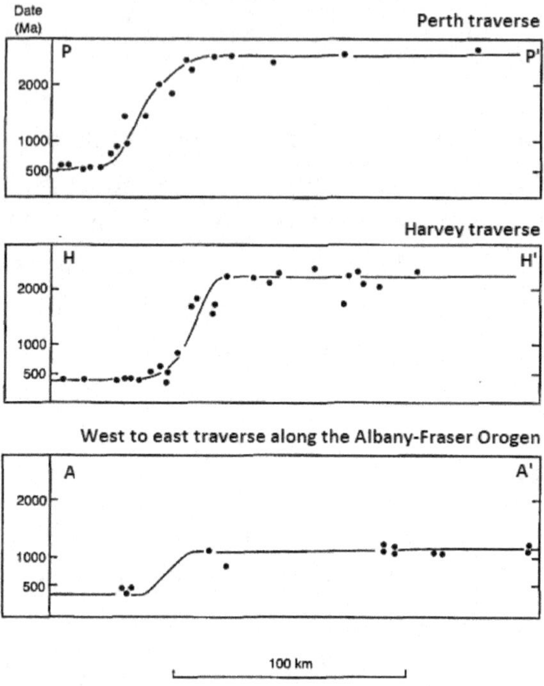

Figure 2. Biotite Rb-Sr radiometric 'age' versus distance sections extending eastward from the Darling Fault (after Libby and De Laeter 1998).

Thermal resetting of radiometric ages is described in greater detail in the literature (Harley et al. 2007; Nyquist et al. 1991).

Libby and De Laeter showed that biotite dates vary systematically along a traverse east from Perth (the Perth traverse; Fig. 2) (Libby and De Laeter 1979). The traverse was divided into three sections, each with a distinctive set of Rb-Sr biotite dates:

1. The western section (closest to the Darling Fault) was shown to have the youngest biotite dates.

2. The middle transition zone, tending to become older toward the east.

3. The eastern section has the oldest 'ages', which are very similar to biotite dates over much of the rest of the Yilgarn Craton.

A second traverse about 100 km to the south of Perth (the Harvey traverse, Fig. 2) established that the trend of younging Rb-Sr biotite dates westward towards the Darling Fault was regional, reproducible, and systematic. This second traverse also defined the trend of the break between biotite to the east, which had typical Yilgarn Craton ages, and biotite to the west, which had younger 'ages'. The regional trend was found not to be parallel to previously described tectonic lineaments, such as the Darling Fault (De Laeter and Libby 1993).

To resolve the question of whether the regional trend extended further south, sampling was extended southward across the Albany-Fraser Orogen to the south coast and eastward beyond Albany. Rb-Sr biotite dates obtained along the Perth and Harvey traverses and along the Albany-Fraser Orogen were projected into cross-sections shown in Figure 2. Janssen et al. 2003 produced an updated map of the three biotite 'age' domains—the western, transitional, and eastern biotite domains (Fig. 3).

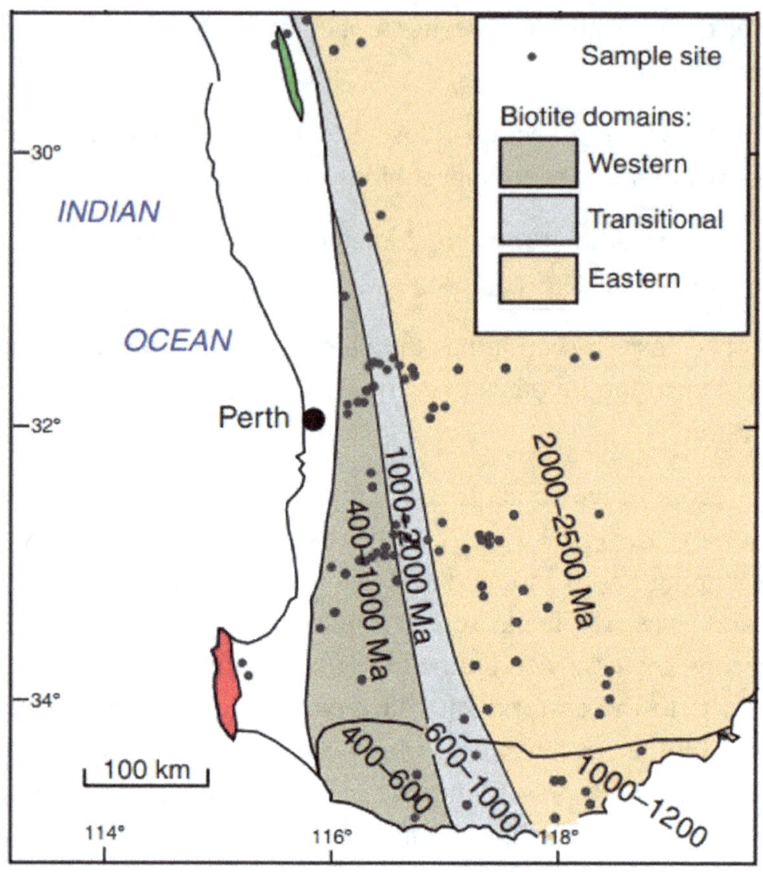

Figure 3. Map showing three biotite 'age' domains in southwestern Australia (after Janssen et al. 2003)

Lu et al. 2015 employed $^{40}Ar/39^{Ar}$ incremental heating experiments on muscovite and biotite grains from sample sites broadly comparable to those sampled by Libby and De Laeter's Perth traverse for Rb-Sr biotite analysis. Similar trends were obtained by $^{40}Ar/^{39}Ar$ biotite 'age' dating—oldest dates for the more interior Yilgarn Craton, with 'ages' decreasing abruptly to a narrow transitional zone before decreasing further along the western margin of the craton.

In light of $^{40}Ar/^{39}Ar$ data in the western margin of both the Yilgarn Craton and the Albany-Fraser Orogen, young biotite 'ages' have been interpreted to result principally from hydrothermal fluid alteration (Lu 2016). Younger biotite $^{40}Ar/^{39}Ar$ 'ages' from the western margin of the craton are consistent with a late Neoproterozoic tectonic event between Greater India and Australia (Fig. 4) (Lu et al. 2015; Kroner and Stern 2004). Moreover, paleomagnetic studies indicate that 'Greater India' was in a position adjacent to Western Australia in the late Neoproterozoic (Fig. 4) (Kroner and Stern 2004; Powell et al. 1993).

Petrographic observations indicate that most biotite grains in the transitional zone and western margin are severely chloritized and contain abundant titanite inclusions. These may have been caused by fluid-induced recrystallisation during an episodic hydrothermal and/or tectonic event (Lu 2015). Petrographic and chemical studies indicate that the biotite from each domain differs markedly in composition and origin, that is magmatic to the east versus hydrothermal to the west (Lu 2016).

The general northerly trend of late Proterozoic mafic dykes close to the Darling Fault (Myers 1990b) is consistent with an east-west extensional regime necessary for the development of the Leeuwin Complex (Myers 1990b). These sub-vertical dykes are known as the Boyagin dyke swarm and increase in abundance towards the Darling Fault (Fig. 5). The Rb-Sr radiometric 'age' of 590–560 Ma together with the pattern and spatial distribution of these dykes in the southwestern part of the Yilgarn Craton suggests that the Boyagin dyke swarm is related to late Proterozoic orogenic activity (Myers 1990b).

Geophysical data

Magnetotellurics is a passive geophysical method which uses natural time variations of the earth's magnetic and electric fields to measure the electrical conductivity of the subsurface. Depth information is obtained by measuring the time variations over a range of frequencies. High frequencies penetrate the earth to shallow depths only, while low frequencies penetrate deeper. Information is obtained from a few hundred metres depth to hundreds of kilometres depth (ga.gov.au). Magnetotelluric data indicate a conductivity anomaly associated with the Darling Fault Zone, and this anomaly has been imaged as penetrating into the upper mantle (Hoskin et al. 2013). Conductors have been imaged on other lithospheric fault zones worldwide, explained by fluids in the enhanced permeability of the damage zone (Hoskin et al. 2013). Other examples of this are found in places such as China, Japan, India, and Turkey (Zhang 2017).

By the late Neoproterozoic, the tectonic style along the western margin of the Yilgarn Craton appears to have become that of an extensional, rift environment, with granitoid emplacement and then granulite facies metamorphism affecting the Leeuwin Complex (Wilde 1999). A geophysical (seismic and magnetics) traverse across the Darling Fault Zone supports a late Proterozoic rifting model, with evidence of extension affecting the upper 8–10 km of crust along the western margin of the Yilgarn Craton (Middleton et al. 1995). Leeuwin Complex granites have been interpreted to have resulted from intracontinental high-temperature melting in a rift environment (Loiselle and Wones 1979) consistent with the development of rifting associated with the breakup of Rodinia (Wilde 1999).

A Young Earth Bible model

I have previously suggested that the huge land erosion was caused by the enormous (prolonged and global) rain of the Noahic Flood and that this can be correlated with Neoproterozoic sedimentary sequences, with strontium isotope trends indicating Neoproterozoic continental erosion (Dickens 2016). A corollary is that Archean to Mesoproterozoic rocks may be correlated with the first few days of Creation Week (Dickens 2017b).

He set the earth on its foundations (Psalm 104:5a ESV).

Mantle roots of Archean cratons may be considered as the foundations of the earth's crust during Creation Week (possibly on Day 1) (Dickens and Snelling 2008). The Archean Yilgarn Craton was cratonized around 2,600 Ma (radiometric 'age') by the emplacement of extensive granitoids into pre-existing greenstone and high-grade gneissic belts (Wilde 1999; Gee et al. 1981). This is considered to correspond to the Kenoran Event of North America's Superior Province (Stockwell 1982).

And God said, 'Let the waters under the heavens be gathered together into one place, and let the dry land appear.' And it was so (Genesis 1:9 ESV).

The 1,200–1,100 Ma peak in isotopic and geochemical signatures, identified in Western Australia's Albany-Fraser

Orogen, North America's Grenville Province, and global data sets, signifies that the Grenvillian Orogeny represents a unique episode in Earth's history (Van Kranendonk and Kirkland 2013). The Grenvillian Orogeny has been correlated with crustal thickening and the consequent emergence of land on Day 3 of Creation Week (Dickens 2017b; Snelling 2009).

In the six hundredth year of Noah's life, in the second month, on the seventeenth day of the month, on that day all the fountains of the great deep burst forth, and the windows of the heavens were opened (Genesis 7:11 ESV).

… by His knowledge, the deeps broke open (Proverbs 3:20a ESV).

The Bible clearly states that on a specific day, there was simultaneous worldwide fracturing of the earth's crust as the fountains burst forth. The phrases "fountains of the great deep burst forth" and "deeps broke open" imply rifting and fracturing of the earth's crust. The text implies that water flowed from within the earth through the fountains, and rain fell. Much of the water for the Noahic Flood may have come from various depths within the earth, with the mantle being the major water source (Dickens and Snelling 2008).

The term 'Pan-African' is used to describe much of the global tectonic (including rifting), magmatic, and metamorphic activity of Neoproterozoic to earliest Paleozoic geology. The Pan-African event is interpreted as a tectono-thermal event at around the radiometric 'date' of about 500 Ma ago, during which a number of orogenic belts formed, surrounding older cratons (Kroner and Stern 2004).

The Pan-African event is associated in secular literature with the Neoproterozoic rifting of the Rodinian supercontinent (Wilde 1999). This event is inferred to have initiated with the breaking open of the fountains of the great deep (Dickens 2017b).

The granulite facies metamorphism of the Leeuwin Complex is considered characteristic of the low-pressure metamorphism in Pan-African terranes (Wilde 1999). $^{40}Ar/^{39}Ar$ 'ages' from the Yilgarn Craton's transitional domain may have been reset due to hydrothermal alteration related to Pan-African tectonism, as recorded in the Leeuwin Complex (Lu 2016). In light of $^{40}Ar/^{39}Ar$ data in the western margin of both the Yilgarn Craton and the Albany-Fraser Orogen (Myers 1990a), young biotite 'ages' have been interpreted to result principally from hydrothermal fluid alteration (Lu 2016).

In my early Flood model (Dickens 2017b), the vicinity of the Darling Fault is considered to be a region where continental crust fragmented and the fountains of the great deep broke open. Rb-Sr and Ar-Ar isotope systems, petrography, and magnetotelluric data all point to a regionally extensive and major hydrothermal event around the Darling Fault. Paleomagnetic data, mafic dykes close to the Darling Fault, a seismic traverse across the Darling Fault Zone, and intracontinental high-temperature melting suggest a model of late Proterozoic rifting. This may have been associated with the breakup of Rodinia or some version of a supercontinent. In this study of southwestern Australia, all these pieces of evidence taken together are consistent with the Bible's account of the Flood event initiating as "the fountains of the great deep burst forth".

SUPPLEMENTARY MATERIAL

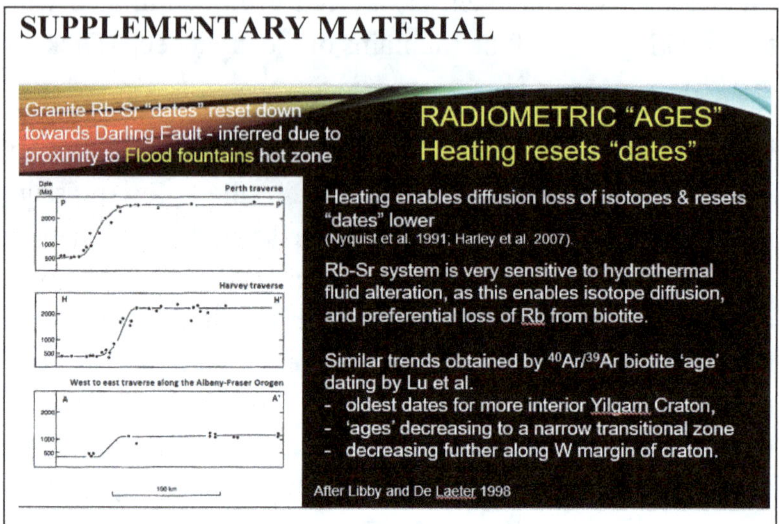

Radiometric "dates" reset towards the Darling Fault Zone, associated with heating.

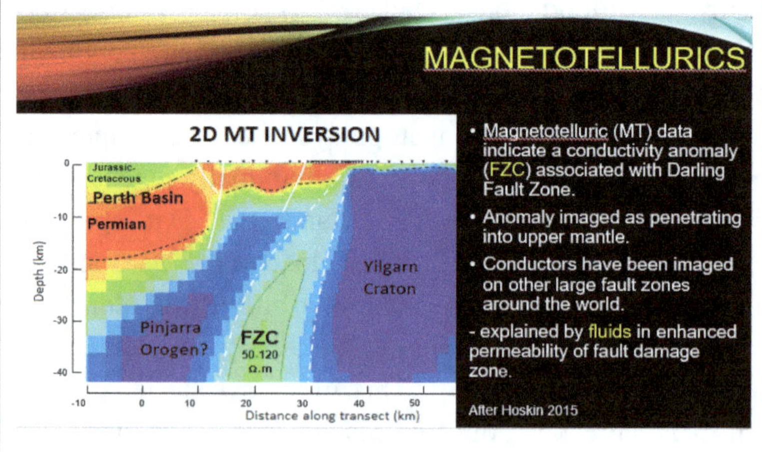

Conductivity anomaly associated with Darling Fault Zone.

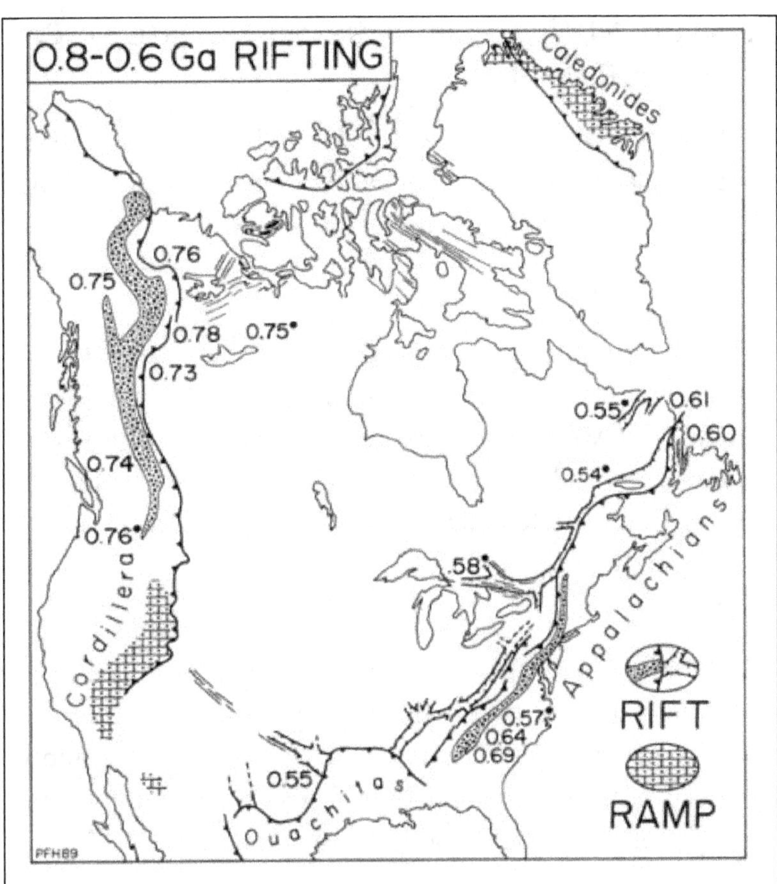

Possible sites of fountains of the great deep in North America (map after Hoffman 1989)

B. STUPENDOUS FLOOD EROSION: THE GREAT UNCONFORMITY

Source: Dickens, H. 2016. The 'Great Unconformity' and Associated Geochemical Evidence for Noahic Flood Erosion. *Journal of Creation* 30 (1): 8–10.

HIGHLIGHTS

The Bible's Flood account describes the greatest rain event ever recorded. Forty days and nights of rain falling on the earth would have caused immense wearing away of landmasses and destruction of land biomes around the globe. Evidence for this denudation is provided by a key stratigraphic surface and by associated geochemical signatures.

The Great Unconformity is the most widely recognised and distinctive stratigraphic surface in the rock record. It is a clear case where uniformitarianism does not apply since extensive peneplanation surfaces are not forming today, but channel erosion is occurring today.

The Great Unconformity commonly separates Precambrian rocks from overlying Cambrian sedimentary strata. Numerous geochemical signatures associated with this boundary indicate continental denudation, enhanced chemical weathering, and changes in global ocean chemistry. Chemical indicators include Ca2+, glauconite, displacive calcite, silicates, and $^{87}Sr/^{86}Sr$.

The evidence is consistent with what would be expected from the erosive effects of enormous rainfall on the land, together with sea level rise, until waters totally covered the continents during the early Noahic Flood:

secular scientists as occurring during 'glaciations'), are more likely mass flow deposits formed in the early stage of Noah's Flood due to enormous rainfall on the

The subsequent decline in the $^{87}Sr/^{86}Sr$ ratio in post-Cambrian strata is considered to be due to the globe being totally covered with oceans, so the Flood's rain no longer directly impacted the land.

3. Evidence of sea level rise includes a universal fining upward sequence observed in Cambrian and Lower Ordovician strata in numerous locations around the world.

4. There are huge volumes of Cambro-Ordovician carbonate globally and this is a Phanerozoic peak for carbonate sediments. This may represent the peak of Noah's Flood.

The Bible's Flood account describes the greatest rain event ever recorded. Forty days and nights of rain falling on the earth (Genesis 7:12) would have caused immense denudation of land masses around the globe. Evidence for this is provided by a key stratigraphic surface and by associated geochemical signatures.

Nature and extent of the 'Great Unconformity'

The term 'Great Unconformity' was originally used to describe the prominent stratigraphic surface exposed in the Grand Canyon that separates the Lower Cambrian Tapeats Sandstone (of the Sauk cratonic sequence) from the underlying Precambrian strata (Granite Gorge Metamorphic Suite and tilted sedimentary rocks of the Grand Canyon Supergroup) (Yochelson 2006).

The Great Unconformity can be traced across North America and globally, including most of today's southern hemisphere landmasses, along with Western Europe and Siberia—this makes it the "most widely recognised and distinctive stratigraphic surface in the rock record" (Peters and Gaines 2012). This surface in most regions separates continental crystalline basement rock from overlying undeformed Cambrian marine fossil -bearing sedimentary rock. It thus records the onset of the denudation of continental crust, followed by the first major marine transgression (Sauk Sequence) and sediment accumulation on the continents (Fig. 1) (Peters and Gaines 2012).

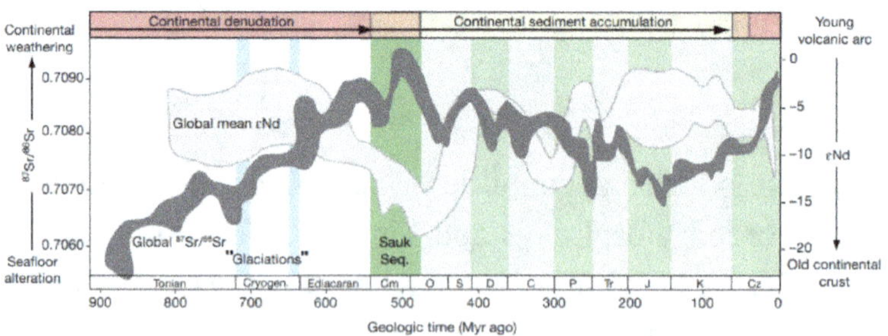

 Figure 1. Summary of major geochemical and sedimentary patterns derived from Upper Proterozoic to Phanerozoic strata (modified from Peters and Gaines 2012)

The Great Unconformity is a clear case where uniformitarianism does not apply. Extensive planation surfaces are not forming today but channel erosion is occurring today (Oard 2008). The very high energy erosion of the global Flood would have had the capacity to wear down Precambrian cratons to simultaneously form the Great Unconformity as a peneplaned surface over tremendous areas of the earth. Most Flood geologists point to this widespread erosional discontinuity in the geological record, known as the Great Unconformity, as indicating the Flood's abrupt onset (Baumgardner 2012).

The Sauk Sequence often has quartz and feldspar-rich basal sands overlying Precambrian basement across North America and North Africa (Peters and Gaines 2012; Clarey 2015). Similarly, basal sandstone units are widespread in the large (2 million km^2 surface area) Australian intracratonic sedimentary basin known as the Centralian Superbasin, which is believed to have formed at the time of the break-up of the Rodinia supercontinent (Allen and Armitage 2012). The Heavitree Quartzite is the basal sandstone unit of the Amadeus Basin, which is, in turn, part of the Centralian Superbasin (Lindsay 1999). The Heavitree Quartzite has been described as an early Flood formation (Walker 2015). In southern Israel, the fossiliferous Cambrian sedimentary strata of the early Flood sit directly on the eroded surface of the crystalline basement of the northernmost Arabian-Nubian Shield (Snelling 2010).

Evidence of sea level rise includes a universal fining upward sequence observed in Cambrian and Lower Ordovician strata in locations across the USA (Sauk Sequence), Greenland, UK, Russia, Australia, Bolivia, and Ghana (Morton 1984). A classic fining upward succession occurs in Grand Canyon Cambrian strata (Austin 1994).

A Flood model has been proposed to explain the erosion of the Great Unconformity and subsequent deposition of the Cambrian Tapeats Sandstone, Bright Angel Shale, and Muav Limestone as floodwaters advanced in areas now known as Nevada, Arizona, and New Mexico (Austin 1994).

Along with tremendous erosion of the exposed continental landmasses, torrential rain would likely have caused huge mass flows to sweep down into the adjacent seas. Upper Proterozoic mixtites, interpreted by secular scientists as occurring during 'glaciations' (Fig. 1), are more likely mass flow deposits formed in the early stage of Noah's Flood due to enormous rainfall on the continents (Wingerden 2003; Sigler and Wingerden 1998; Snelling 2009; Austin and Wise 1994). Other Upper Proterozoic mixtites are found in the Appalachian Mountains, Scandinavia, Russian Platform, Siberia, Caledonian Mountains, northwest China, Brazil, central and southern Africa, and northwest, central and southern Australia (Schermerhorn 1974).

Geochemical signatures consistent with continental denudation

Numerous geochemical signatures indicative of continental denudation have been described from Upper Proterozoic strata (Peters and Gaines 2012; McKenzie et al. 2014).

Strong evidence for an increase in continental erosion and weathering products to the global ocean is provided by measurements of Ca2+ in fluid inclusions (Peters and Gaines 2012). Concentrations of Ca2+ show a precipitous increase from the Upper Proterozoic strata to a peak in the Cambrian strata (Brennan et al. 2004). Much of this near threefold increase in Ca2+ has been attributed to greater chemical weathering of continental crust during the Sauk marine transgression (Peters and Gaines 2012).

The abundance and distribution of the phyllosilicate mineral glauconite, (K,Na)(Fe3+,Al,Mg)2 (Si,Al)4 O10(OH)2, in Cambrian sediments likely required rapid authigenesis due to an unusually large flux of continental weathering products, particularly Fe3+, K+ and H3 SiO4, during the formation of the Great Unconformity (Peters and Gaines 2012). Trough cross-stratified deposits of glauconitic mineral-rich accumulations (glaucarenites, i.e. coarse-grained glauconitic mineral pellets) found in Cambro-Ordovician strata indicate a high-energy environment. The abundance of thoroughly cross-stratified deposits also indicates that, at least on the cross-set scale, individual pellets were deposited and covered by other laminae very rapidly (Chafetz and Reid 2000).

Precipitation of carbonate sediments also reached a peak in the Phanerozoic, as recorded in the Cambrian-Lower Ordovician strata of the Sauk Sequence of North America (Ronov et al. 1980; Walter et al. 2002; Ginsburg 1982). Petrographic textures (displacive growth of calcite crystals within the claystone matrix) and depleted δ13C values provide evidence of rapid direct precipitation of carbonate at the sediment-water interface (Gaines et al. 2012). Calcium carbonate precipitation does not require deep time as has been demonstrated by laboratory studies (Wojtowicz 2001).

Thus, huge volumes of Cambro-Ordovician carbonate globally could have precipitated rapidly, likely within months during the year of Noah's Flood. During the early stage of the Flood, the enormous runoff from continents may have contributed to the drawdown of carbon dioxide described for the Cryogenian (Berner 2006), since chemical weathering of silicate rocks is a major carbon dioxide sink (Berner et al. 1983; Kump et al. 2000).

^{87}Sr is a radiogenic daughter isotope of ^{87}Rb and is found in silicate rocks such as granite. The abundance of radiogenic ^{87}Sr relative to 'common' ^{86}Sr in a sample of sediment is related to the amount of sediment that originated from the erosion of continental crust as opposed to that originating from the ocean. The observed increase in Upper Proterozoic strontium isotope ratios ^{87}Sr $/^{86}$Sr (Fig. 1) has been explained by accelerated rates of erosion during the so-called Pan-African orogeny, and high crustal erosion rates have been inferred from Cambrian ^{87}Sr $/^{86}$Sr values (Derry et al. 1994).

The subsequent decline in the ^{87}Sr $/^{86}$Sr ratio in post-Cambrian strata indicates greater oceanic influence and a time of accumulation of sediments on the continents (Fig. 1) as more of the Sauk Sequence began to be deposited, reducing the direct erosive impact on landmasses. The radiometric 'timespan' for the Upper Proterozoic to Cambrian increase in ^{87}Sr $/^{86}$Sr ratio is approximately 400 Ma (Fig. 1), but in the biblical framework, the actual time elapsed would have been of the order of weeks to months.

Final comment

The erosional surface represented by the Great Unconformity is found on continents around the globe and is an exceptional boundary in earth history. This surface commonly separates Precambrian rocks from overlying Cambrian sedimentary strata. Continental denudation, enhanced chemical weathering, and changes in global ocean chemistry are indicated by numerous geochemical signatures associated with this boundary. The evidence is consistent with what would be expected from the effects of enormous rainfall and rising Flood waters on the continents during the early Noahic Flood.

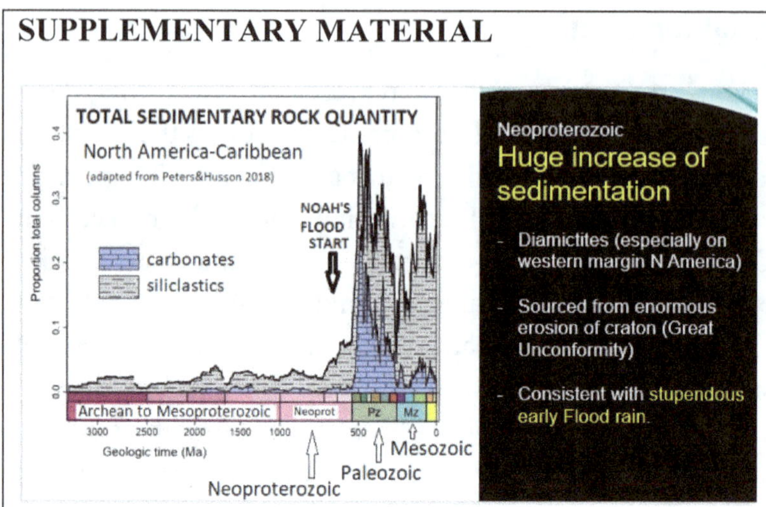

Huge increase in sedimentation in the Neoproterozoic and Phanerozoic.

Powerful erosion of Oroville Dam spillway.

Enormously powerful and destructive continental erosion

- The modern-day canyon formed in the spillway of California's Oroville Dam demonstrates that water is powerful enough to rapidly erode even hard crystalline rock (Walker 2017).

- The Noahic rain event (Genesis 7:12) was the greatest rain event ever recorded in the history of the earth. Erosion was consequently immense and powerful enough to erode and peneplane hard crystalline basement rocks around the globe and wear mountains down (Dickens 2017b; Dickens 2018b).

- The 40 days and nights of global rain during Noah's Flood may have resulted in effects orders of magnitude greater than what happened at the Oroville Dam spillway, e.g., erosion of Grenville mountains to their roots.

- I infer an enormous erosion of land and water flows associated with the early Flood year's rain (Dickens 2016). Erosion would have been enhanced by energetic downslope water flows from highland areas to lowland areas. In the Mackenzie Mountains of the Canadian Cordillera (western continental margin), the Neoproterozoic strata is over 10 km thick. This huge thickness of strata is consistent with enormous rain in the early Flood year. Water and entrained detritus flowed downward towards the continental margins where there is now thick Neoproterozoic strata.

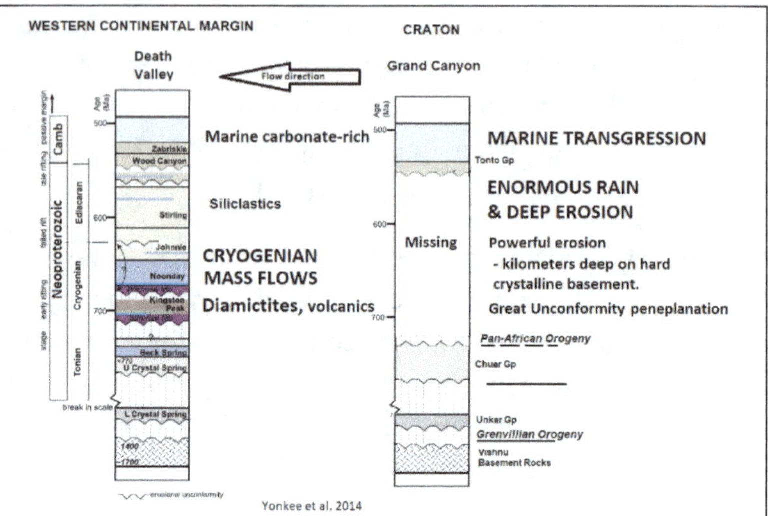

Enormous erosion and deposition indicated by stratigraphy of the Grand Canyon and Death Valley.

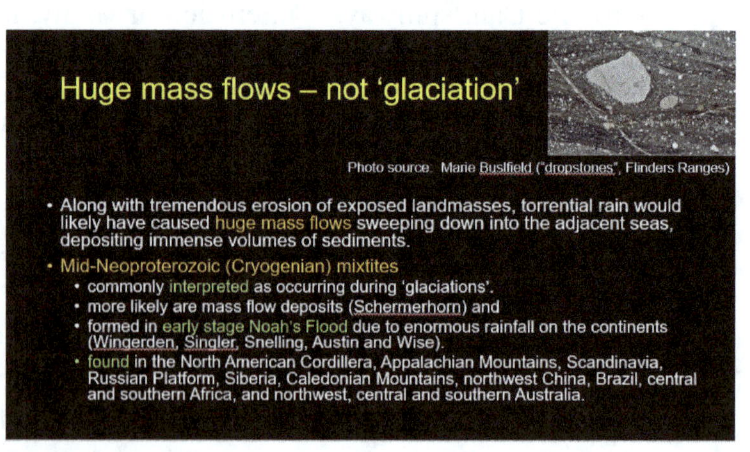

Cryogenian mixtites as mass flow deposits.

C. FLOOD AND AFTERMATH

1. Five stages of the early Flood year

Source: Dickens, H. and Hutchison, A. 2021. Geochemical and related evidence for early Noah's Flood year. *Journal of Creation* 35(1):78-88.

HIGHLIGHTS

"Ascertaining the dynamic earth process causes of enormous Neoproterozoic continental denudation followed by Phanerozoic sedimentation, and relating those dynamics to the timing and spatial distribution of marine transgression and biogeochemical change", has been said to be a challenge for geoscience.

However, this paper addresses the challenge by proposing a five-stage time sequence for the early part of Noah's Flood year, with an emphasis on geochemistry. Early Flood year processes include the fountains bursting forth, enormous rain causing stupendous erosion of land, and concurrent sea level rise until eventually all the earth's land was covered.

The Neoproterozoic to Cambrian stratigraphy of the Mackenzie Mountains of northwest Canada was used as a case study.

Stages in an interpreted early Flood year process model based on stratigraphy:

1. Intracratonic basin – Extensional tectonic regime associated with Flood fountains bursting forth. Hydrothermal fluids. Copper sulphide and CaSO4 precipitation.

2. Diamictites-bearing and volcanics – Rapitan overturn of deeper anoxic waters with upwelling currents to more oxygenated waters. Hydrothermal-derived FeII oxidised to FeIII. Rapitan phosphatic BIF with hydrothermal and detrital components. Phosphorus inferred from dissolved pre-Flood land vertebrates. Enormous rain eroding and depositing clastic sediments. Submarine landslides (not "glacials") on continental margin.

3. Mature siliclastics – upwelling waters bring anoxic deeper water material up above wave base, causing their oxidation. Not an NOE.

4. Immature siliciclastics and volcanics—$^{87}Sr/^{86}Sr$ increased to its peak in the Cambrian due to enormous continental erosion caused by rain and then declined when all the land was covered by water.

5. Carbonate-rich – sea level now completely covered the land - the first continental-scale marine transgression of the Phanerozoic.

$^{87}Sr/^{86}Sr$ ratio and sedimentary thickness curves correlate because both curves are a function of runoff. Runoff and therefore the thickness and volume of sediment, is related to tectonism and rainfall. We refute the assertion that the lateral extent, volume, and thickness of megasequences relates to the height of sea level.

The rapidity of basic chemical reactions involved is consistent with a young-earth creationist understanding of Earth's history.

Abstract

This paper proposes a five-stage time sequence for the early part of Noah's Flood year, with an emphasis on geochemistry. Early Flood year processes include the fountains bursting forth, enormous rain, and sea level rise. The Neoproterozoic to Cambrian stratigraphy of the Mackenzie Mountains of northwest Canada is well described in the literature. This location is used as a key example of strata inferred to have formed during the early Flood year. Neoproterozoic stratigraphy is subdivided upwards into Tonian, Cryogenian, and Ediacaran strata.

Introduction

Early Flood year geological activity included major volcanics, huge amounts of continental erosion, deposition of sheet sandstones, mass flows, banded iron formations with high phosphate content, high volumes of nutrients, and the burial of diverse marine invertebrates. Chemical parameters used in this study include $^{87}Sr/^{86}Sr$ ratios, oxygen levels, lithology types, carbon isotopes, carbonate formation, the order of precipitation of barium and iron, phosphorus levels, sulfur isotopes, organic matter burial, and molybdenum isotope ratios.

Explaining the cause-effect relationships of the rock record at the interface between the Precambrian and Phanerozoic rocks is a complex task:

"Determining the geodynamic causes of extensive Neoproterozoic continental denudation followed by Phanerozoic sedimentation, and linking those dynamics to the timing and spatial distribution of marine transgression and biogeochemical change, is now a challenge for geoscience." (Peters and Gaines 2012).

This paper seeks to address this challenge by invoking a framework of the early stages of the Flood year based on correlating inferred common geochemical processes to the biblical and geological records. Therefore, geochemistry should help clarify events and processes operative during the early phase of Noah's Flood year.

An anti-creationist geologist said: "Sedimentation in the past has often been very rapid indeed and very spasmodic. This may be called the Phenomenon of the Catastrophic Nature of the Stratigraphical Record."(Ager 1973).

Many chemical reaction rates increase exponentially with increasing temperature (Laidler 1984). As such, chemical reactions can occur very rapidly under conditions such as hydrothermal activity. Even at room temperature, many chemical precipitation reactions necessary for mineral formation occur almost instantly (Kennedy 1990). The rapidity of the basic chemical reactions involved is consistent with a young-earth creationist understanding of Earth's history.

Broadly speaking, the initial Flood deluge would have caused enormous erosion of the land, and concurrently, the sea level rose until eventually, all of the earth's land was covered (Dickens 2016). This initial enormous erosion of land is an important aspect of the Flood year that must be recognized in conjunction with the marine transgressions of the Flood year (Dickens 2017b). The Cordilleran stratigraphy of North America, and particularly the Mackenzie Mountains of Canada published by such researchers as Colpron et al. 2002 (Fig. 1) and Hoffman and Halverson 2011 (Fig. 2), serve as a good illustration of how these processes could rapidly form Neoproterozoic to Cambrian strata during the early stages of the Flood year. The abundant published studies written on this region that have geochemical relevance make it an especially useful example for closer analysis.

Discussion

The following is a proposed Flood model for the Mackenzie Mountains (Fig. 1) in five stages in approximate time order for the early Noahic Flood year. We maintain that the generally accepted secular deep-time 'radiometric ages' used in this paper are not absolute ages. In addition, we assert that the events described occurred some thousands of years ago but in a similar order as the referenced radiometric dates.

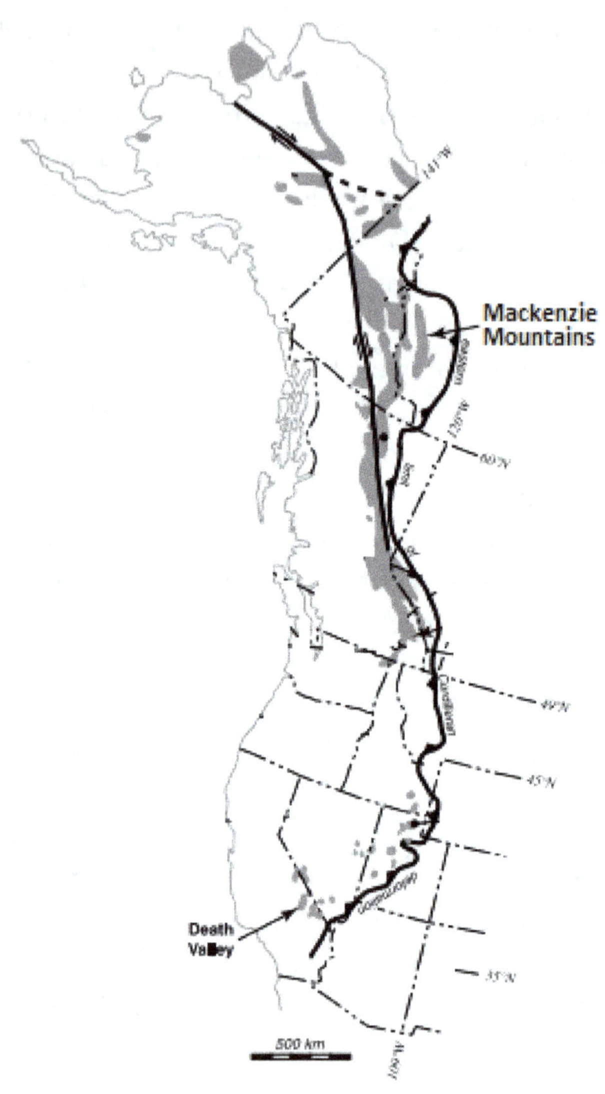

Figure 1. Distribution of late Neoproterozoic strata in western North America, showing the location of the Mackenzie Mountains in north-west Canada (after Colpron et al. 2002)

140

<u>Stage 1</u>

A. <u>Pre-Flood sediments</u>

The stratigraphic section of the Tonian Mackenzie Mountains Supergroup adapted from Hoffman and Halverson 2011 (Fig. 2) illustrates how the supergroup likely represents pre-Flood deposition in a large epicratonic basin (Martel et al. 2012) (Stage 1) (Yonkee et al. 2014). Detrital zircon provenance studies indicate that the Katherine Group quartz arenite was in part delivered by a continent-crossing early Neoproterozoic river system draining the mountains of Grenville Province in the south-east of North America (Rainbird et al. 1997). The Little Dal Group has giant microbial carbonate reefs (Martel et al. 2012) and the presence of sulfate 'evaporite' indicates the action of hydrothermal springs. These features suggest the presence of a hydrothermal biome on the pre-Flood continental shelf (Wise 2003).

B. <u>Initial tectonism and volcanism</u>

Consistent with Genesis 7:11 and Proverbs 3:20a, Noah's Flood may have been initiated by God causing the mantle to heat in a cataclysmic global thermal-tectonic episode, cracking open the earth's crust and driving out water to the earth's surface. Secular scientists have found evidence of episodic rifting events at the margins of North America between 0.8 and about 0.6 Ga. These are thought to record the fragmentation of a Neoproterozoic supercontinent (Bond et al. 1984; Hoffman 1989). This is consistent with the breaking open of the crust by the fountains of the great deep, followed by further continental extension and then ocean formation.

Mafic volcanic rocks record widespread igneous activity during regional rifting along western North America (Yonkee et al. 2014) and the Cryogenian breakup of the supercontinent. Researchers have inferred that large continental flood basalts were emplaced when the supercontinent began to break up. A major example of this volcanism is northern Canada's Franklin Large Igneous Province, which is over 2 million km^2 in area (Cox et al. 2016).

^{87}Sr is a radiogenic daughter isotope of ^{87}Rb and is found in silicate rocks such as granite, which are a significant part of the continental crust. The abundance of radiogenic ^{87}Sr relative to 'common' ^{86}Sr in a sample of sediment is related to the amount of sediment that originated from the erosion of continental crust. Lowered ^{87}Sr/^{86}Sr values indicate hydrothermal and oceanic sources. In north-west Canada, a low ^{87}Sr/^{86}Sr value in early Neoproterozoic strata (ca. 830 Ma) has been correlated with a large input of juvenile crust and the Pan-African event (Asmerom et al. 1991). The Pan-African event relates to massive rifting on the Cordilleran and Appalachian margins of North America, as well as immense continental erosion and enormous water flows (Dickens 2018b). In northwest Canada, breaking open of the crust enabled extensive volcanism, which intruded as far as the top of the Mackenzie Mountains Supergroup, where it formed pillow basalt lavas (Hoffman and Halverson 2011) (Fig. 2).

The Little Dal Group (at the top of the Mackenzie Mountains Supergroup—Fig. 2) is inferred to be the highest pre-Flood formation in the Mackenzie Mountains (Fig. 1).

The basalt which intruded the Little Dal Group (Fig. 2) is inferred to have formed as part of an ongoing extensional regime while the early Flood year fountains were active. Extension and intracratonic basin deposition (Stage 1 of Fig. 2) is thought to have occurred contemporaneously with the intrusion of the Franklin and Gunbarrel large igneous province dike swarms of northern Canada (Yonkee et al. 2014).

The Coates Lake Group (the lowest section within the Windermere Supergroup—Fig. 2) is inferred to have been deposited on top of the Little Dal Group at the very beginning of the Flood year. The sandstone and siltstone-rich unit may have formed from sediments eroded from the land by the massive rainfall. A layer of sulfate (Hoffman et al. 2017) within the Coates Lake Group formed when the heat from magma, welling up because of the igneous activity concurrent with the fountains erupting, led to $CaSO_4$ precipitating from the waters. Along with the magma came hydrothermal fluids rich in CO_2. Widespread and prolonged rain and fountains pouring forth (Genesis 7:11–12) caused enormous runoff. Dead organisms and other nutrients carried in the runoff provided food for microbes, which then helped convert the CO_2 to carbonates (Fig. 2, Stage 2). The laminated, stromatolitic nature of the carbonate layer at the top of the Coates Lake Group supports this interpretation of its formation (Macdonald et al., 2018; Snelling and Purdom, 2013).

The Coates Lake Group likely represents deposition in embayments of a rift system (Martel et al. 2012). It hosts significant strabound copper deposits in a series of half-grabens, which we suggest are related to the first stage of the supercontinent breakup (Ootes et al., 2013). Chloride brines may have leached copper from the underlying Little Dal Basalt, and then passed through reducing sulfate-bearing strata of the Coates Lake Group, which triggered the precipitation of copper sulfides (Ootes et al. 2013). This hypothesis is supported by the fetid, black carbonates of the Copper Cap Formation, which is the top part of the Coates Lake Group (Hoffman and Halverson 2011). The coarse-grained limestones have abundant sparry calcite cement with $\delta C13$ values near zero. These $\delta C13$ values suggest that the source of the sparry calcite cement is at least in part from CO_2 produced by methane fermentation of organic material in the substrata (Ross and Oana 1961). The reducing nature of these carbonates could have enabled the precipitation of the copper sulfide.

Enormous rainfall impacted the North American continent at this stage, causing increased erosion and the mass-flow deposition of coarser sediments, forming diamictite along with sandstone, siltstone, and mudstone (Fig. 2, Stage 2). These sediments characterize the Rapitan through the Icebrook formations of Figure 2. The Rapitan and Icebrook formations have respectively been correlated worldwide with the supposedly 'glacial' Sturtian and Marinoan strata (Narbonne et al. 2014). The finer-grained shale, sandstone, siltstone, and limestone of the Twitya Formation and the Keele Formation, which overlay the diamictite of the Rapitan, suggest a rising sea level.

The basal Twitya Formation has a cap carbonate overlying the Rapitan Group (Fig. 2) (Hoffman et al. 2017). δ13C values suggest a somewhat higher input of inorganic carbon to the carbonates of the Keele and Ravensthroat formations compared to the carbonate in the Coates Lake Group. This indicates a fresh input of inorganic carbon from volcanic hydrothermal fluids containing carbon dioxide, which led to oversaturation of carbonate and precipitation of calcite and aragonite, some of which later underwent diagenic dolomitization (James et al. 2001; Shields 2005). However, the still increasing $^{87}Sr/^{86}Sr$ ratio indicates a significant amount of this carbon may be from continental carbonates that were eroded into the basin as well. It has been proposed that some cap carbonates formed both by microbially mediated precipitation during algal blooms under low salinity conditions and by direct precipitation of aragonite onto the seafloor (Shields 2005). The presence of flakestone provides additional evidence for extensive calcium carbonate precipitation.

<u>Stage 2</u>

A. <u>Enormously powerful and destructive continental erosion</u>

The Noahic rain event (Genesis 7:12) was the greatest rain event ever recorded in the history of the earth. Erosion was consequently immense and powerful enough to erode and peneplane hard crystalline basement rocks around the globe and wear mountains down (Dickens 2017b; Dickens 2018b). The modern-day canyon formed in the spillway of California's Oroville Dam demonstrates that water is powerful enough to rapidly erode even hard crystalline rock

(Walker 2017). We infer an enormous erosion of land associated with the early Flood year's rain (Dickens 2016).

The significant Neoproterozoic ^{87}Sr/^{86}Sr isotope ratio increase as reported by Peters and Gaines 2012 and reproduced in figure 3 is consistent with enormous erosion of notably radiogenic continental crust1, (Dickens 2016; Dickens 2017b; James et al. 2001; Dickens and Snelling 2015; Mackenzie et al. 2014) during the Pan-African event (Derry et al 1994). The 'radiometric timespan' for this increase in ^{87}Sr/^{86}Sr ratio is approximately 0.4 Gyr (between 0.9 Ga and 0.5 Ga, i.e. early Neoproterozoic to mid-Cambrian—Fig. 3), but in the biblical framework, the actual time elapsed would have been of the order of weeks to months. This 'radiometric timespan' likely represents the time from the initiation of Noah's Flood (associated with fountains hydrothermal activity) and massive continental erosion caused by rain, to a time of greater oceanic influence with accumulation of sediments on the continents as the Sauk sequence began to be deposited (Dickens 2016; Dickens 2018b). ^{87}Sr/^{86}Sr ratios in Cambrian sedimentary carbonates are the highest of Phanerozoic strata (Veizer and Compston 1974; Veizer et al. 1999). High crustal erosion rates have been inferred from Cambrian ^{87}Sr/^{86}Sr values in north-west Canada (Asmerom et al. 1991). The large supplies of clastic sediments that flooded into basins imply high rates of erosion of the basin hinterlands, which in turn can explain the progressive rise in ^{87}Sr/^{86}Sr (Fig. 3).

Detritus resulting from continental erosion was entrained in flowing water, which produced Neoproterozoic sedimentary cover sequences (Dickens 2018b). This included thick sedimentary successions found in North America's Cordilleran region. Zircon grains of Grenvillian age (1.0–0.9 Ga) were recovered from lower Neoproterozoic sedimentary basins in north-western Canada, more than 3,000 km away from the nearest source in the Grenville Province on the other side of the continent (Rainbird et al. 1997). The pre-Flood earth and its people were destroyed during the Flood year (Genesis 6:13) in the sense of its topography and people being totally wiped away (Matthew 24:39). This drastic transformation began with an enormous erosional event from the early Flood year's prolonged and globally extensive rain. Early in Noah's Flood year, even high mountains were eroded down and peneplaned. Today's Grenville, Mazatzal, and Yavapai provinces in south-eastern North America are considered to be examples of the roots of eroded mountains (Dickens 2017b).

B. <u>Cryogenian mass flows</u>

Enormous torrential rain is inferred to be responsible for the initial massive subaerial sheet erosion of the continental landmasses. This was followed by huge submarine mass flows, depositing immense volumes of sediments, as the Flood advanced (Dickens 2018b). In contrast to lower Neoproterozoic sheet sandstones, mid-Neoproterozoic (Cryogenian) sequences contain poorly sorted diamictites, so-called 'glacial' deposits, (Hoffman 1989) especially on continental margins such as North America's Cordilleran (Sigler and Wingerden 1998; Snelling 2009; Wingerden 2003). These 'glacials' are instead considered to represent submarine landslide deposits (Sigler and Wingerden 1998; Snelling 2009; Wingerden 2003) along active tectonic zones as the marine transgression of the Flood year progressed. Cryogenian deposits are mainly poorly sorted immature clastic sediments, with lesser volcanic rocks.

Cryogenian 'glacials' have a close association with sedimentary rocks formed in warm climates (Young 2013). Warm, not cold conditions have been interpreted from associated kaolinite, diaspore, redbeds, dolomite, and limestone with phytolites (Dickens and Snelling 2008), as well as abundant carbonates with stromatolites and carbonate ooids (Hallam 1981). Flakestone, a very distinctive fine-grained carbonate facies with its characteristic broken-up clasts, is an indicator of the action of stormy seas (Tucker 1992) and not an ice-covered sea. Structures interpreted as giant wave ripples (generated by sea surface waves) have been observed in cap carbonate rocks from the Mackenzie Mountains, as well as Australia, Brazil, Namibia, and Svalbard (Allen and Hoffman 2005). Waves would not have been possible in an ice-covered ocean. The ubiquitous association of Neoproterozoic iron formations with thick successions containing numerous levels of rounded dropstones in Canada, Australia, Brazil, and Namibia indicates that mixing across a redoxcline occurred repeatedly during a sustained interval of energetic hydrological cycling, which is incompatible with a globally static ice cover (Shields 2005). We regard the Cryogenian Snowball Earth hypothesis as seriously flawed.

Transfer of atmospheric carbon dioxide to the ocean during rifting would enable rapid precipitation of calcium carbonate in warm surface waters, producing the cap carbonate rocks over Cryogenian diamictites which are observed globally

(Shields 2005). Carbon dioxide build-up from active Flood fountains is believed to have contributed to the rapid precipitation of calcium carbonate discussed earlier.

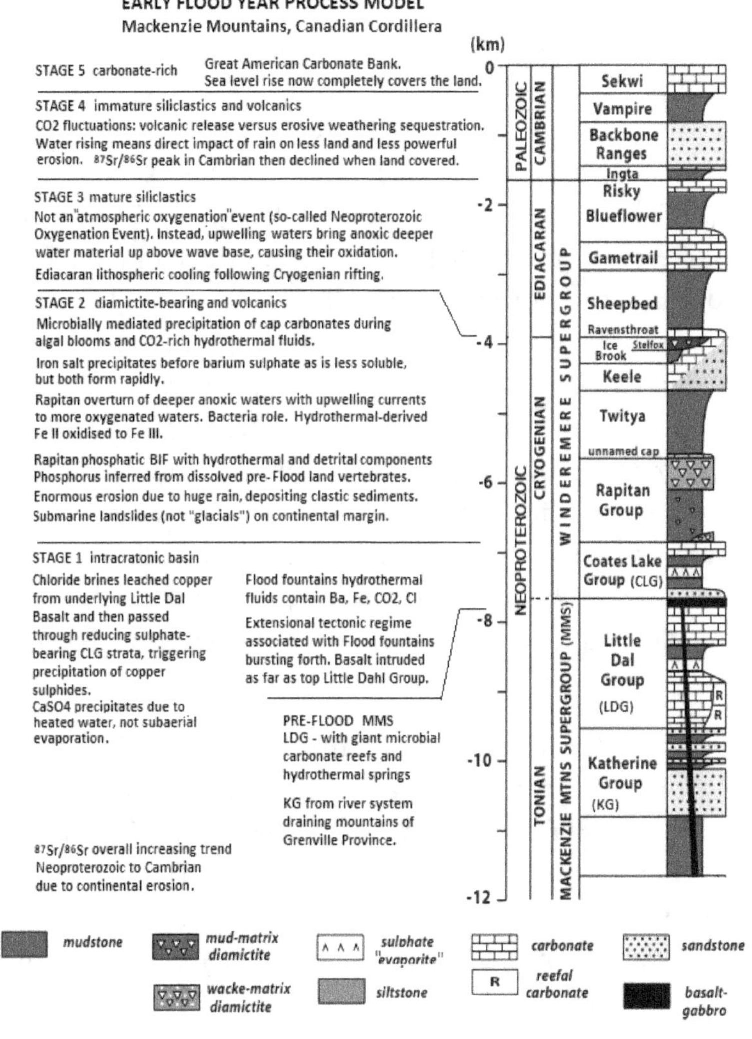

Figure 2. Composite stratigraphic section of Neoproterozoic to Cambrian strata in the Mackenzie Mountains, Canadian

Cordillera (section based on Hoffman and Halverson 2011; Stages in the North American Cordilleran margin from Yonkee et al. 2014), together with an interpreted early Flood year process model.

Massive erosion and deposition due to early Flood year rain is inferred to have rapidly laid down Cryogenian strata. Submarine landslides are indicated by diamictites in the Rapitan Group and Ice Brook Formation. The Rapitan Group (Fig. 2) consists of diamictite, debris flow deposits, turbidites, siltstone, shale, sandstone (including arkosic sandstone), and volcanics, as well as banded iron formation (Dickens 2018b; Baldwin et al. 2012; Frazier and Schwimmer 1987; Cox et al. 2013). Rapitan iron formations are found in extensional grabens that are associated with the initial breakup of the supercontinent, and are commonly found in association with mafic volcanics. Geochemical data indicates that Rapitan iron formations resulted from mixing between hydrothermal and detrital components, while rare earth element data indicates substantial interaction with seawater (Cox et al. 2013).

Overlying the Rapitan Group are more Cryogenian strata, including shallower-water carbonate and siliciclastic strata of the Keele Formation and the "glacial-related" Ice Brook Formation (Fig. 2) (Ootes et al. 2013). The Ice Brook Formation has 'hotel-size' megabreccia (Fig. 2). These so-called 'glacials' may represent a second phase of mass flows early in Noah's Flood year.

The geochemistry of cap carbonates around the world carries a strong hydrothermal signal (Young 2013). Consistent with this, Canadian Neoproterozoic diamictites are marked by negative δ13C carbonate and correspondingly depleted δ13C organic and lower $^{87}Sr/^{86}Sr$ (Walter et al. 2000). Dissolved CO2 from hydrothermal fluids and volcanic activity would have provided a significant source of inorganic carbon, overshadowing even the effect of massive burial of organic carbon that was occurring throughout the Flood year. The $^{87}Sr/^{86}Sr$ ratio of hydrothermal fluid is lower than that of seawater and continental crust (Antonelli et al. 2017; Jamieson et al. 2016).

There is an overall Neoproterozoic to the Cambrian trend of rising $^{87}Sr/^{86}Sr$ values due to enormous continental erosion (Fig. 3). However, at times, the hydrothermal input caused some dips in the overall trend of increasing $^{87}Sr/^{86}Sr$ values for Neoproterozoic strata.

C. Cryogenian barium, iron, and phosphorus occurrence

The most specific and typical feature of Cryogenian strata globally is the occurrence of so-called 'glaciogene' rocks from two stratigraphic levels. The upper or Marinoan 'glacial' is usually overlain by sediments with a higher concentration of barium. In the Mackenzie Mountains example (Fig.1), Ravensthroat dolostone caps the Ice Brook Formation (Fig. 2) and contains a layer of $BaSO_4$ (Hoffman et al. 2017). The lower or Sturtian 'glacial' (such as the Rapitan in Figure 2) is commonly associated with sheet deposits of iron ores and basic volcanics (Walter et al. 2000).

This appearance of a barium layer several levels above an iron formation is common (Walter et al. 2000). We believe this indicates that all the Cryogenian sedimentary layers (between the iron and the barium) must have been deposited

151

rapidly. Hydrothermal fluids characteristically contain iron, barium, and sulfide. If these are mixed with seawater above the wave base, atmospheric oxygen could oxidize iron and sulfide. Iron oxide deposition in the form of hematite in both Sturtian and Marinoan strata implies a build-up of ferrous (Fe2+) iron in seawater and subsequent mixing of deeper, suboxic water with shallower, more oxidizing water (Shields 2005).

Fe_2O_3 is significantly less soluble than $BaSO_4$. However, both are highly insoluble and would be expected to precipitate from the water almost as quickly as they formed (Kennedy 1990; Ball and Nordstrom 1991). The presence of the iron oxides stratigraphically beneath the barium sulfate suggests bacterial action increased the rate of Fe oxidation. The oxidation rate of both Fe(II) and sulfide is variable based on pH and bacterial action (Morgan and Lahav 2007; Luther et al., 2011). Despite the lower solubility of Fe_2O_3, if the $BaSO_4$ formed first, it would precipitate first. In this specific environment, the presence of Fe(III) oxides below $BaSO_4$ indicates that the oxidation of the iron was concurrent with or preceded the oxidation of the sulfide, suggesting bacterial action may have encouraged the conversion of Fe(II) to Fe(III). However, it is unlikely that the sulfate took significantly longer to form than the iron oxides. This suggests that the layers between the Rapitan and Ravensthroat were deposited very quickly.

Venting of hot fluids into cold neutral seawater causes rapid quenching and supersaturation, enabling the immediate precipitation of colloidal particles of ferrous hydroxide and hydrous ferrous silicate. The episodic character and rapid deposition of turbidity and density currents, lasting a few hours to days, is in direct contrast to the slow deposition of annual micro-laminations over millions of years inferred by earlier models for the origin of banded iron formations (Lascelles 2013).

During and immediately after the older, Sturtian 'glacial', the deeper parts of the ocean are inferred to be anoxic and with sufficient ferrous iron to sequester very large amounts of sulfur derived from bacterial reduction of sulfate. A huge shift in the sulfur isotopic composition was global, and this is inferred to have been accompanied by the reduction of as much as half the sulfate in the anoxic parts of the oceans (Walter et al. 2000).

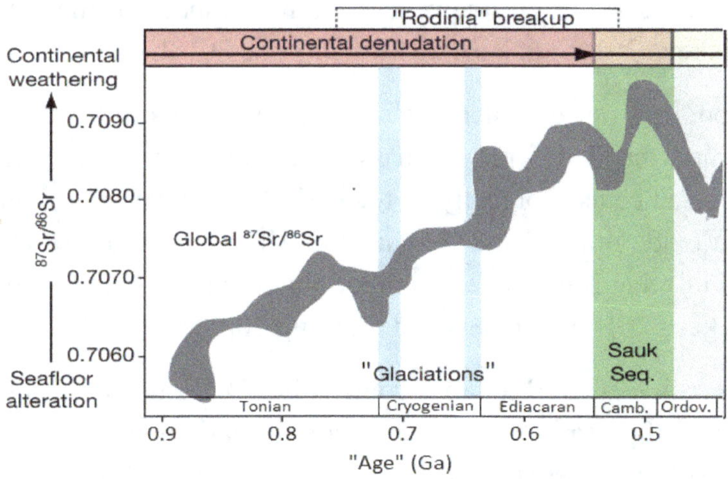

Figure 3. Summary of major geochemical and sedimentary patterns derived from Neoproterozoic to Ordovician strata. There is a shift from widespread continental denudation to widespread sedimentation on the continents (after Peters and Gaines 2012).

We infer that:

• The observed increase in the Neoproterozoic strontium isotope ratio $^{87}Sr/^{86}Sr$ can be explained by accelerated rates of denudation due to the impact of the early Flood's rain on the supercontinent and to associated Pan-African event tectonism. The Sturtian (S) and Marinoan (M) supposed 'glaciations' are instead times of massive mass flows due to enormous runoff caused by the colossal rain of the early Flood year (Dickens 2016; Dickens 2017b; Dickens 2018b).

• The subsequent decline in the $^{87}Sr/^{86}Sr$ ratio in post-Cambrian strata is associated with the first continental-scale marine transgression of the Phanerozoic (Peters and Gaines 2012). The supercontinent was covered by the ocean so that the Flood's rain no longer had a direct impact on the land (Dickens 2016; Dickens 2017b; Dickens 2018b).

A pouring out of volcanics and associated hydrothermally formed banded iron formations in the Neoproterozoic occurred catastrophically in the early Flood year. The main iron oxide mineral in Rapitan-type BIF is hematite (Fe_2O_3) and this may have appeared blood-coloured (Dickens 2017a, Dickens 2018b; Dickens and Snelling 2008).

The rift-related Rapitan Group (Fig. 2) hosts billions of tonnes of phosphatic stratiform iron formations (Ootes et al. 2013) and associated diamictite. Rapitan Group iron formation, in common with other Cryogenian iron formations, has much higher phosphate contents than Paleoproterozoic and Archean iron formations (Hoffman and Halverson 2011). This indicates unusually high dissolved phosphate concentrations and is related to high rates of primary productivity and organic carbon burial (Planavsky et al. 2010).

The greatest global phosphogenic episode in geologic history occurred in Late Precambrian and Cambrian times (Northolt et al. 1989). It is noteworthy that all continents except Antarctica, to date, are known to have Precambrian-Cambrian transition sedimentary phosphate. These phosphorite deposits are generally found stratigraphically above Cryogenian diamictites, as well as generally below shelly fossils (Dickens and Snelling 2008). Precambrian-Cambrian transition phosphorite is associated with catastrophic ocean water mixing (deep anoxic and shallow oxic oceanic waters), as inferred from sulfur isotopes (Cook 1992; Cook and Shergold 1984).

Upwelling of hydrogen sulfide-rich deep ocean water to become surface waters at the Precambrian-Cambrian transition is indicated by the basal Cambrian black shale molybdenum isotope signal (Wille et al. 2008). Upwelling currents are inferred to have supplied phosphate-rich waters to continental shelves where phosphorites were deposited around the world (Tucker 1992). The very active Flood fountains of the great deep would have caused catastrophic mixing of deep and shallow waters (Dickens and Snelling 2015).

Stage 3: Ediacaran: oxidation/reduction

It has been claimed that there was a rise in atmospheric oxygen in the Ediacaran (late Neoproterozoic) and that this was related to tectonism (Williams et al. 2019). This inferred episode of increased atmospheric oxygen is called in the secular literature the "Neoproterozoic Oxygenation Event" (NOE) (Dickens 2018b). However, in a YEC model of Earth's history, the atmosphere already had to have oxygen levels comparable to modern times since the Earth was full of human and animal life.

We do not believe the so-called NOE interval represents a massive increase in atmospheric oxygen. Rather, the increase in oxidized species in the stratigraphic record may simply indicate the movement of elements in a reduced state (such as S-2, Fe_2+, and CH_4), from deeper water to above wave base where they underwent oxidation by atmospheric oxygen. The very active Flood fountains of the great deep could have caused catastrophic mixing of deep and shallow waters (Dickens and Snelling 2015). Across the globe, it is likely that anoxic seafloor sediment was brought to the surface while near-surface material was suddenly buried. We infer that the resulting near-surface oxidation of reduced sediments was the source of the supposed NOE.

Simultaneously, buried organic carbon would have undergone decay, depleting waters of oxygen and creating localized reducing conditions in some areas and at some time periods. Careful study of the redox proxies used to support the NOE, such as $\delta^{82/76}Se$ values (Von Strandmann et al. 2015), redox-sensitive element enrichment and sulfur isotope ratios (Sahoo et al. 2016), cerium-anomaly values (Wallace et al. 2017) and $\delta238U$ (Lau et al. 2017) all reveal just such a pattern.

Rather than one dramatic and steady oxygenation event, the evidence shows multiple cycles of both oxidation and reduction, with a general pattern of oxygenated surface waters overlaying anoxic waters characterized by organic decay (Sahoo et al. 2016) This pattern is consistent with trends in δ13C for these sediments (Lau et al. 2017). Rather than a single oxygenation event, the Neoproterozoic waters were characterized by a complex and fluctuating redox chemistry, while the atmosphere maintained a relatively high oxygen content, similar to today.

Stage 3 (Ediacaran) (Fig. 2) is considered to represent lithospheric cooling following Cryogenian rifting (Yonkee et al. 2014). Ediacaran strata in the Mackenzie Mountains include shale and turbidites of the Sheepbed Formation, carbonate strata of the Gametrail Formation, thick terrigenous, clastic strata of the Blueflower Formation, and carbonate-dominated rocks of the Risky Formation (Ootes et al. 2013). Based on sedimentary facies, these Ediacaran formations are thought to have formed in marine environments with water depths ranging from deep (continental-slope) to shallow (areas of wave action) (Martel et al. 2012).

Mass mortality and a sudden decrease in biological productivity prior to the 'Cambrian explosion' (the lowermost appearance of shelly fossils in the stratigraphic record) have been inferred from a negative δ13C global geochemical anomaly in carbonate-containing black shale at the Precambrian-Cambrian transition. Kimura and Watanabe 2001 claimed that this corresponds to the widespread development of an oxygen-deficient (anoxic) shallow marine environment—a "Strangelove ocean" (Hsu et al. 1985). We suggest that this relates to the consumption of oxygen in shallow waters due to the presence of dissolved organic material undergoing decomposition. This dissolved organic material has been inferred to include that derived from pre-Flood animals and some shelly invertebrates (Dickens and Snelling 2015). Vertebrate decomposition uses oxygen from the surroundings (Weigelt 2009), creating anoxic conditions.

<u>Stage 4: Immature siliclastics and volcanics</u>

This stage is characterised by continuing erosion as evidenced by the increasing $^{87}Sr/^{86}Sr$ ratio trend for North America which reached a peak within Cambrian strata (Peters and Gaines 2012) (Fig. 3). As mentioned in Stage 1, the abundance of radiogenic ^{87}Sr relative to 'common' ^{86}Sr in a sample of sediment is related to the amount of sediment that originated from erosion of continental crust as opposed to that originating from the ocean. In other words, the strontium isotope ratio $^{87}Sr/^{86}Sr$ is linked to runoff caused by erosion. This runoff, in turn, is related to the amount of rainfall and to tectonism. At times of lower rainfall, there is less runoff, and conversely, with more rainfall, more runoff occurs (Hallam 1992). "Tectonic setting is the principal controlling factor of lithology, chemistry, and preservation of sediment accumulations in their depocenters, the sedimentary basins." (Veizer and Mackenzie 2014). In summary, the greater the topographic relief due to tectonism, and with more rain, the more the runoff and greater volume and thickness of sediment deposited.

In the Mackenzie Mountains, the Neoproterozoic strata are over 10 km thick (Fig. 2). This huge thickness of strata is consistent with the effects of Pan-African event break-up tectonism, active fountains of the great deep and enormous rain in the early Flood year, commencing with Stage 1. Water and entrained detritus flowed downward towards the continental margins, where there are now thick Neoproterozoic strata. Sea level in the pre-Flood seas would have risen at the same time as the adjacent land was being massively eroded until, eventually, the whole globe was covered with water, and the rain no longer directly impacted the land. Sea level rise indicated by North America's Sauk Megasequence is inferred to follow the initial break-up of the supercontinent (Ford and Golonka 2003).

The continuity of the basal Sauk sandstone layer across North America is a testimony to the extent and uniformity of the first great marine transgression of the Phanerozoic (Clarey 2019). In the Mackenzie Mountains of Cordilleran, Canada, this sandstone is represented by the Backbone Ranges Formation (Martel et al. 2012) (Fig. 2). Lower Cambrian strata correspond to the onset of the first major Phanerozoic marine transgression preserved extensively in North America at the base of the transgressive Sauk Megasequence, which culminated in the Great American Carbonate Bank (Peters 2006).

Marine transgressive deposits can be recognised through an upward deepening of facies (Cattaneo and Steel 2003). In addition to North America, evidence of sea level rise is provided by a universal fining upward sequence that has been observed in other Cambrian and Lower Ordovician (Sauk Megasequence) strata around the world, including Greenland, UK, Russia, Australia, Bolivia, and Ghana (Morton 1984). A classic fining upward succession occurs in Grand Canyon Cambrian strata (Tapeats Sandstone then

Bright Angel Shale). Similarly, in Stage 4 of the Cambrian of the Mackenzie Mountains, the Backbone Ranges Formation sandstone is succeeded by the Vampire Formation mudstone (Fig. 2). "Global or worldwide marine transgression" is the descriptor in the secular literature (Cook and Shergold 1984). This is another way of saying global flooding!

Fluctuations in carbon dioxide levels during Stage 4 are considered to be related to the fluctuating opposing influences of volcanic release (McKenzie et al. 2014) versus consumption with the weathering process (Peters and Gaines 2012). It has been inferred that, during Stage 4, rifting of the supercontinent and associated volcanism led to separation and transition to drift with the opening of an ocean basin in the west of Cordilleran North America (Yonkee et al. 2014).

<u>Stage 5: Early Paleozoic sea and carbonates</u>

Subsidence histories of passive margins are a key indicator of worldwide continental extension and then ocean formation beginning at 0.6 Ga (Bond et al. 1984). Cambrian (through Devonian) strata of the Mackenzie Mountains were deposited on Neoproterozoic strata in a developing passive margin which underwent thermal subsidence (Yonkee et al. 2014). An expansive Paleozoic siliciclastic-carbonate passive margin was established (Martel et al. 2012), beginning with Stages 4 and 5 (Fig. 2). We acknowledge and commend the great amount of work that fellow creationists Tim Clarey and co-workers have done in mapping the thickness and extent of megasequences on several continents (Clarey and Werner 2018). This data compilation was used to infer a sea level curve based on the assertion that the lateral extent, volume, and thickness of the megasequences relate to the height of the sea level (Clarey 2019). For instance, they inferred that the lesser lateral extent and volume of sediment in the Sauk Megasequence indicates minimal flooding (Clarey and Werner 2017). However, these assertions regarding height of sea level and amount of flooding are refuted by numerous lines of evidence. $^{87}Sr/^{86}Sr$ ratio and sedimentary thickness curves correlate (Cupps and Clarey 2020) because both curves are a function of runoff. As mentioned in Stage 4, runoff and therefore the thickness and volume of sediment is related to tectonism and rainfall.

The great thickness of Neoproterozoic strata (over 10 km in Stages 1–3) (Fig. 2) due to rain and powerful tectonism was followed by much thinner Cambrian strata (Stages 4 and 5) (Fig. 2). During marine transgressions, such as in the Cambrian, the coastline moved landwards and the marine area enlarged. This is accompanied by a reduced sediment influx to the basin (Cattaneo and Steel 2003). Water rising in Stage 4 meant less area with direct impact by rain and so less sediment influx and less powerful erosion. Times of sea level rise over land are marked by an excess of carbonates over siliclastics (Hallam 1992). This can be seen in Stage 5 with the Great American Carbonate Bank.

Major oil companies find sea level curves to be invaluable in petroleum exploration since they provide useful models to help predict the location of reservoir rocks and petroleum source rocks. Researchers at Exxon were among the first to develop global sea level curves using seismic stratigraphy, based on oil exploration seismic and well data from around the world (Vail et al. 1977). The Exxon sea level curve rises in the Cambrian to a peak at the end Cambrian. Subsequently, others refined Exxon's curve and interpreted the global sea level to have risen in the Cambrian to an Ordovician peak (Hallam 1984; Haq and Schutter 2008).

Haq and Shutter used reference geological sections from North America, Australia, northern and southern Africa, north-western Europe, and China to develop their curve for the Paleozoic. This augmented earlier results from subsurface data and the stratigraphic interpretation method of Exxon. Quantitative data from paleontology demonstrated increased diversity of plankton and pelagic organisms with higher sea levels (Haq 1991). The global Cambrian to Ordovician increase in marine invertebrate genera has been related to increased habitat area as the rising sea level transgressed the land (Hallam 1992; Hannisdal and Peters 2011). During sea level rise and maximum flooding of continental shelves, increased biological productivity, combined with greater preservational potential for organic matter in the expanded and deeper lower oxygen zone, make such sediments most likely locations for petroleum source rocks (Haq 1991). In addition to seismic stratigraphy, Hallam used additional techniques such as paleogeographic mapping, the occurrence of depth-related invertebrate and algal groups, glauconite concentration and facies correlation to develop sea level curves for the Phanerozoic (Hallam 1984).

Drowning of cratons has been inferred from lithofacies changes in uppermost Proterozoic and Cambrian strata around the world. Peritidal carbonate platforms were drowned, followed in places by phosphorites and then black shales, which form in deeper water (Brasier and Lindsay 2001). This drowning of cratons has been inferred to correlate with the time Noah's Ark rose and floated on the waters (Dickens and Snelling 2015). Consistent with the above-discussed independent lines of evidence (seismic stratigraphy, fossils, and sedimentary facies), the decline in $^{87}Sr/^{86}Sr$ ratio after the peak in Cambrian strata1 (Fig. 3) is inferred to be due to ocean formation (Bond et al. 1984), such that the enormous rain of Noah's Flood no longer directly impacted the land (Dickens 2016; Dickens 2018b). In other words, by Stage 5 rising water in the early Flood year covered the land.

Deposition of the Sauk Megasequence of north-western Canada occurred along a complex segment of the rifted western margin of North America (Pyle 2012). The Great American Carbonate Bank comprises the carbonates (and related siliciclastics) of the Sauk Megasequence, which were deposited on and around the North American continent during the Cambrian through the earliest Middle Ordovician, forming one of the largest carbonate-dominated platforms of the Phanerozoic (Derby et al. 2012). Although the term 'Great American Carbonate Bank' is understood to have originally just been used for the North American continent, the term has also been used elsewhere, such as in western South America (Keller 2012), as well as Scotland and Greenland (Raine and Smith 2012). Cambrian carbonate-rich strata, such as the Sekwi Formation of the Mackenzie Mountains (Fig. 2), accumulated in an extensive shallow epicontinental sea as siliciclastic sources were covered during the Sauk marine transgression (Yonkee et al. 2014).

While carbonates were forming throughout the Flood, precipitation of carbonate sediments reached a peak in the Cambrian-Lower Ordovician strata of the Sauk sequence of North America (Walker et al. 2002). Petrographic textures (displacive growth of calcite crystals within the claystone matrix) and depleted δ13C values provide evidence of rapid direct precipitation of carbonate at the sediment-water interface (Peters and Gaines 2012). The 'Cambrian explosion' of organisms with carbonate skeletons and the proliferation of bioturbating organisms are coincident with the onset of a carbon cycle with isotopic fluctuations damped in both frequency and amplitude (Walter et al. 2000).

The Cambrian-Lower Ordovician peak in carbonate formation may possibly have been enhanced by the input of fresh rainwater along with high concentrations of carbon dioxide. Although we infer that Flood waters had completely covered the land, continuing rain may have contributed a significant amount of freshwater, which is more favourable for carbonate precipitation than seawater. Simultaneously, CO_2 input may have peaked as the Cambrian has been inferred to have the highest modelled atmospheric carbon dioxide concentrations of the Phanerozoic (Berner 2006).

Conclusions

Geochemical processes played a significant role early in Noah's Flood year. We have proposed a time sequence of early Noah's Flood year, including various items of evidence, with an emphasis on the geochemistry of North America. Early Flood year processes discussed include fountains bursting forth, enormous rain, and the timing of sea level rise.

The Neoproterozoic to Cambrian stratigraphy of the Mackenzie Mountains of north-west Canada is used as an example (Fig. 1). Early Flood year geological products are inferred to include volcanics, huge continental erosion, sheet sandstones, mass flows, banded iron formations with high phosphate content, nutrients, and marine invertebrate diversity.

Backed up by evidence, we infer key differences to current common secular views of Neoproterozoic geological history:

- So-called 'evaporites' in Little Dal Group and Coates Lake Group formed by hydrothermal means, rather than by subaerial evaporation.

- Cryogenian diamictites formed by mass flows rather than by 'glaciation' and a 'Snowball Earth'.

- Neoproterozoic oxidation of sediments due to vigorous upwelling and mixing of suboxic sediments associated with energetic Flood fountains, rather than the 'Neoproterozoic Oxygenation' of the atmosphere.

- Deep-time is unnecessary and unrealistic for geochemical reactions (such as the formation of BIF and copper sulfide orebodies), particularly under hydrothermal conditions.

Key inferences in time order:

1. Mackenzie Mountains Supergroup represents pre-Flood deposition in a large epicratonic basin. Katherine Group quartz arenite was in part delivered by a continent-crossing early Neoproterozoic river system draining the

mountains in the southeast of North America. Sulfate 'evaporites' of the Little Dal Group indicate the action of hydrothermal springs in a hydrothermal biome on the preFlood continental shelf.

2. The bursting forth of Flood fountains is indicated by extensional tectonism and associated large igneous province activity and intrusives into the Mackenzie Mountains Group.

3. Early Flood year's enormous rain caused huge continental erosion, consistent with the Sr ratio trend upwards from the Neoproterozoic to Cambrian. This erosion was powerful enough to wear down crystalline basement rocks.

4. Supposed 'glacials' in the Cryogenian strata (Rapitan Group and Ice Brook Formation) are considered to have formed as mass flow deposits associated with downslope water movement in early Noahic Flood times.

5. Rapitan phosphatic BIF formed hydrothermally in association with volcanic activity.

6. Carbonate-rich marine Cambrian strata formed in North America and some other continents as the sea transgressed the land.

7. The Sr ratio decreased post-Cambrian as the land was covered by water, and the rain was not directly impacting the land.

8. Cambrian to Ordovician increasing sea level and increase in marine invertebrate diversity.

A possible application for further investigation is to use geochemistry to help distinguish other phases of the Flood event year, such as marine regression and drying phases.

[see Dickens, H. 2023. Receding Noahic Flood Waters Led to Seafloor Spreading: A Proposed Geological Model. In J.H. Whitmore (editor), *Proceedings of the Ninth International Conference on Creationism*, pp. 446-477. Cedarville, Ohio: Cedarville University International Conference on Creationism. DOI: 10.15385/jpicc.2023.9.1.25]

Journal of Creation Editor's comment: It is possible that the immense Neoproterozoic to Cambrian erosion of the land and related intense abrasion was not favourable for the preservation of land animal fossils (Brett and Baird 1986).

Journal of Creation Editor's comment: The authors suggest that at least some terrestrial vertebrates were abraded away, dissolved, and then incorporated in Cryogenian phosphatic iron formation and in Ediacaran-Cambrian transition sedimentary phosphate deposits. This is arguably part of the blotting out process referred to in Genesis 6:7, 7:4 and 7:23. See Dickens and Snelling 2015.

Extensive Neoproterozoic continental denudation due to enormous Flood rain was followed by Phanerozoic sedimentation as sea level rose to cover the supercontinent.

2. Further stages of the Flood and its aftermath

Source: Dickens, H. and Hutchison, A. 2021. Reply to Letter to the Editor regarding the article Geochemical and related evidence for early Noah's Flood year. *Journal of Creation* 35(2):16-21.

We emphasized continental erosion and hydrothermal activity, and Neoproterozoic to Ordovician strata, since we were considering the early Flood Year's rain and fountain activity once the supercontinent fragmented. The following sections consider matters regarding stages that continued beyond the early Flood.

1. Stupendous continental erosion

The early Flood's rain on the supercontinent and associated Pan-African event tectonism caused enormous erosion, consistent with the increasing $^{87}Sr/^{86}Sr$ ratio in the Neoproterozoic. At the same time, the sea level rose in the adjacent seas due to the rain.

The Hebrew word *mabbul*, translated as Flood, has been referred to as the 40-day marine transgression at the Flood onset (Boyd 2016). We consider that Cryogenian through Cambrian strata was formed by this *mabbul*.

Enormous and abrasive Neoproterozoic continental erosion may help explain the lack of air-breathing land vertebrate fossils in the early Paleozoic.

2. The Zonation Fossil Model is not plausible

The increasing Neoproterozoic $^{87}Sr/^{86}Sr$ ratio is consistent with enormous continental erosion due to the 40 days and nights of rain and resulting detritus. The rain was sufficient to peneplane hard crystalline basement rocks (schist and granite) seen in the Grand Canyon. It was not a tranquil mabbul (Flood). The severity of erosion and mass flows makes it unlikely that anyone could escape by going uphill. Modern day examples of rain-triggered mass flows down mountains would be tiny in comparison to what happened early in the Flood Year.

3. Earth's complete flooding began early in the Flood year

Fountains bursting forth, windows of heaven opening and rain falling on Earth for 40 days and nights are recorded at the very beginning of the Flood account (Genesis 7:11-12, 17). This was the source of the bulk of the water that eroded the pre-Flood land and flooded the earth.

The decline in the $^{87}Sr/^{86}Sr$ ratio in post-Cambrian strata is associated with continental-scale marine transgression of the Phanerozoic. The supercontinent was covered by the global ocean so that the Flood's rain no longer had a direct erosive impact on the land. Marine carbonate dominance peaked during the Great American Carbonate Bank in the Late Cambrian and Early Ordovician and is unrivalled in North America's Phanerozoic (Peters 2006). The Great Ordovician Biodiversification Event occurred at a time of peak sea level (Hallam 1992).

Drowning of cratons has been inferred from lithofacies changes in Neoproterozoic and Cambrian strata around the world. Peritidal carbonate platforms were drowned, followed in places by phosphorites and then black shales, which formed in deeper water (Brasier and Lindsay 2001). This drowning of cratons has been inferred to correlate with the time Noah's Ark rose and floated on the waters (Genesis 7:17). A classic fining upward succession indicating marine transgression occurs in Grand Canyon strata (Cambrian Tapeats Sandstone then Bright Angel Shale, followed by a sequence dominated by marine carbonates up to the end Mississippian). Water continued to cover the earth up to day 150. This is consistent with the dominance of marine carbonates up to the end of Mississippian (Sauk, Tippecanoe and Kaskasia megasequences).

4. Marine covering, then waters receding and drying

Post-Cambrian decline in $^{87}Sr/^{86}Sr$ represents the influence of oceanic conditions on the craton and less direct erosive impact by rain - this includes marine transgression followed by marine regression.

There is a prominent mid-Carboniferous unconformity in cratonic sequences around the world. In North America it marks the Mississippian-Pennsylvanian boundary (Hallam 1992). Spectacular karst paleorelief is found at the top Mississippian, for example, the Redwall Limestone of the Grand Canyon. Karst occurs *on land* where limestone has eroded due to the action of slightly acidic rainwater. Sea level drop accelerated from the end of Mississippian to the lowest point at the end of Permian.

The Triassic has numerous indicators of drying, such as the widening of arid and semiarid belts of Pangea (Chumakov and Zharkov 2003) and the dominance of evaporites in North America's Absaroka megasequence.

5. Today's oceans opening later

The opening up of today's oceans is believed to have occurred later – evident from Mesozoic and Cenozoic stratigraphy. It is important not to conflate the two periods of initial fragmentation by fountains of the great deep and later seafloor spreading.

Today's oceans began opening up (seafloor spreading) significantly, and so coastline length increased (Kocsis and Scotese 2021) in the Jurassic, and with new seafloor, the $^{87}Sr/^{86}Sr$ ratio declined. Henry Morris indicated that since the word for "divided" used in connection with the division of languages (Hebrew *parad*) was different from that used in the days of Peleg (Hebrew *palag*) when the earth was divided (Genesis 10:25), there existed the possibility that two different dividings were in view, one being that of the nations, the other a physical division of the continents (Morris 1984).

6. Post-Flood mountain-building and runoff

The Cretaceous onward overriding increase in the $^{87}Sr/^{86}Sr$ ratio can be related to significant continental erosion and runoff associated with the development of today's greatest mountain ranges (for example, the Alpine-Himalayan, Cordillera and Andes). In North America, the great volume of Zuni and Tejas megasequences coincides with Cordilleran mountain-building.

Tectonic setting

"Tectonic setting is the principal controlling factor of lithology, chemistry, and preservation of sediment accumulations in their depocenters, the sedimentary basins."(Veizer and Mackenzie 2014). Throughout Earth's history, continental tectonism has occurred on a variety of scales and in a variety of regions. It is a key factor in mountain-building, sedimentary basin formation and filling, and relative sea level changes. It needs to be factored into regional geological history models (Veizer and Mackenzie 2014).

The diverse composition and provenance of North American Phanerozoic sandstones have been evaluated as a function of changing tectonic settings. These sandstones have been related to orogenies including the Taconic, Acadian, Allegheny, Nevadan, and Laramide, along with ancestral Rockies development (Dickinson et al. 1983). To date, it seems that the role of successive continental orogenies has been largely overlooked in models encompassing the entire Flood Year.

Sediment area and volume not related to sea level height

The assertion that sediment area and volume (Clarey and Werner 2018) relate to sea level height lacks corroborating evidence. This view, in effect, does not take into account matters such as the reduced sediment influx during marine transgression (Cattaneo and Steel 2003), varying rock successions (Peters 2006), lithologic associations (Sloss 1964) and the role of continental orogenies.

The great thickness of Neoproterozoic strata (some 10 km in Stages 1–3 of our paper is not related to the height of sea level. It was due to the early Flood Year's enormous continental erosion caused by 40 days and nights of stupendous rain, along with tectonism associated with fountains bursting forth.

Stratigraphy is far more than just physical dimensions. Other stratigraphic data includes marine carbonates versus terrigenous clastics, biota types, diversity and geographical distribution, fining upward succession, geochemical trends, unconformities, sedimentary facies and lithologic associations. These data need to be considered along with the tectonic setting.

Factors influencing the areal extent and volume of sedimentary sequences include:

- With greater rain and higher topographic relief due to tectonism (such as mountain building), there is increased continental erosion and runoff, to then be deposited as sediment.

- In contrast, during marine transgression, the coastline moves landwards and the marine area enlarges. This is accompanied by a *reduced* sediment influx to the basin (Cattaneo and Steel 2003). In addition, sediment thickness in today's oceans averages less than 1 km and the water depth has no obvious correlation with sediment thickness (www.britannica.com/science/ocean-basin/Deep-sea-sediments).

- North American Cambrian to Mississippian cratonic sedimentary successions (Sauk, Tippecanoe and Kaskasia megasequences) are dominated by marine carbonates (Clarey and Werner 2018). These megasequences have smaller volumes and areas, consistent with their dominantly marine lithologies and marine fossils (Clarey and Werner 2018). Times of sea level rise over land are marked by an excess of carbonates over siliclastics. This can be especially seen with the Great American Carbonate Bank.

- In contrast, North American post-Paleozoic cratonic successions (upper Absaroka, Zuni and Tejas megasequences) are dominated by terrigenous classics (Peters 2006). This is consistent with runoff associated with great continental mountain building, especially on the Cordilleran margin.

The $^{87}Sr/^{86}Sr$ ratio and the sedimentary thickness and volume curves (asserted to be a sea level curve) (Cupps and Clarey 2020) correlate because both curves are a function of runoff.

Stratigraphy and sea level

Hallam 1981 referred to "restoring stratigraphy to its rightful place as the core discipline of geology." Hallam is a respected facies interpreter. His description of the characteristics of wind-blown deposits was used to show that the Coconino Sandstone is not wind-deposited (Borsch et al. 2018). We referred to Hallam's Phanerozoic eustatic sea level curve, which took into account not only seismic stratigraphy (initially developed by oil companies) but also techniques such as paleogeographic mapping, the occurrence of depth-related invertebrate and algal groups, glauconite concentration and facies correlation to develop sea level curves for the Phanerozoic.

Some significant items in Hallam's first-order sea level curve:

- There are two first-order supercycles, with peaks in the Ordovician and Cretaceous.

- The sea level rose in the Cambrian to its highest sea level in the Ordovician. This peak coincides with a peak in biodiversity known as the Great Ordovician Biodiversification Event (Servais and Harper 2018). This can be related to the increased area of marine habitat (Hallam 1981). The second highest sea level peak is in the Cretaceous. This is consistent with less than a globe-covering ocean but with interior seaways, such as the Western Interior Seaway in North America, the Eromanga Sea in Australia, and trans-Asian and trans-African interior seaways (Hay et al. 1993).

The lowest sea level is at the end of the Permian and coincides with the greatest mass extinction of biota.

D. NEOPROTEROZOIC OXYGEN: WHAT'S UP?

Source: Dickens, H. and Hutchison, A. 2020. No to NOE: Neoproterozoic Oxygen in the Early Flood Year. *Journal of Creation Theology and Science Series C: Earth Sciences* 10:1-4 (Creation Geology Society Annual Conference Abstracts 2020).

HIGHLIGHTS

It has been claimed that there was a "Neoproterozoic Oxygenation Event" that enabled the early evolution of animal life. However, in a biblical young Earth history framework, there was sufficient oxygen early in Earth history to support land and sea life, which were subsequently buried and fossilised during the Flood Year.

- A number of chemical proxies for the redox environment of sediments are briefly discussed. Chemical data indicate a dynamic environment with phases of both oxidation and reduction.

- Increase in oxidized species in the Neoproterozoic stratigraphic record indicates the movement of elements in a reduced state (such as S^{-2}, Fe^{2+}, and CH_4), from deeper water to above wave base and to the surface where they underwent oxidation by atmospheric oxygen.

- We conclude that near-surface oxidation of reduced sediments was the source of the supposed NOE and that Neoproterozoic sediments have been misinterpreted as indicators of significant atmospheric oxygenation.

It has been claimed that there was a Neoproterozoic rise in atmospheric oxygen (Och and Shields-Zhou 2012). This inferred episode is called the "Neoproterozoic Oxygenation Event" (NOE) (Dickens 2018b). The timing and magnitude of the NOE remains poorly determined (Och and Shields-Zhou, 2012), along with its alleged unidirectional increase and supposed enabling evolution of early animal life (Sahoo et al. 2016). However, in a biblical young Earth history framework, there was sufficient oxygen early in Earth history to support land and sea life, which were subsequently buried and fossilised during the Flood Year.

The redox environment of ancient sediments is inferred from a number of proxies. Chemical data indicate a dynamic environment with phases of both oxidation and reduction. The $\delta 13C$ value of carbonates shows significant variations throughout the Neoproterozoic. Uranium isotope evidence for global marine oxygenation and return to anoxic conditions suggests that Neoproterozoic oxygenation was not an irreversible, stepwise increase in oxygenation. At least one major interval of oxygenation after the deposition of Sturtian strata was followed by a return to widespread anoxia prior to the deposition of Marinoan strata. (Lau et al. 2017). Similarly, cerium depletion studies (Wallace et al. 2017) suggest there was protracted and irregular oxygenation increase that extended well into Phanerozoic strata. Integrated data for sulfur isotope patterns in pyrite, iron speciation analysis, and redox-sensitive elements from euxinic shales of a deep-water section in South China, indicate multiple oxygenation events in overall anoxic strata (Sahoo et al. 2016).

The overall increase in the $^{87}Sr/^{86}Sr$ ratio in Neoproterozoic to Cambrian marine sediments indicates erosion of more radiogenic continental crust and an influx of resulting detritus to the ocean (Peters and Gaines 2012). This is consistent with massive erosion caused by stupendous rain early in the Flood Year, and resulting deposition of Neoproterozoic sediments (Dickens 2018b). A massive influx of organic carbon from completely abraded animals would have created anoxic zones where decay consumed oxygen. However, an increase in oxidized species in the Neoproterozoic stratigraphic record indicates the movement of elements in a reduced state (such as S-2, Fe2+, and CH4), from deeper water to above wave base and to the surface where they underwent oxidation by atmospheric oxygen. Precambrian-Cambrian transition phosphorite is associated with catastrophic ocean water mixing (deep anoxic and shallow oxic oceanic waters) as inferred from sulphur isotopes (Cook 1992). This is consistent with the action of very energetic fountains of the great deep. (Dickens and Snelling 2015).

We conclude that near-surface oxidation of reduced sediments was the source of the supposed NOE and that Neoproterozoic sediments have been misinterpreted as indicators of significant atmospheric oxygenation. There was no massive change in atmospheric oxygen levels, but there was a massive global upheaval early in Noah's Flood.

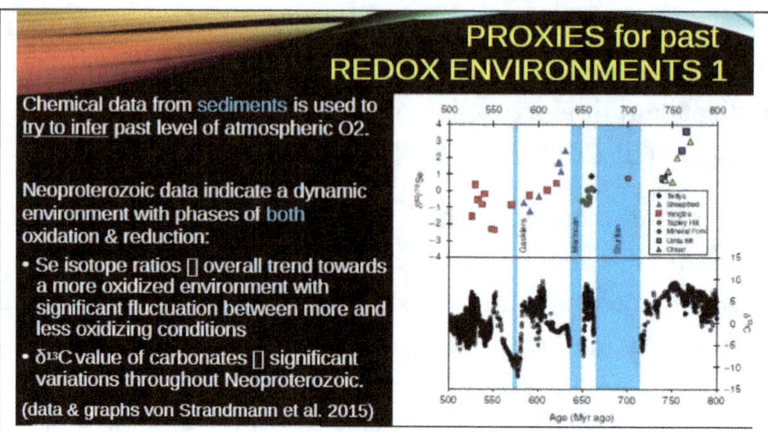

Neoproterozoic chemical data indicate significant variations – phases of both oxidation and reduction.

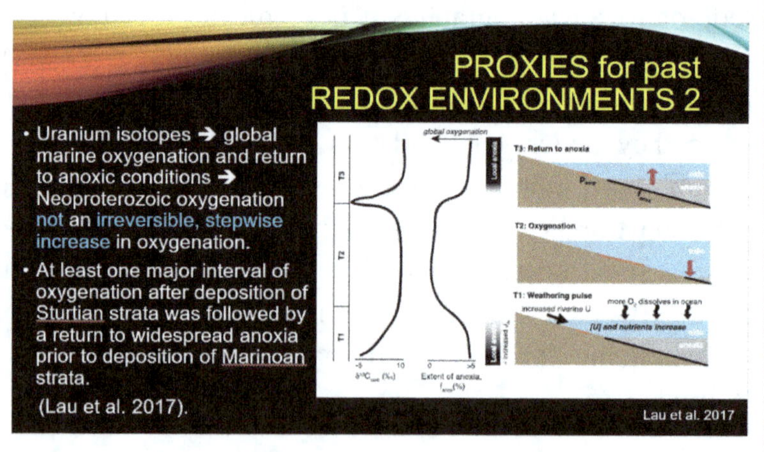

Neoproterozoic example of a major interval of oxygenation followed by a return to widespread anoxia.

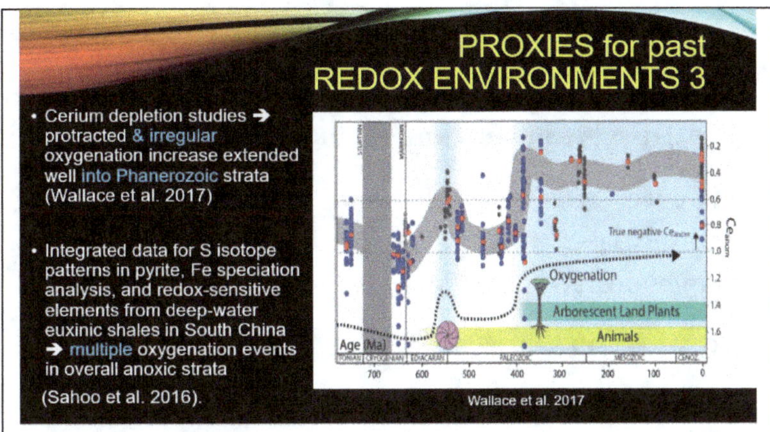

Indication that irregular oxygenation increase extended into the Phanerozoic.

E. DESTRUCTION OF EVIL MANKIND AND ALL LAND ANIMALS NOT ON THE ARK

1. Dissolved bones and all in early Flood!

Source: Dickens, H., and Snelling, A.A. 2015. Terrestrial Vertebrates Dissolved Near Flood Fountains. *Answers Research Journal* 8: 437–447.

HIGHLIGHTS

The focus of this paper is the relationship between the Flood fountains, mass flows (represented by Neoproterozoic mixtites) and great volumes of phosphorites which are located stratigraphically around the Precambrian-Cambrian transition and generally above the Neoproterozoic mixtites in localities around the globe.

In the judgement of the Noah's Flood, the Bible describes the blotting out of life that had the breath of life and nostrils. This implies the inclusion of fully land vertebrates (reptiles, birds, and mammals including man). These animals breathe with lungs supported by a backbone, and bone is a unique characteristic of the skeletons of vertebrates. Phosphorite (marine sedimentary phosphate) and vertebrate bones have essentially the same composition—calcium phosphate.

The breaking up of the fountains of the great deep that initiated the Flood was accompanied by enormous rainfall. This caused immense runoff from the pre-Flood land surfaces, resulting in mass flows (rather than "glacials") down slopes from land into the seas to form Neoproterozoic mixtites. The Cambrian peak in modelled

---

partial pressure of atmospheric carbon dioxide may correspond with maximum pressure release and a maximum output of carbon dioxide associated with the fountains of the great deep breaking forth early in Noah's Flood.

"Blotting out" process - terrestrial vertebrate bones (and invertebrate shells) were dissolved under volcanic acidic conditions in the vicinity of the Flood fountains, and the dissolution would have been assisted by abrasive and erosive currents. Skeletal fragments in some Cambrian sediments have been described as attesting to abrasion by current activity and abrasion of organisms with phosphatic hard parts (such as trilobites and brachiopods) to form pelletal phosphorites has also been described.

Thus, these vertebrates were not annihilated in the sense of going to nothing. Instead, some chemical evidence remained. Massive phosphorite is associated with a worldwide marine transgression, and catastrophic ocean water mixing (deep anoxic and shallow oxic oceanic waters) as inferred from sulphur isotopes. Flood fountains of the great deep bursting forth would have caused catastrophic mixing of deep and shallow waters.

UPDATE BY DICKENS   (see also III. C.1. and E.2)

Harry Dickens' original intention when developing the paper was to say that all pre-Flood land animals and people's flesh and bones were dissolved. He now believes even more so that abrasion and dissolution in the Neoproterozoic was the principal fate of land vertebrates, and not decomposition or burial. Fully land animal skeletal material first appears in the Upper Paleozoic. The Upper Paleozoic is inferred to be a time of receding Flood waters, with widespread drying in the Triassic (Dickens 2024). The drying and tectonic activity may correlate with the exit of land animals from Noah's ark, with some animals subsequently being buried and fossilised.

Acidic fountains may have had a role in the dissolution of land vertebrates, for example, in the Mackenzie Mountains (refer to evidence such as Rapitan phosphatic BIF in paper III. C.). However, Harry now believes that enormous erosion alone would be sufficient to abrade away land vertebrates in the Neoproterozoic.

The early Flood erosion was powerful enough to peneplane hard crystalline rocks (eg granite and schist of the basal Grand Canyon) and to erode the Grenville Mountains (Himalayan size) to their roots. In both cases the PT regime of minerals now exposed at the surface indicates many km depth of erosion. The 'Great Unconformity' (first named for its occurrence in the Grand Canyon, but traceable across North America) provides evidence for the enormous erosion of continental crust as Flood rain impacted the land. Thus, Harry believes that it would be likely for land animals' flesh and bone (much softer than granite and schist) to have been abraded away in the Neoproterozoic. In addition, there would be no chance of escape by going uphill against huge erosive torrents and mass flows.

Abstract

The Bible's Flood account describes fountains bursting forth followed by enormous rain, global sea level rise, the death and the blotting out of air breathing land animals, along with man. The following model is proposed:

1. The initial Flood stage was characterized by the venting of acidic water and rainfall, together with high energy erosion and deposition. Upper Proterozoic mixtites[1] formed from mass flows downslope from land into the seas.

2. The blotting out process meant the death of terrestrial vertebrates (land animals) everywhere, as well as the dissolution of vertebrate bones (and invertebrate shells) under acidic and erosive conditions in the vicinity of volcanic fountains.

3. On shelfal areas at greater distances from the fountains, ocean chemistry was more normal, that is, slightly alkaline. This enabled dissolved bones (and shells) to precipitate out as amorphous phosphorite deposits. All continents except Antarctica, to date, are known to have Precambrian-Cambrian transition phosphorites and these phosphorite deposits are generally found stratigraphically above Upper Proterozoic mixtites.

Thus this paper highlights geochemical evidence within a biblical Flood framework and proposes that terrestrial vertebrates close to the Flood fountains were dissolved and then precipitated out to form Precambrian-Cambrian transition sedimentary phosphate deposits.

Keywords: blotted out, terrestrial vertebrates, Flood fountains, Upper Proterozoic mixtites, dissolution, chemical processes, geochemistry, bones, phosphorite, northwest Queensland, Cambrian, metals, isotope ratio, sea level, pH

Introduction

Although the radiometric date for the base of the Cambrian has been revised by secular scientists, the relative position of Precambrian and Cambrian strata remains observable and mappable, and recognized by geologists (including a number of young-earth creationists) worldwide. Cambrian strata are recognized by the lowermost appearance of shelly fossils (of nearly every major invertebrate animal group).

Rocks of the Precambrian-Cambrian transition point to one of the greatest upheavals in the earth's history. This transition is widely regarded by geologists as of great importance in terms of phosphogenesis, ocean chemistry, tectonism, volcanism, erosion, deposition, sea level rise, and the fossil record (Brasier 1992; Cook and Shergold 1984; Halverson et al. 2009; Knoll and Walter 1992; McKenzie et al. 2014; Peters and Gaines 2012; Tucker 1992). The authors believe that the strata of the Precambrian-Cambrian transition and their chemical signature have immense significance when interpreted in terms of the onset of the Noahic Flood.

This paper elaborates on a paragraph in an earlier paper (Dickens and Snelling 2008):

In the vicinity of active acidic volcanic fountains the abrasive power of jets of water with entrained sediment assisted the solution of vertebrate bones and flesh. Abrasion

would have provided finer grained material which would have assisted the chemical solution process. The dissolved material may have subsequently precipitated out as massive phosphorite deposits at localities around the Precambrian-Cambrian sequence boundary.

The focus of this paper is the relationship between the Flood fountains, mass flows (represented by Upper Proterozoic mixtites) and phosphorites which are located stratigraphically above the Upper Proterozoic mixtites. Scientists with an old-age worldview do not recognize the connection between Proterozoic rock-hosted ore deposits, Upper Proterozoic mixtites, and Cambrian phosphorites found in locations such as northwest Queensland. This is because their deep time perspective entails the belief that there are many millions of years of time gaps between the formation of each of these three sets of geological deposits.

Geochemistry has the potential to greatly refine and enhance young-earth creation models of geology and the Bible, and in the case of the paper under review, to model effects early in Noah's Flood.

Event Sequence

Cataclysmic judgment foretold

And God said to Noah, "I have determined to make an end of all flesh, for the earth is filled with violence through them. Behold, I will destroy them with the earth." (Genesis 6:13 ESV)

So the Lord said, "I will blot out man whom I have created from the face of the land, man and animals and creeping things and birds of the heavens, for I am sorry that I have made them." (Genesis 6:7 ESV)

For behold, I will bring a flood of waters upon the earth to destroy all flesh in which is the breath of life under heaven. Everything that is on the earth shall die. (Genesis 6:17 ESV)

The breath of life implies the inclusion of land vertebrates (amphibians, reptiles, birds, and mammals including man). These animals breathe with lungs supported by a backbone, and bone is a unique characteristic of the skeletons of vertebrates (Pough, Heiser, and McFarland 1989, 57). Phosphorite (marine sedimentary phosphate) and vertebrate bones have essentially the same composition—calcium phosphate (Cook and Shergold 2005; Martin 2007).

Land animals and man in the vicinity of the Flood fountains were not to be annihilated in the sense of going to nothing. Instead, their life and structures were to be destroyed. *"Destroy them with the earth"* meant that the crust of the earth itself also was to be transformed but not reduced to nothing by way of the Flood.

Flood Tectonism

In the six hundredth year of Noah's life, in the second month, on the seventeenth day of the month, on that day all the fountains of the great deep burst forth, and the windows of the heavens were opened. (Genesis 7:11 ESV)

by His knowledge the deeps broke open, . . . (Proverbs 3:20a ESV)

On a specific day, there was simultaneous worldwide fracturing of the earth's crust as the fountains burst forth.

"Fountains of the great deep burst forth" and "deeps broke open" imply rifting and fracturing of the earth's crust. The text implies that water flowed from within the earth through the fountains, and rain fell. Volcanic material would have accompanied these eruptions as the crust ruptured, releasing pressure from the rocks underneath (Schmandt et al. 2014). Much of the water for the Noahic Flood likely came from various depths within the earth, with the mantle being the major water source (Bergeron 1997; Pearson et al. 2014; Schmandt et al 2014).

The Precambrian-Cambrian transition was characterized by rifting and continental extension (Ilyin 1990). Rifting and basin development are associated with supercontinent breakup. Reconstruction of the Rodinia supercontinent was based on the recognition of correlatable Upper Proterozoic rifted passive margins (Evans 2013). Plume-related extensional events are indicated by reconstructions of voluminous mafic magmatism along the margins of paleo-continents where numerous mafic dyke swarms were inferred to form as hot rock rose through the earth during continental rifting (Pisarevsky et al. 2008).

A model of catastrophic plate tectonics during the global Flood has been proposed as follows (Austin et al. 1994). Flooding of the continents began with meters per second subduction of slabs of pre-Flood mafic oceanic floor along thousands of kilometers of pre-Flood continental margins. Flow induced in the mantle would have produced rapid extension along linear belts in the seafloor and corresponding rapid horizontal movement of the broken-apart continents. Upwelling magma jettisoned steam into the atmosphere causing intense global rain.

Most of the volume of modern volcanic gases is water in the form of water vapor (steam) as well as carbon dioxide. Other main volcanic gases include sulphur dioxide, hydrogen chloride, hydrogen sulphide, and hydrogen fluoride (Macdonald 1972; Sigurdsson et al. 2015). Volcanic gas aerosols include sulfuric acid and hydrochloric acid droplets with absorbed halide salts, so volcanic gas emissions are acidic and may contribute to acid rain (McGee et al. 1997) (see Fig. 1).

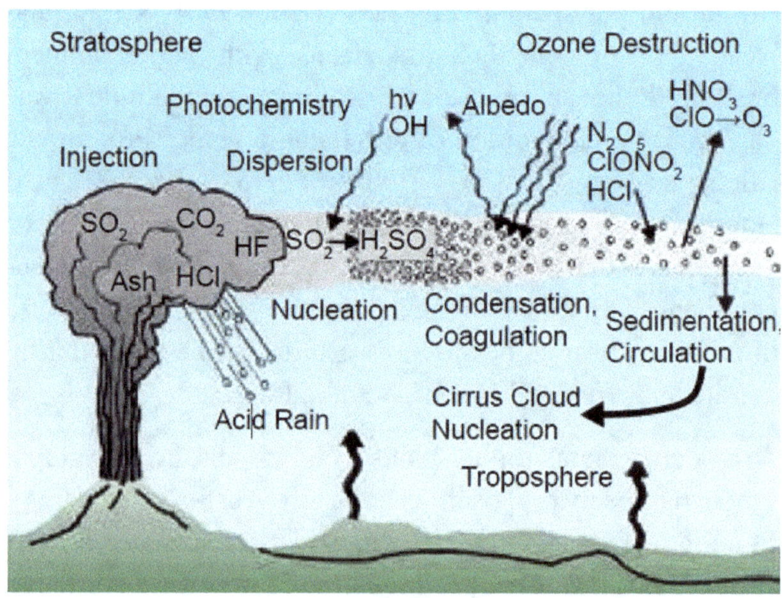

Figure 1. Schematic of chemical effects from volcano injection of aerosols and gases into the atmosphere (after McGee et al. 1997).

Plate tectonic activity is inferred to have raised the level of carbon dioxide in the atmosphere and seawater through increased volcanism and subduction zone metamorphism. Tectonic outgassing is a major source of carbon dioxide and rapid carbon dioxide fluxes from large igneous province volcanism can cause dramatic environmental perturbations. Major pulses of volcanism and magmatism have been indicated by Cambrian strata based on zircon "age" data (McKenzie et al. 2014). The Cambrian had the highest modelled atmospheric carbon dioxide concentrations of the Phanerozoic (Berner 1990, 2006) (see Fig. 2), "suggesting an extraordinary event at that time" (Cook 1992). This peak in partial pressure of atmospheric carbon dioxide may correspond with the maximum pressure release and maximum output of carbon dioxide associated with the fountains of the great deep breaking forth early in Noah's Flood.

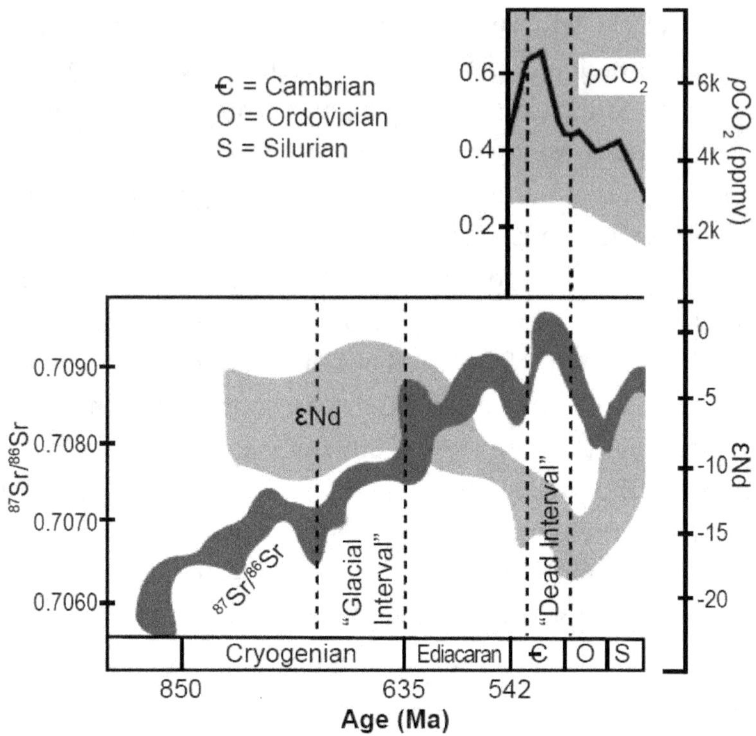

Figure 2. Upper Proterozoic to Lower Paleozoic seawater strontium and neodymium isotopic trends, and partial pressure of atmospheric carbon dioxide (after McKenzie et al. 2014).

Detrital zircon "age" data indicate spatially extensive Ediacaran-Cambrian continental arc volcanism. Zircon is a common accessory mineral in felsic-intermediate igneous rocks and convergent margins with continental arcs produce voluminous felsic-intermediate magmas with high zircon abundance. The marked increase in "end-Cryogenian" detrital zircon in global distributions supports a major increase in continental arc volcanism at the "end of the "glacial"" interval (McKenzie et al. 2014).

Chemical effects decrease with increasing distance from modern erupting volcanoes (McGee et al. 1997). Thus, in Noah's Flood, we believe that marine life would likely have been able to survive in higher proportions at increasing distances away from the fountains of the great deep.

A number of Precambrian-Cambrian transition black shales have been found to contain highly anomalous metal contents (Cook 1992; Donnelly, Shergold, and Southgate 1988; Wille et al. 2008; Xu et al. 2011). This includes highly metalliferous black shales over inferred carbonate shelves of South China, India, and Arabia (Brasier 1992). These metals are consistent with volcanic/fumarolic input into the system (Cook 1992). In addition, most metal deposits hosted in Proterozoic sedimentary and volcanic rocks can be shown to have formed in tectonic environments characterized by rifting (Sawkins 1983). Thus input of metals into Precambrian-Cambrian transition rocks and Proterozoic host rocks is believed to have occurred during the initial rifting and volcanism early in the Flood.

Continental Erosion and Mass Flows

And rain fell upon the earth forty days and forty nights. (Genesis 7:12 ESV)

and they were unaware until the flood came and swept them all away, so will be the coming of the Son of Man. (Matthew 24:39 ESV)

This rain event was the greatest rain event ever recorded. Erosion was consequently immense. The tremendous runoff from continents during the early stage of the Flood would have been responsible for the drawdown of carbon dioxide described for the Cryogenian (Berner 2006), as chemical weathering of silicate rocks is a major carbon dioxide sink (Berner, Lasaga, and Garrels 1983; Kump, Brantley, and Arthur 2000).

The rise in Upper Proterozoic strontium isotope ratios $^{87}Sr/^{86}Sr$ (see Fig. 2) has been explained by accelerated rates of erosion associated with uplift during the so-called Pan-African orogeny (Derry et al. 1994). $^{87}Sr/^{86}Sr$ ratios (measured from shells) in Cambrian sedimentary carbonates are the highest of Phanerozoic strata (Veizer and Compston 1974; Veizer et al. 1999) (see Fig. 2) and high crustal erosion rates have been inferred from Cambrian $^{87}Sr/^{86}Sr$ values (Derry et al. 1994). The large supplies of clastic sediments that flooded into basins imply high rates of erosion of the basin hinterlands, which in turn may explain the progressive rise in $^{87}Sr/^{86}Sr$, as well as the very negative neodymium isotope ratio $\varepsilon Nd(t)$ in the Cambrian[2] (see Fig. 2). Rubidium (Rb) is common in the crust's silicate minerals (Faure and Powell 1972). ^{87}Sr is a radiogenic daughter isotope of ^{87}Rb. Therefore the abundance of radiogenic ^{87}Sr relative to "common" ^{86}Sr in a sample of sediment is related to the amount of sediment that originated from continental crust as opposed to that originating from the ocean. Similarly, a negative $\varepsilon Nd(t)$ is related to the fractionation of neodymium isotopes observed in crustal rocks compared to a standard.

Skeletal fragments in some Cambrian sediments have been described as attesting to abrasion by current activity (Donnelly, Shergold, and Southgate 1988). Abrasion of organisms with phosphatic hard parts (such as trilobites and

194

brachiopods) to form pelletal phosphorites has also been described (Cook and McElhinny 1979).

Along with massive erosion of the continental landmasses, enormous torrential rain would have caused huge mass flows sweeping down from landmasses into the seas, depositing immense volumes of sediments. Upper Proterozoic mixtites of the North American Cordillera have been interpreted as submarine mass flow deposits (Austin and Wise 1994; Sigler and Wingerden 1998; Snelling 2009; Wingerden 2003) formed in the initial phase of the Flood rather than as glacial deposits. Upper Proterozoic mixtites are widespread and are found in other regions, such as the Appalachian Mountains, Caledonian Mountains, Scandinavia, Russian Platform, Siberia, northwest China, Brazil, central and south Africa, and northwest, central and southern Australia (Schermerhorn 1974).

The Cryogenian was so named in the mainstream scientific literature because abundant mixtites were interpreted as being formed in a cold glacial environment. The "snowball earth" concept has even been put forward based on interpreted equatorial latitudes for claimed Upper Proterozoic "glacial" rock units and on data indicating collapsed biological productivity (Arnaud, Halverson, and Shields-Zhou 2011; Hoffman et al. 1998; Shields 2005). However, Upper Proterozoic mixtites more likely represent mass flows down slopes adjacent to active tectonic areas since they occur by preference in thick mobile belt successions or unstable platforms, and not in the thin sequences developed in stable environments (Schermerhorn 1974). These mixtites formed along active tectonic zones

(Austin and Wise 1994; Sigler and Wingerden 1998; Young 1995). Under a mass flow hypothesis, tectonically elevated borderlands would have provided freshly eroded material and the gradient necessary to transport it into adjacent basins. The mass flows in this environment would commence as subaerial flows, until entering the sea where they spread out as coastal fans, depositing their loads on loss of momentum (Schermerhorn 1974). Classic Upper Proterozoic "tillites" may be better interpreted as mass flow deposits (Oard 1997).

The occurrence of carbonate beds above, below, and within mixtite beds sets Upper Proterozoic mixtite formations apart from the claimed Middle Precambrian and Permo-Carboniferous glacial formations, and the genuine Pleistocene glacial formations (Schermerhorn 1974). The abundance of Proterozoic carbonates with stromatolites and ooids suggests a relatively warm rather than a cold climate prevailed at the time of deposition (Hallam 1981). Flat-pebble breccias also suggest warm depositional conditions, as they are formed in modern environments by the erosional rip-up of finely layered sedimentary rock (Brasier 1992; Roehl and Choquette 1985).

Transfer of atmospheric carbon dioxide to the ocean has been interpreted as enabling rapid precipitation of calcium carbonate in warm surface waters, producing the cap carbonate rocks over Upper Proterozoic mixtites which are observed globally (Shields 2005). It has been proposed that cap carbonates formed primarily by microbially mediated precipitation during algal blooms under low salinity conditions (Shields 2005). In addition, the presence of very distinctive fine-grained carbonate facies (flakestone) provides evidence for extensive calcium carbonate precipitation (Tucker 1992). Carbon dioxide build-up from active Flood fountains is believed to have contributed to this rapid precipitation of calcium carbonate.

Structures interpreted as giant wave ripples (generated by sea surface waves) have been observed in cap carbonate rocks from Australia, Brazil, Canada, Namibia, and Svalbard (Allen and Hoffman 2005). A flakestone facies, with its characteristic broken-up clasts, is a further indicator of the action of stormy seas (Tucker 1992). Waves would not have been possible in an ice-covered ocean. Instead giant tsunami waves would have resulted from Flood tectonism, especially in shallow seas (Snelling 2009).

Sea Level Rise and Death of Terrestrial Vertebrates

The flood continued for forty days on the Earth. The waters increased and bore up the ark, and it rose high above the earth. The waters prevailed and increased greatly on the earth, and the ark floated on the face of the waters. And the waters prevailed so mightily on the earth that all the high mountains under the whole heaven were covered. The waters prevailed above the mountains, covering them fifteen cubits deep. (Genesis 7:17–20 ESV)

They were eating and drinking and marrying and being given in marriage, until the day when Noah entered the ark, and the flood came and destroyed them all. (Luke 17:27 ESV)

Sea level rise has been associated with volcanism and tectonism (Schopf 1980; Tucker 1992). Supercontinent rifting is inferred to have created a large number of epicontinental seas (shallow seas lying upon continental areas) at low latitudes, enabling deep phosphorus-rich ocean waters to be moved into shallow shelfal environments (Donnelly et al. 1990).

Drowning of cratons has been inferred from the uppermost Proterozoic and Cambrian strata. Peritidal carbonate platforms were drowned, followed in places by phosphorites and black shales (Brasier and Lindsay 2001). Evidence of sea level rise includes an upward fining sequence observed in Cambrian strata, which has been interpreted as a deepening succession in locations such as the USA, Greenland, the United Kingdom, Russia, Australia, Bolivia, and Ghana (Morton 1984). These occurrences include an upward fining sequence found exposed in the Grand Canyon's Cambrian strata (Austin 1994). "Global or worldwide marine transgression" is the descriptor in the secular literature (Brasier 1982; Cook and Shergold 1984; Matthews and Cowie 1979). This is another way of saying global flooding! Sea levels rose during the Flood as substantial volumes of water from the fountains were added to the earth's surface and as the new warmer basaltic oceanic crust rose isostatically (Austin et al. 1994). We believe that the drowning of cratons correlates with the time the Ark rose and floated on the waters.

Seismic stratigraphic studies indicate that Ordovician strata had the highest sea level of the Paleozoic (Haq and Schutter 2008). We consider this to signify a peaking of the Flood waters. Consistent with this is the decrease of the $^{87}Sr/^{86}Sr$ ratio following the peak in Cambrian strata (see Fig. 2), which has been explained by a drop in the rate of erosion, decrease in silicate weathering rate, and/or the influence of rift-related hydrothermal activity (Nicholas 1996). After the earth, with its mountains, was totally covered by water, rain would no longer impact the land, and so there would not be the same degree of continental erosion, as described in the previous section, "Continental erosion and mass flows."

Blotting Out

And all flesh died that moved on the earth, birds, livestock, beasts, all swarming creatures that swarm on the earth, and all mankind. Everything on the dry land in whose nostrils was the breath of life died. He blotted out every living thing that was on the face of the ground, man and animals and creeping things and birds of the heavens. They were blotted out from the earth. Only Noah was left, and those who were with him in the ark. (Genesis 7:21–23 ESV)

The key Hebrew word "*machah*" (מחה) has a general meaning of destroy, as well as more specific meanings such as blot out or wipe away. Other meanings of "*machah*" include erasing from a book, removing the memory of a people (such as the Amalekites), blotting out sins, and wiping as one wipes a dish (Fouts and Wise 1998). Further aspects of the meaning of the word "*machah*" and which are relevant to the effects of the Flood fountains include:

- Full of marrow (Strong 2007)—this is quite relevant as vertebrate bones contain marrow.

- Abrasion—to stroke or rub; by implication, to erase; also to smooth (Strong 2007).

- Washing—erasing writing from a scroll was normally effected by washing (Van Gemeren 1997).

Land vertebrates, including man, have nostrils which admit and expel air for respiration in conjunction with the mouth. The blotting-out process meant the death of all land vertebrates in the Flood (*Genesis 7:23*). We believe that these vertebrates had three different fates—dissolution, decomposition, and burial.

Many terrestrial vertebrate bones (as well as invertebrate shells) would have dissolved, particularly in near-surface acidic waters, in the vicinity of the Flood's volcanic fountains. This fate is the particular focus of this paper. The vertebrates close to the Flood fountains were not annihilated in the sense of going to nothing. Instead some evidence remained (Fouts and Wise 1998). When the pH of sediment solutions drops below 7, bone minerals will rapidly dissolve (Berna, Matthews, and Weiner 2004). Thus acidic volcanic waters would dissolve bones. In the vicinity of the active fountains of the great deep, the blotting out process is inferred to include the dissolution of vertebrate skeletal phosphate. Widespread development of nutrient-enriched waters during the Precambrian-Cambrian transition has been indicated (Brasier and Lindsay 2001). $\delta^{13}C$ is a measure of the ratio of the two stable isotopes of carbon—^{13}C and ^{12}C. Organic matter preferentially takes up the lighter isotope ^{12}C. $\delta^{13}C$ varies as a function of biological productivity and organic carbon burial. The Precambrian-Cambrian transition throughout much of Asia is marked by a sharp change in the carbon-isotope ratio $\delta^{13}C$, suggesting that "As major phosphogenic events straddle this turning point in $\delta^{13}C$, huge fluxes in nutrient supply may have occurred . . ." (Brasier 1990a, 1990b; Cook 1992). The death and dissolution of terrestrial vertebrates in the Flood waters would have contributed greatly to this nutrient supply!

Another fate of land vertebrates would have been the decomposition of corpses in surface waters. Mass mortality, and a sudden decrease in biological productivity, prior to the "Cambrian explosion" (the lowermost appearance of shelly fossils in the stratigraphic record) has been inferred from a negative $\delta^{13}C$ geochemical anomaly in carbonate-containing black shale, which is found around the globe at the Precambrian-Cambrian transition. It has been claimed that this corresponds to the widespread development of an oxygen-deficient shallow marine environment (Kimura and Watanabe 2001)—a "Strangelove ocean" (Hsu et al. 1985). We suggest that this relates to the consumption of oxygen in shallow waters due to the presence of bloated, decomposing corpses of drowned animals. This would have occurred in areas further away from the effects of the acidic Flood fountains since putrefying bacteria are sensitive to acid, and acidic waters delay the onset of putrefaction (Weigelt 2009). Hydrogen forms during vertebrate decomposition and captures oxygen from the surroundings (Weigelt 2009), creating anoxic conditions.

Away from the effects of the acidic fountains, many vertebrates would have suffered a third fate—rapidly buried by sediment and subsequently fossilized. Terrestrial vertebrate fossils are found in the Upper Paleozoic and overlying strata (Tree of Life Web Project 2008).

Phosphorites Precipitate

The chemical conditions under which bone can recrystallize in place as phosphate are restricted and lie in a narrow alkaline pH range (Berna, Matthews, and Weiner 2004). At greater distances from the fountains, including shallow shelfal areas, ocean environments would likely have been more alkaline. This would have enabled the precipitation of dissolved bones[4] to contribute to amorphous phosphorite deposits around the Precambrian-Cambrian transition. Every continent except Antarctica is known to have Precambrian-Cambrian transition phosphorites (Cook 1992). Deposits known to have billions of tons of phosphorite are found in northwest Queensland, Vietnam, China, Mongolia, Russia, and Kazakhstan (Cook and Shergold 1984; Notholt, Sheldon, and Davidson 1989). In addition, significant deposits are found in Africa and South America (Cook 1992) (see Fig. 3).

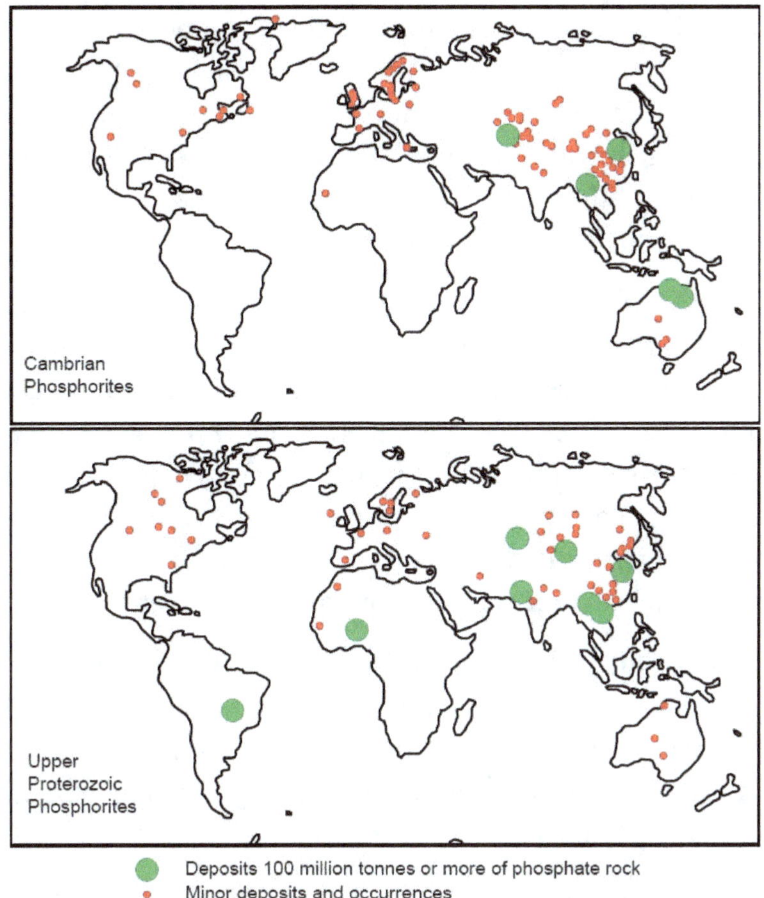

Figure 3. Worldwide distribution of Precambrian-Cambrian transition phosphorite deposits (after Cook 1992). Cook's lower map was labelled Precambrian phosphorites but these phosphorites are more specifically Upper Proterozoic phosphorites.

The phosphorite is associated with a worldwide marine transgression, and catastrophic ocean water mixing (deep anoxic and shallow oxic oceanic waters) as inferred from sulphur isotopes (Cook 1992; Cook and Shergold 1984).

Upwelling of hydrogen sulphide-rich deep ocean water to become surface waters at the Precambrian-Cambrian transition is indicated by the basal Cambrian black shale molybdenum isotope signal (Wille et al. 2008). The Flood fountains of the great deep bursting forth would have caused catastrophic mixing of deep and shallow waters.

We infer that during the Flood, dissolved phosphate from vertebrate bones was moved by currents away from the fountains to shelfal areas. Shoreward transport and entrapment of phosphate grains in shallow nearshore zones may have helped form high-grade phosphate deposits (Cook and Shergold 1984). Bacteria may have had a role in the precipitation of phosphorite deposits under anoxic conditions in numerous locations around the world.

Petrographic evidence has confirmed the presence of bacterial structures, including microbial mats (Nathan et al. 1993). Phosphate abundance in sediments may correlate with the abundance and activity of large sulphur bacteria (Schulz and Schulz 2005).

Paleomagnetism indicates mainly equatorial latitudes for Upper Proterozoic phosphorites (Cook and McElhinny 1979) as well as for Upper Proterozoic mixtites (Arnaud, Halverson, and Shields-Zhou 2011).

In numerous locations around the world, there is a general upward stratigraphic trend of Upper Proterozoic mixtites followed by phosphorites. This succession is mappable in many locations (Cook 1992; Ross 2013). Walther's Law of the Correlation of Facies states that the vertical succession of facies reflects lateral changes in the environment

(Middleton 1973). Conversely, it states that when a depositional environment "migrates" laterally, sediments of one depositional environment come to lie on top of another. A classic example of this law is the vertical stratigraphic succession that typifies marine transgressions (Stanley 1999). Thus Upper Proterozoic mixtites may have formed in deeper water than the phosphorites as the sea transgressed landwards during the Noahic Flood.

Case Study—Northwest Queensland, Australia

Northwest Queensland is very significant in a global context for its economic importance as a world-class mineral province. The following provides a biblical framework for the chemical processes inferred in the formation of the region's giant metallic ore deposits together with the adjacent huge phosphorite deposits.

The principal structural divisions in northwest Queensland are the Proterozoic Mount Isa Orogen and the mainly Paleozoic Georgina Basin (Geological Survey of Queensland 2012). Figure 4 is a map which shows numerous metallic ore deposits of the Mount Isa Orogen together with the many sedimentary phosphate deposits of the Georgina Basin on the margin of the Mount Isa Orogen (Geological Survey of Queensland 2012). We consider that these metallic ore deposits and phosphate deposits formed in association with activity by the fountains of the great deep. We infer that the fountains of the great deep occurred at sites of the breakup of the Rodinia supercontinent. This would include the region of eastern Australia, with its Mount Isa Orogen.

Figure 4. Map of northwest Queensland showing metallic ore deposits of the Mount Isa Orogen and phosphorite deposits of the adjacent Georgina Basin (after Geological Survey of Queensland 2012).

Mount Isa Orogen

Mount Isa Orogen rocks outcrop over an area of some 50,000 km^2 (19,305 mi^2), roughly centered on the town of Mount Isa. This orogen consists of mainly marine sediments, felsic and mafic volcanics, granites and mafic intrusives (Blake 1987; Palfreyman 1984).

The Mount Isa Orogen is a world-class base metals province and contains giant sediment-hosted orebodies. These orebodies include Mount Isa (copper, lead, zinc, and silver), Cannington, Hilton, Century, George Fisher North, Lady Loretta (lead, zinc, and silver), and Ernest Henry (copper and gold) (Lyons et al. 2006; Palfreyman 1984). Sediment-hosted silver-lead-zinc orebodies generally comprise accumulations of sulphide and sulphate minerals interbedded with anoxic and sulphidic marine sediments (Jell 2013).

These major stratiform zinc-lead-silver deposits exhibit many similar geological features. Host rocks are organic-rich black siltstone/shales (interpreted as formerly seafloor mud) that formed under anoxic conditions. The deposits are located adjacent to several major regional faults (Large et al. 2005). These faults likely acted as conduits for the transport of hot metalliferous sedimentary brines from deep in the basin system. Laterally extensive strata-bound iron-manganese carbonate halos indicate significant volumes of hydrothermal fluids have interacted with seafloor and sub-seafloor sediments. Numerical modelling demonstrates that the deposits are probably formed by free convection of marine waters and basinal brines during basin rifting events (Large et al. 2005).

Sedimentary exhalative deposits hosted in northern Australia's Proterozoic rocks formed from relatively oxidized fluids that encountered reduced conditions at the site of mineralization (Lyons et al. 2006). In addition, seawater is alkaline enough to induce instability in metal complexes (Tarling 1981).

We infer that the relatively oxidized hot acidic oreforming fluids were flowing in association with active Noahic Flood fountains of the great deep. Interaction with anoxic, cool, reduced deep seafloor sediments, and more alkaline seawater made it possible for base metal sulfides to be deposited on the seafloor. Rapid ore formation is inferred from lead isotopes and from the rapid temperature drop as plumes carrying metals enter the sea (Snelling 1984). However, in near surface acidic waters close to the fountains, vertebrate bones would have dissolved as described previously in the "Blotted out" section of this paper

Georgina Basin

The Georgina Basin is a large sedimentary basin straddling the Queensland/Northern Territory border. The basin's area is approximately 330,000 km^2 (127,413 mi^2) of which about 144,000 km^2 (55,598 mi^2) is in Queensland. The Georgina Basin contains sediments that range from Upper Proterozoic to Lower Paleozoic and are in excess of 4500 m (14,763 ft) in thickness. Basin fill consists mainly of Cambrian and Ordovician marine sedimentary rocks— essentially carbonate rocks with minor sandstone and siltstone (Jell 2013). Anomalous geochemical signals, including trace metal enrichment, have been recorded in the Cambrian rocks of the Georgina Basin (Donnelly, Shergold, and Southgate 1988). This is consistent with the idea that at a distance from the fountains, there was still some slight evidence of the fountain's activity.

Northwest Queensland's known phosphate rock resources of 3 billion tons lie in large phosphorites hosted by Cambrian rocks in the Georgina Basin (Jell 2013). Mixtites such as the

Little Burke "Tillite" and the Mount Birnie Beds are found stratigraphically below the phosphorites in the basin (Jell 2013; Palfreyman 1984).

Extensive phosphorite deposits are mined at Phosphate Hill. This deposit is located 140 km (87 mi) south-southeast of Mount Isa. It is a world-class rock phosphate resource that is close to the surface and easy to access and mine. This deposit is one of a generally north-south, 6 km (3.7 mi) long string of similar deposits distributed over an area of some 180 km^2 (69 mi^2). The phosphorite is hosted by the Cambrian Beetle Creek Formation (so named due to the presence of abundant trilobites) sequence. This sequence is in a 30 km (18 mi) wide by 100 km (62 mi) long, north-south elongated graben within the southern Mount Isa Orogen. Most of the phosphorite occurs in particulate form as pellets and minor replacement of fossil fragments, commonly as inclusions in the pellets (Porter 2011).

We infer that vertebrate bones were dissolved in acidic waters associated with Flood fountains in the region of Mount Isa Orogen and that dissolved bones helped form the phosphorite deposits of the Georgina Basin.

Conclusion

In localities around the globe, great volumes of phosphorite in massive beds are found stratigraphically around the Precambrian–Cambrian transition, and generally above Upper Proterozoic mixtites.

The breaking up of the fountains of the great deep that triggered the Flood was accompanied by enormous rainfall. This caused immense runoff from the pre-Flood land surfaces, resulting in mass flows down slopes from land into the seas to form Upper Proterozoic mixtites.

Terrestrial vertebrate bones (and invertebrate shells) were dissolved under acidic conditions in the vicinity of the Flood fountains. However, at greater distances from the fountains the ocean chemistry was more normal, that is, slightly alkaline. This resulted in the dissolved bones being precipitated on adjacent shelfal areas contributing to amorphous phosphorite deposits around the Precambrian-Cambrian transition, and stratigraphically above Upper Proterozoic mixtites.

Chemical processes would have affected the pre-Flood world in the vicinity of the Flood fountains. These processes would have left their signature in the form of the distribution of minerals seen today. It is hoped that this paper may encourage further work to improve and refine our understanding of chemical processes in space and time in areas where the Flood's fountains may have been active.

SUPPLEMENTARY MATERIAL

It was only once the sea transgressed the land (Matthews and Cowie 1979) that macrofossils (marine invertebrates) were formed and preserved (Brett and Baird 1986).

Fully terrestrial land vertebrate fossils are not recorded below Upper Paleozoic strata. (Laurin 2011). The first appearance of land animal fossils may be associated with the exit of land animals from the ark, and their subsequent burial in regional terrestrial flooding episodes.

2. Abraded away in early Flood!

Source: Dickens, H. and Hutchison, A. 2021. The Flood Swept Away Pre-Flood Lives! *Journal of Creation Theology and Science Series C: Earth Sciences* 11:1-4 (Creation Geology Society Annual Conference Abstracts 2021).

HIGHLIGHTS

The Hebrew word *mabbul*, translated as Flood, has been referred to as the Flood onset's 40 days of water, which swept away. Consistent with this, Jesus spoke of people being suddenly and violently swept or taken away by the Noahic Flood.

Stratigraphic and chemical evidence demonstrate that the judgement of Noah's Flood was extremely severe. This may explain why no human skeletons have been recognized in Flood rocks. The evidence we have cited suggests that Neoproterozoic erosive slurries were exceedingly destructive and people caught in them were not fossilized but abraded away.

Due to extraordinary abrasive power and hydrothermal acidity, land vertebrates and their bones (essentially $CaPO_4$) could have abraded into solution. This may have increased the concentration of light Ca isotopes, which were preferentially fractionated into rapidly precipitating cap carbonates. Much of the massive Neoproterozoic to Cambrian transition phosphorites may have come from continental erosion, plus incorporated dissolved vertebrate phosphate.

Cryogenian banded iron formations are unlike older BIFs in that they are found with diamictites and are phosphatic. The iron is considered a hydrothermal component related to Flood fountains. The detrital component is considered to represent detritus stemming from continental erosion. The diamictites are considered to represent submarine mass flows rather than cold glacial environments. The isotopic composition of enriched Hg concentrations in late Neoproterozoic/early Cambrian rocks is consistent with a volcanic origin.

Powerful Neoproterozoic kilometres of deep erosion and denudation is demonstrated by the Great Unconformity. The overall Neoproterozoic to mid-Cambrian trend of increasing $^{87}Sr/^{86}Sr$ ratio is also consistent with continental denudation, and Si isotope studies point to waters that were saturated in Si by the end of the Neoproterozoic, consistent with unprecedented continental erosion.

The Hebrew word *mabbul*, translated as Flood, has been referred to as the Flood onset's 40 days of water, which swept away (Boyd 2016). Consistent with this, Jesus spoke of people being suddenly and violently swept (ESV and CSV) or taken (KJV and NASV) away by the Flood (Matthew 24:39). While we acknowledge that there are alternative views on correlating stratigraphy with the Flood, this paper uses evidence from Cryogenian to mid-Cambrian strata that we correlate with the *mabbul* (Dickens and Hutchison 2021, and discussion with Tim Clarey in "Letters to the Editor" in *Journal of Creation*, 35(21). 2021).

The term Cryogenian pertains to mid-Neoproterozoic strata and is largely based on the interpretation of diamictites as representing cold glacial environments. However, we consider that these diamictites represent submarine mass flows consistent with this *mabbul* (Dickens and Hutchison 2021). Cryogenian strata have non-uniformitarian geochemistry and lack skeletal fossils.

The Great Unconformity is well exposed in the Grand Canyon, but this geomorphic surface, which records continental denudation followed by sediment accumulation, can be traced across today's continents (Peters and Gaines 2012). Hard Precambrian crystalline rocks such as schist and granite found in Grand Canyon have been peneplaned and eroded down tens of kilometers (Karlstrom et al. 2021). The Grenville Mountains eroded to a similar depth (Dickens 2018b). Furthermore, Si isotope studies point to waters that were saturated in Si by the end of the Neoproterozoic (Gao et al. 2020), consistent with unprecedented continental erosion. The overall Neoproterozoic to mid-Cambrian trend of increasing $^{87}Sr/^{86}Sr$ ratio is also consistent with continental denudation (Peters and Gaines 2012).

Cryogenian banded iron formations are unlike older BIFs in that they are found with diamictites and are phosphatic. The iron is considered a hydrothermal component related to Flood fountains, while the detrital component is considered to represent detritus stemming from continental erosion (Dickens and Hutchison 2021).

The isotopic composition of enriched Hg concentrations in late Neoproterozoic/early Cambrian rocks is consistent with a volcanic origin. This enrichment correlates with the total organic content of the sediments (Fan et al. 2020; Zhou et al. 2021). The destructive power of the early stages of the Flood drove organic material into the waters at the same time that volcanic processes were adding mercury.

Due to extraordinary abrasive power and hydrothermal acidity, land vertebrates and their bones (essentially $CaPO_4$) could have abraded into solution (Dickens and Snelling 2015). This may have increased the concentration of light Ca isotopes, which were preferentially fractionated into rapidly precipitating cap carbonates, resulting in their $^{44}Ca/^{40}Ca$ ratio being significantly lower than other Cryogenian rocks (Kaseman et. al. 2014; Sawaki et. al 2014). Much of the massive Neoproterozoic to Cambrian transition phosphorites may have come from continental erosion, plus incorporated dissolved vertebrate phosphate (Dickens and Snelling 2015).

Stratigraphic and chemical evidence demonstrate that the judgement of Noah's Flood was extremely severe. This may explain why no human skeletons have been recognized in Flood rocks. The evidence we have cited suggests that Neoproterozoic erosive slurries were exceedingly destructive and people caught in them were not fossilized, but abraded away.

IV. CONCLUSIONS OF ANTHOLOGY

The Bible, especially chapters one and seven of the book of Genesis, provides a high view historical record of the formation and transformation of the early Earth. This anthology describes geological features inferred to have been produced by processes in the early Creation Week and early Noah's Flood.

You cannot observe deep time. Today's slow radiometric decays, which have only been measured for a little over a century, are commonly extrapolated with uniformitarian faith to millions and billions of years. In contrast, many geological products are known to not require deep time (Ager 1973). Numerous examples were mentioned where uniformitarianism does not apply in the Precambrian.

This anthology provides an explanation for two challenges for secular geoscience: the origin of the four Precambrian "age" clusters and why enormous Neoproterozoic continental denudation was followed by Phanerozoic sedimentation.

Interpretation of the four global radiometric date clusters of the Precambrian, and thus thermal-tectonic events, was used to infer geological correlation with the biblical record of the first three Days of Creation Week and of early Noah's Flood. These "age" peaks imply the episodic nature and non-uniformitarian nature of crustal processes. I consider that God instigated heating events which provided the immense energy required for cataclysmic continent-scale geological processes during early Creation Week and in initiating

Noah's Flood. I infer that Archean to Mesoproterozoic basement provinces formed as continental crust grew in the early Creation Week. During the early Flood, massive tectonism as well as immense continental erosion and enormous water flows delivered detritus to form the Neoproterozoic sedimentary cover.

Multiple lines of evidence have been provided for an example where fountains of the great deep may have fragmented the crust and burst forth, at the commencement of the Flood.

The stupendous power of erosion caused by the rain of early Noah's Flood has been underestimated in YEC literature. It is considered that immense erosion of the land (including hard crystalline rocks like granite and schist) and related abrasion/blotting out was not favorable for the preservation of fossils. The abraded bone may have been incorporated in Late Precambrian-Cambrian transition phosphorites and Rapitan phosphatic BIF. There would be no escape for land animals and people by going uphill against extremely strong abrasive currents. It was only once the sea transgressed the land ("Cambrian transgression") that marine macrofossils had a chance to be formed and be more readily preserved.

Near surface oxidation of reduced sediments early in the Flood upheaval was inferred to be the source of the supposed Neoproterozoic Oxygenation Event and Neoproterozoic sediments have been misinterpreted as indicators of significant atmospheric oxygenation.

V. REFERENCES

Ager, D.V. 1973. *The Nature of the Stratigraphical Record.* John Wiley, New York.

Alabi, A.O., Camfield, P.A. and D.I. Gough. 1975. The North American Central Plains conductivity anomaly. *Geophysical Journal Royal Astronomical Society* 43:815–833.

Allen, P.A. and Armitage, J.J. 2012. *Cratonic Basins, in Tectonics of Sedimentary Basins: Recent Advances*, Edited by Busby, C. and Azor, A, Blackwell Publishing.

Allen, P.A., Eriksson, P.G., Alkimim, F.F., Betts, P.G., Catuneanu, O., Mazumder, R., Meng, Q., and Young, G.M. 2015. Classification of basins, with special reference to Proterozoic examples. In *Precambrian Basins of India: Stratigraphic and Tectonic Context*, eds. Mazumder, R. and Eriksson, P.G., pp. 5-28. Geological Society, London, Memoirs 43.

Allen, P.A. and Hoffman, P.F. 2005. Extreme winds and waves in the aftermath of a Neoproterozoic glaciation, *Nature* 433:123–127.

Anhaeusser, C.R. 1975. Precambrian Tectonic Environments. In *Annual Review of Earth and Planetary Sciences* 3, no. 1:31-53.

Antonelli, M.A., Pester, N.J., Brown, S.T., and DePaolo, D.J. 2017. Effect of paleoseawater composition on hydrothermal exchange in midocean ridges, *PNAS* 114(47):12413–12418.

Arnaud, E., Halverson, G.P., and Shields-Zhou, G. eds. 2011. *The Geological Record of Neoproterozoic Glaciations*. Geological Society Memoir No. 36. London, United Kingdom: Geological Society of London.

Ashwal, L.D. 2010. The temporality of anorthosites. *The Canadian Mineralogist* 48, no. 4:711-728.

Baldwin, G.J., Turner, E.C. and Kamber, B.S. 2012. A new depositional model for glaciogenic Neoproterozoic iron formations: Insights from the chemostratigraphy and basin stratigraphy of the Rapitan iron formation. *Canadian Journal of Earth Sciences* 49:455-476.

Asmerom, Y., Jacobsen, S.B., Knoll, A.H., Butterfield, N.J., and Swett, K. 1991. Strontium isotopic variations of Neoproterozoic seawater: implications for crustal evolution, *Geochimica et Cosmochimica Acta* 55:2883–2894.

Austin, S.A., A creationist view of Grand Canyon strata; in: Austin, S.A. 1994. *Grand Canyon, Monument to Catastrophe*, Institute for Creation Research, Santee, CA.

Austin, S. A., Baumgardner, J.R., Humphreys, D.R., Snelling, A.A., Vardiman, L. and Wise, K.P. 1994. Catastrophic Plate Tectonics: A Global Flood Model of Earth History. In *Proceedings of the Third International Conference on Creationism*. Edited by R. E. Walsh, 609–621. Pittsburgh, Pennsylvania: Creation Science Fellowship.

Austin, S.A. and Wise, K.P. 1994. The Pre-Flood/Flood Boundary: As Defined in Grand Canyon, Arizona and Eastern Mojave Desert, California; in: Walsh, R.E. (Ed.), *Proceedings of the Third International Conference on*

Creationism, Creation Science Fellowship, Inc., Pittsburgh, PA, pp 37–47.

Bai, S-B, Cheng, C., Wang, J., Thiebes, B. and Zhang, Z. 2013. Regional Scale Rainfall- and Earthquake-Triggered Landslide Susceptibility Assessment in Wudu County, China. *Journal of Mountain Science* 10 (5): 743–753.

Baldwin, G.J., Turner, E.C., and Kamber, B.S. 2012. A new depositional model for glaciogenic Neoproterozoic iron formation: Insights from the chemostratigraphy and basin configuration of the Rapitan iron formation, *Canadian Journal of Earth Sciences* 49(2):455–476.

Ball, J.W. and Nordstrom, D.K. 1991. WATEQ4F—User's manual with revised thermodynamic data base and test cases for calculating speciation of major, trace and redox elements in natural waters, *U.S.G.S. Open-File Report* 90-129, Menlo Park, CA.

Barley, M.E., Pickard, A.L., Hagemann, S.G. and Folkert, S.L. 1999. Hydrothermal origin for the 2 billion year old Mount Tom Price giant iron ore deposit, Hamersley Province, Western Australia. *Mineralium Deposita* 34:784–789.

Barley, M.E., Pickard, A.L. and Sylvester, P.J. 1997. Emplacement of a large igneous province as a possible cause of banded iron formation 2.45 billion years ago, *Nature* 385:55–58.

Baumgardner, J. 2012. Could most of the earth's U, Th, and K have been in the mantle prior to the Flood? J. *Creation*, 26(3), 47–48.

Bekker, A., Kaufman, A.J., Karhu, J.A. and Eriksson, K.A. 2005. Evidence for Paleoproterozoic cap carbonates in North America. *Precambrian Research* 137:167-206.

Bekker, A., Slack, J.F., Planavsky, N., Krapez, B., Hofmann, A., Konhauser, K.O., and Rouxel, O.J. 2010. Iron formation: The sedimentary product of a complex interplay among mantle, tectonic, oceanic, and biospheric processes, *Economic Geology* 105:467–508.

Bergeron, L. 1997. Deep Waters. *New Scientist* 155, no. 2097: 22-26.

Berna, F., A. Matthews, and S. Weiner. 2004. Solubilities of Bone Mineral from Archaeological Sites: The Recrystallization Window. *Journal of Archaeological Science* 31 (7): 867–82.

Blake, D. H. 1987. *Geology of the Mount Isa Inlier and Environs, Queensland and Northern Territory. Bulletin 225.* Canberra, Australia: Bureau of Mineral Resources, Geology and Geophysics.

Bloch, J. D., Timmons, J.M., Crossey, L.J., Gehrels, G.E. and Karlstrom, K.E. 2006. Mudstone Petrology of the Mesoproterozoic Unkar Group, Grand Canyon, U.S.A.: Provenance, Weathering, and Sediment Transport on Intracratonic Rodinia. *Journal of Sedimentary Research* 76 (9–10): 1106–1119.

Bond, G.C., Christie-Blick, N. and Kominz, M.A. 1984. Break-up of a supercontinent between 635 Ma and 555 Ma: New evidence and implications for continental histories. *Earth and Planetary Science Letters* 70:325-345.

Borsch, K., Whitmore, J.H., Strom, R. and Hartree, G. 2018. The significance of micas in ancient cross-bedded sandstones. In Proceedings of the Eighth International Conference on Creationism, ed. J.H. Whitmore, Pittsburgh, Pennsylvania: Creation Science Fellowship 306-326.

Boyd, S.W. 2016. The Last Week before the Flood: Noah on Vacation or Working Harder than Ever? *Answers Research Journal* 9:197–208.

Bradley, D.C. 2011. Secular trends in the geologic record and the supercontinent cycle. *Earth-Science Reviews* 108:16-33.

Brasier, M. D. 1982. Sea Level Changes, Facies Changes and the Late Precambrian–Early Cambrian Evolutionary Explosion. *Precambrian Research* 17 (2): 105–23.

Brasier, M. D. 1990a. Nutrients in the Early Cambrian. *Nature* 347 (6293): 521–22.

Brasier, M.D. 1990b. Phosphogenic Events and Skeletal Preservation Across the Precambrian-Cambrian Boundary Interval. In *Phosphorite Research and Development*. Edited by A. J. Notholt and I. Jarvis. *Geological Society of London, Special Publication* 52: 289–303.

Brasier, M.D. 1992. Global Ocean-Atmosphere Change Across the Precambrian-Cambrian Transition. *Geological Magazine* 129 (2): 161–68.

Brasier, M.D., and Lindsay, J.F. 2001. Did Supercontinent Amalgamation Trigger the 'Cambrian Explosion'? In *Ecology of the Cambrian Radiation*. Edited by R. Riding and A. Zhuravlev, 69–89. New York, New York: Columbia University Press.

Brennan, S.T., Lowenstein, T.K. and Horita, J. 2004. Seawater chemistry and the advent of biocalcification, *Geology* 32:473–476.

Brett, C.E. and Baird, G.C. 1986. Comparative Taphonomy: A Key to Paleoenvironmental Interpretation Based on Fossil Preservation. *Palaios* 1:207-227)

britannica.com/science/ocean-basin/Deep-sea-sediments

Brown, M. 2007. Metamorphic condition in orogenic belts: A record of secular change. *International Geology Review* 49:193-234.

Burke, K., Windley, J.F. and Kidd, W.S.F. 1976. Dominance of horizontal movements, arc and microcontinental collisions during the Later Permobile Regime. In *The early history of the Earth*, ed. B.F. Windley, pp. 113-130. London, Wiley.

Cameron, E.M. 1988. Archean gold: Relation to granulite formation and redox zoning in the crust. *Geology* 16:109–112.

Campbell, I.H., and Taylor, S.R. 1983. No water, no granites - No oceans, no continents. *Geophysical Research Letters* 10:1061–1064.

Carey, S.W. 1976. *The Expanding Earth.* Amsterdam: Elsevier, 488 pp..

Cartigny, P., Chinn, I., Viljoen, K.S. and Robinson, D. 2004. Early Proterozoic ultrahigh pressure metamorphism: Evidence from microdiamonds. *Science* 304:853-855.

Cattaneo, A. and Steel, R.J. 2003. Transgressive deposits: a review of their variability, *Earth Science Reviews* 62:187–228.

Chafetz, H.S. and Reid, A. 2000. Syndepositional shallow-water precipitation of glauconite minerals, *Sedimentary Geology* 136:29–42.

Ciborowski, J., and Kerr, A.C. 2016. Did mantle plume magmatism help trigger the Great Oxidation Event? *Lithos* 246-247:128-133.

Clarey, T. 2015. Reading African strata, *Acts & Facts* 44(9).

Clarey, T.L. 2019. A rock-based global sea level curve, *Acts and Facts* 48(2):9–10. 31 January 2019.

Clarey, T.L. and Werner, D.J. 2017. The sedimentary record demonstrates minimal flooding of the continents during Sauk deposition, *Answers Research Journal* 10:271–283.

Clarey, T.L. and Werner, D.J. 2018. Use of sedimentary megasequences to re-create pre-Flood geography; in: Whitmore, J.H. (Ed.), *Proceedings of the Eighth International Conference on Creationism*, Creation Science Fellowship, Pittsburgh, PA, pp. 351–372.

Clark, C., Fitzsimmons, I.C.W., Healy, D. and Harley, S.L. 2011. How Does the Continental Crust Get Really Hot? *Elements* 7 (4): 235–240.

Colpron, M., Logan, J.M., and Mortensen, J.K. 2002. U-Pb zircon age constraint for late Neoproterozoic rifting and initiation of the lower Paleozoic passive margin of western Laurentia, *Canadian J. Earth Sciences* 39(2):133–143.

Condie, K.C. 2018. A planet in transition: The onset of plate tectonics on Earth between 3 and 2 Ga? *Geoscience Frontiers* 9, no.1:51-60.

Condie, K.C., Arndt, N., Davaille, A. and Puetz, S.J. 2017. Zircon age peaks: Production or preservation of continental crust?. *Geosphere* 13(2):227-234.

Condie, K.C., and Aster, R.C. 2010. Episodic zircon age spectra of orogenic granitoids: The supercontinent connection and continental growth. *Precambrian Research* 180:227-236.

Condie, K.C., Belousova, E., Griffin, W.L. and Sircombe, K.N. 2009. Granitoid events in space and time: Constraints from igneous and detrital zircon age spectra. *Gondwana Research* 15:228 –242.

Cook, P.J. 1992. Phosphogenesis around the Proterozoic-Phanerozoic transition, *J. Geological Society of London* 149(4):615–620.

Cook, P.J., and McElhinny, M.W. 1979. A Re-Evaluation of the Spatial and Temporal Distribution of Sedimentary Phosphate Deposits in the Light of Plate Tectonics. *Economic Geology* 74 (2): 315–30.

Cook, P.J. and Shergold, J.H. 1984. Phosphorus, phosphorites and skeletal evolution at the Precambrian-Cambrian boundary, *Nature* 308:231–236, 15 March 1984.

Cook, P.J., and Shergold, J.H. 2005. *Phosphate Deposits of the World.* Vol. 1. *Proterozoic and Cambrian Phosphorites.* London, United Kingdom: Cambridge University Press.

Cox, G.M., Halverson, G.P., Minarik, W.G., Le Heron, D.P., Macdonald, F.A., Bellefroid, E.J., and Strauss, J.V. 2013. Neoproterozoic iron formation: An evaluation of its temporal, environmental and tectonic significance. *Chemical Geology* 362:232–249.

Cox, G.M., Halverson, G.P., Poirer, A., Le Heron, D., Strauss, J.V. and Stevenson, R. 2016. A model for Cryogenian iron formation. *Earth and Planetary Science Letters* 433:280-292.

Cuney, M. 2010. Evolution of uranium fractionation processes through time: Driving the secular variation of uranium deposit types. *Economic Geology* 105:553–569.

Cupps, V.R. and Clarey, T.L. 2020. Flood evidence from sea levels and strontium, *Acts and Facts* 49(3):9.

Davidson, A. 1995. A Review of the Grenville Orogen in Its North American Type Area. *AGSO Journal of Australian Geology and Geophysics* 16 (1/2): 3–24.

Davidson, A. 1998. An overview of Grenville Province geology, Canadian Shield. In *Geology of the Precambrian Superior and Grenville Provinces and Precambrian fossils in North America*, ed. S.B. Lucas and M.R. St-Onge, pp. 205-270. Volume C-1, Geology of North America series, Geological Society of America.

Dehler, C., Gehrels, G., Porter, S., Heizler, M., Karlstrom, K., Cox, G., Crossey, L. and Timmons, M. 2017. Synthesis of the 780–740 Ma Chuar, Uinta Mountain, and Pahrump (ChUMP) Groups, Western USA: Implications for Laurentia-Wide Cratonic Marine Basins. *Geological Society of America Bulletin* 129 (5–6): 607–624.

De Laeter, J.R. and Libby, W.G. 1993. Early Palaeozoic biotite Rb-Sr dates in the Yilgarn Craton near Harvey, Western Australia, *Australian J. Earth Sciences* 40:445–453.

Derby, J., Fritz, R., Longacre, S., Morgan, W., and Sternbach, C. (Eds.), 2012. Great American Carbonate Bank: The geology and economic resources of the Cambrian–Ordovician Sauk Megasequence of Laurentia, *AAPG Memoir* 98.

Derry, L.A., M.D. Brasier, R.M. Corfield, A.Y. Rozanov, and A.Y. Zhuralev. 1994. Sr and C isotopes in Lower Cambrian carbonates from the Siberian craton: A paleoenvironmental record during the 'Cambrian explosion'. *Earth and Planetary Science Letters* 128:671-681.

Deynoux, M., Affaton, P., Trompette, R. and Villeneuve, M. 2006. Pan-African Tectonic Evolution and Glacial Events Registered in Neoproterozoic to Cambrian Cratonic and Foreland Basins of West Africa. *Journal of African Earth Sciences* 46 (5): 397–426.

Dickens, H. 2016. The 'Great Unconformity' and associated geochemical evidence for Noahic Flood erosion. *Journal of Creation* 30(1):8-10.

Dickens, H. 2017a. Banded Iron Formations formed rapidly. *Journal of Creation* 31(2):14–16.

Dickens, H. 2017b. Colossal water flows during early Creation Week and early Flood. *Answers Research Journal* 10:221–235.

Dickens, H. 2018a. Evidence for Flood fountains adjacent to the cratonic margin of southwestern Australia. *Journal of Creation.* 32(1):16-20.

Dickens, H. 2018b. North American Precambrian geology—a proposed young earth biblical model; in: Whitmore, J.H. (Ed.), *Proceedings of the Eighth International Conference on Creationism,* Creation Science Fellowship, Pittsburgh, PA, pp. 389–403.

Dickens, H. 2024. *Receding Noah's Flood as trigger for seafloor spreading. Receding Then Spreading (RTS) Flood Model.* Lambert Academic Publishing. ISBN: 978-620-6-15135-7.

Dickens, H. and Hutchison, A. 2021a. Geochemical and related evidence for early Noah's Flood year. *Journal of Creation* 35(1):78-88.

Dickens, H. and Hutchison, A. 2021b. Letters to the Editor. *Journal of Creation* 35(2):18-21.

Dickens, H. and Hutchison, A. 2021c. The Flood Swept Away Pre-Flood Lives! *Journal of Creation Theology and Science Series C: Earth Sciences* 11:1-4 (Creation Geology Society Annual Conference Abstracts 2021).

Dickens, H., and Snelling, A.A. 2008. Precambrian geology and the Bible: a harmony. *Journal of Creation* 22(1):65-72.

Dickens, H., and Snelling, A.A. 2015. Terrestrial vertebrates dissolved near Flood fountains. *Answers Research Journal* 8:437-447.

Dickinson, W.R, Beard, L.S., Brakenridge, G.R., Erjavec, J.L., Ferguson, R.C., Inman, K.F., Knepp, R.A., Lindberg, F.A. and Ryberg, P.T. 1983. Provenance of North American Phanerozoic sandstones in relation to tectonic setting. *Geological Society of America Bulletin* 94:222-235,.

Donnelly, T.H., Shergold, J.H. and Southgate, P.N. 1988. Anomalous Geochemical Signals from Phosphatic Middle Cambrian Rocks in the Southern Georgina Basin, Australia. *Sedimentology* 35 (4): 549–70.

Donnelly, T.H., Shergold, J.H., Southgate, P.N. and Barnes, C.J. 1990. Events Leading to Global Phosphogenesis Around the Proterozoic/Cambrian Boundary. *Geological Society of London, Special Publications* 52 (1): 273–87.

Douglas, R.J.W., ed. 1970. *Geology and Economic Minerals of Canada*. Geological Survey of Canada, Economic Geology Report no. 1.

Engel, A.E.J., and Kelm, D.L. 1972. Pre-Permian global tectonics: A Tectonic test, *Bulletin of Geological Society of America* 83:2325-2340.

Eriksson, P.G., Banerjee, S.O., Catuneanu, P.L., Corcoran, K.A., Eriksson, E.E., Hiatt, M., Laflamme, M., Lenhardt, N., Long, D.G.F., Miall, A.D. Mints, M.V., Pufahl, P.K., Sarkar, S., Simpson, E.L. and Williams, G.E. 2013. Secular changes in sedimentation systems and sequence stratigraphy. *Gondwana Research* 24(2):468–489.

Evans, D.A.D. 2013. Reconstructing Pre-Pangean Supercontinents. *Geological Society of America Bulletin* 125 (11–12): 1735–1751.

Evans, K.A., McCuaig, T.C., Leach, D., Angerer, T. and Hagemann, S.G. 2013. Banded iron formation to iron ore: A record of the evolution of Earth environments? *Geology* 41(2):99-102.

Eyles, N. 2008. Glacio-epochs and the supercontinent cycle after ~3.0 Ga: Tectonic boundary conditions for glaciation. *Paleogeography, Paleoclimatology, Paleoecology* 258:89-129.

Eyles, N. and Januszczak, N. 2004. 'Zipper-Rift': A Tectonic Model for Neoproterozoic Glaciations During the Breakup of Rodinia after 750 Ma. *Earth-Science Reviews* 65 (1–2): 1–73.

Fan, H., Fu, X., Ward, J.F., Yin, R., Wen, H. and Feng, X. 2020. Mercury isotopes track the cause of carbon perturbations in the Ediacaran ocean. *Geology* 49:248-252.

Farquhar, J., Wu, N., Canfield, D.E. and Oduro, H. 2010. Connections between sulfur cycle evolution, sulfur isotopes, sediments, and base metal sulfide deposits. *Economic Geology* 105:509–533.

Faure, G., and Powell, J.L. 1972. *Strontium Isotope Geology*. Berlin, Germany: Springer-Verlag.

Fedo, C.M., Sircombe, K.N. and Rainbird, R.H. 2003. Detrital Zircon Analysis of the Sedimentary Record. *Reviews in Mineralogy and Geochemistry* 53 (1): 277–303.

Fedo, C.M., Young, G.M., Nesbitt, H.W. and Hanchar, J.M. 1997. Potassic and sodic metasomatism in the Southern Province of the Canadian Shield: Evidence from the Paleoproterozoic Serpent Formation, Huronian Supergroup, Canada. *Precambrian Research* 84:17-36.

Fedo, C.M., Sircombe, K.N. and Rainbird, R.H. 2003. Detrital zircon analysis of the sedimentary record. *Reviews in Mineralogy and Geochemistry* 53, no. 1:277-303.

Ford, D. and Golonka, J. 2003. Phanerozoic paleogeography, paleoenvironment and lithofacies maps of the circum-Atlantic margins, *Marine and Petroleum Geology* 20:249–285.

Fouts, D.M., and Wise, K.P. 1998. Blotting Out and Breaking Up: Miscellaneous Hebrew Studies in Geocatastrophism. In *Proceedings of the Fourth International Conference on Creationism*. Edited by R. E. Walsh, 217–28. Pittsburgh, Pennsylvania: Creation Science Fellowship. Geological Survey of Queensland. 2012. *Queensland's Mineral, Petroleum and Energy Operations and Resources Map*. June 2012.

Frazier, W.J., and Schwimmer, D.R. 1987. *Regional Stratigraphy of North America*. New York, New York: Plenum Press.

ga.gov.au/scientific-topics/disciplines/geophysics/magnetotellurics

Gaillard, F., Scaillet, B. and Arndt, N.T. 2011. Atmospheric oxygenation caused by a change in volcanic degassing pressure. *Nature* 478:229- 232.

Gaines, R.R., Hammarlund, E.U., Hou, X., Qi, C., Gabbott, S.E., Zhao, Y., Peng, J. and Canfield, D.E. 2012. Mechanism for Burgess Shale-type preservation, *PNAS* 109(14):5180–5184.

Gao, P., Li, S., Lash, G.G., He, Z., Xiao, X., Zhang, D., and Hao, Y. 2020. Silicification and Si cycling in a silica-rich ocean during the Ediacaran-Cambrian transition. *Chemical Geology* 552: 119787.

Garrels, R.M. 1987. A model for the deposition of the microbanded Precambrian iron formations. *American Journal of Science* 287:81–106.

Gee, R.D., Baxter, J.L., Wilde, S.A., and Williams, I.R. 1981. Crustal development in the Archaean Yilgarn Block, Western Australia, *Geological Society of Australia, Special Publication* 7:43–56.

Geological Survey of Western Australia. 1990. *Geology and Mineral Resources of Western Australia*: Western Australia Geological Survey, Memoir 3, 827 pp.

George, J. and Varghese, G. 2005. Intermediate colloidal formation and the varying width of periodic precipitation bands in reaction-diffusion systems, *Journal of Colloid and Interface Science* 282:397–402.

Ginsburg, R.N. 1982. Actualistic depositional models for the Great American Bank (Cambro-Ordovician); in: *Eleventh International Congress on Sedimentology*, Abstracts of Papers, International Association of Sedimentologists, McMaster University, Hamilton, Ontario, Canada, p. 114.

Gower, C.F., Kamo, S. and Krogh, T.E. 2008. Indentor Tectonism in the Eastern Grenville Province. *Precambrian Research* 167 (1–2): 201–212.

Gross, G.A. 1996. Lake Superior-type iron-formations; in: Eckstrand, O.R., Sinclair, W.D., and Thorpe, R.I. (Eds.), *Geology of Canadian Mineral Deposit Types*, Geological Survey of Canada, Geology of Canada 8:54–66.

Groves, D.I., Vielreicher, R.M., Goldfarb, R.J., and Condie, K.C. 2005. Controls on the heterogeneous distribution of mineral deposits through time; in: McDonald, I., Boyce, A.J., Butler, I.B., Herington, R.J., and Polya, D.A. (Eds.), *Mineral Deposits and Earth Evolution*, Geological Society, London, Special Publications, 248:71–101.

Hallam, A. 1981. *Facies interpretation and the stratigraphic record*, W.H. Freeman and Co. Ltd., Oxford, England. 291 pp.

Hallam, A. 1984. Pre-Quaternary sea-level changes, Annual Review of *Earth and Planetary Sciences* 12:205–243.

Hallam, A. 1992. *Phanerozoic Sea-Level Changes*, Columbia University Press, New York.

Halverson, G.P., Hurtgen, M.T., Porter, S.M. and Collins. A.S. 2009. Neoproterozoic-Cambrian Biogeochemical Evolution. In *Neoproterozoic-Cambrian Tectonics, Global Change and Evolution: A Focus on Southwestern Gondwana.* Edited by C. Gaucher, A. N. Sial, G. P. Halverson, and H. E. Frimmel. *Developments in Precambrian Geology* 16: 351–65.

Hamilton, W.B. 2003. An alternative earth. *GSA Today* 13, no. 11:4-12.

Hamilton, W.B. 2007. Earth's first two billion years – The era of internally mobile crust. In *4-D Framework of Continental Crust*, eds. R.D. Hatcher Jr., M.P. Carlson, J.H. McBride, and J.R. Martínez Catalán, pp 233-296. Geological Society of America Memoir 200.

Hamilton, W.B. 2011. Plate tectonics began in Neoproterozoic time, and plumes from deep mantle have never operated. *Lithos* 123(1-4):1-20.

Hanly, A.J., Kyser, T.K., Hiatt, E.E., Marlatt, J. and Foster, S. 2006. The uranium mineralization potential of the Paleoproterozoic Sioux Basin and its relationship to other basins in the southern Lake Superior region. *Precambrian Research* 148(1-2):125-144.

Hannisdal, B. and Peters, S.E. 2011. Phanerozoic earth system evolution and marine biodiversity, *Science* 334:1121–1124.

Haq, B.U. 1991. Sequence stratigraphy, sea-level change, and significance of the deep sea, *Special Publications of the International Association of Sedimentologists* 12:3–39.

Haq, B.U. and Schutter, R. 2008. A chronology of Paleozoic sea-level changes, *Science* 322:64–68.

Harley, S.L., Kelly, N.M. and Moller, A. 2007. Zircon behaviour and the thermal histories of mountain chains. *Elements* 3:25-30.

Hawkesworth, C.J., B. Dhuime, A.B. Pietranik, P.A. Cawood, A.I.S. Kemp, and C.D. Storey. 2010. The generation and evolution of the continental crust. *Journal of the Geological Society, London* 167(2):229-248.

Hawkesworth, C.J., Cawood, P.A. and Dhuime, B. 2016. Tectonics and crustal evolution. *GSA Today*. 26, no. 9:4-11.

Hay, W.W., Eicher, D.L. and Diner, R. 1993. Physical oceanography and water masses in the Cretaceous Western Interior Seaway, *in* Caldwell, W.G.E. and Kauffman, E.G., eds., Evolution of the Western Interior Basin. *Geological Association of Canada. Special Paper* **39**:297-318.

Hofmann, H.J. 1998. Synopsis of Precambrian fossil occurrences in North America. In *Geology of the Precambrian Superior and Grenville Provinces and Precambrian fossils in North America*, eds. S.B. Lucas and M.R. St-Onge, pp. 271-376. C-1, Geology of North America series, Geological Society of America.

Hofmann, H.J. 2000. Archean stromatolites as microbial archives. *Microbial Sediments* 315-327.

Hoffman, P.F. 1989. Precambrian geology and tectonic history of North America In *The Geology of North America; An Overview*, eds. A.W. Bally and A.R. Palmer, pp 447-512. Geological Society of America.

Hoffman, P.F. 1990. Old and young mantle roots. *Nature* 347:19–20.

Hoffman, P.F. 1998. United Plates of America, The birth of a craton: Early Proterozoic assembly and growth of

Laurentia. *Annual Review of Earth and Planetary Sciences* 16:543-603.

Hoffman, P.F., Abbot, D.S., Ashkenazy, Y., Benn, D.I., Brocks, J.J., Cohen, P.A., Cox, G.M., Creveling, J.R., Donnadieu, Y., Erwin, D.H., Fairchild, I.J., Ferreira, D., Goodman, J.C., Halverson, G.P., Jansen, M.F., Le Hir, G., Love, G.D., Macdonald, F.A., Maloof, A.C., Partin, C.A., Ramstein, G., Rose, B.E.J., Rose, C.V., Sadler, P.M., Tziperman, E., Voigt, A., and Warren, S.G. 2017. Snowball Earth climate dynamics and Cryogenian geology-geobiology, *Science Advances* 3(11):1–43.

Hoffman, P.F. and Halverson, G.P. 2011. Neoproterozoic glacial record in the Mackenzie Mountains, northern Canadian Cordillera; in: Halverson, A.E., Halverson, G.P., and Shields-Zhou, G. (Eds.), The Geological Record of Neoproterozoic Glaciations, *Geological Society, London, Memoirs* 36:397–411.

Hoffman, P. F., Kaufman, A.J., Halverson, G.P. and Schrag, D.P. 1998. A Neoproterozoic Snowball Earth. *Science* 281 (5381): 1342–46.

Hoskin, T.E., Regenauer-Lieb, K., and Jones, A.G. 2013. Conductivity models for the North Perth Basin, Western Australia, *American Geophysical Union, Fall Meeting 2013*, abstract.

Hsu, K.J., Oberhänsli, H., Goa, J.Y., Shu, S., Haihong, C., and Krähenbühl, U. 1985. 'Strangelove Ocean' before the Cambrian explosion, *Nature* 316(6031):809–811.

Humphreys, D. R. 2005. Young Helium Diffusion Age of Zircons Supports Accelerated Nuclear Decay. In *Radioisotopes and the Age of the Earth: Results of a Young-Earth Creationist Research Initiative*. Edited by Larry Vardiman, Andrew A. Snelling, and Eugene F. Chaffin, 25-100. El Cajon, CA: Institute for Creation Research, and Chino Valley, AZ: Creation Research Society.

Humphreys, D.R. 2011. Argon diffusion data support RATE's 6,000-year helium age of the earth. *Journal of Creation* 25(2):74-77.

Ielpi, A. and Rainbird, R.H. 2016a. Highly Variable Precambrian Fluvial Style Recorded in the Nelson Head Formation of Brock Inlier (Northwest Territories, Canada). *Journal of Sedimentary Research* 86 (3): 199–216.

Ielpi, A., and Rainbird, R.H. 2016b. Reappraisal of Precambrian sheet-braided rivers: Evidence for 1.9 Ga deep-channelled drainage. *Sedimentology* 63(6):1550-1581.

Ielpi, A., Rainbird, R.H., Greenman, J.W. and Creason, C.G. 2015. The 1.9 Ga Kilohigok Paleosol and Burnside River Formation, Western Nunavut: Stratigraphy and Gamma-Ray Spectrometry. *Summary of Activities, Canada-Nunavut Geoscience Office* 1–10.

Iizuka, T., Hirata, T., Komiya, T., Rino, S., Katayama, I., Motoki, A. and Maruyama, S. 2005. U-Pb and Lu-Hf Isotope Systematics of Zircons From the Mississippi River Sand: Implications for Reworking and Growth of Continental Crust. *Geology* 33 (6): 485–488.

Iizuka, T., Komiya, T. and Maruyama, S. 2007. The early Archean Acasta Gneiss Complex: Geological, geochronological and isotopic studies and implications for early crustal evolution. In *Precambrian Ophiolites and Related Rocks*. eds. M.J. van Kranendonk, R. Hugh Smithies and V.C. Bennett, pp. 1-22. Developments in Precambrian Geology, Vol. 15, no. 1. Elsevier.

Ilyin, A.V. 1990. Proterozoic Supercontinent, Its Latest Precambrian Rifting, Breakup, Dispersal Into Smaller Continents, and Subsidence of Their Margins: Evidence from Asia. *Geology* 18 (12): 1231–34.

International Commission on Stratigraphy, *International Stratigraphic Chart*, 2004.

Irving, E., McGlynn, J.C. and Morgan, G.E. 1976. Proterozoic magnetostratigraphy and the tectonic evolution of Laurentia. *Philosophical Transactions of the Royal Society* 280, no. 1298:433-467.

Jones, A.G., Ledo, J. and Ferguson, I.J. 2005. Electromagnetic images of the Trans-Hudson orogeny: The North American Central Plains anomaly revealed. *Canadian Journal of Earth Sciences* 42:457-478.

James, N.P., Narbonne, G.M., and Kyser, T.K. 2001. Late Neoproterozoic cap carbonates: Mackenzie Mountains, northwestern Canada: precipitation and global glacial meltdown, *Canadian J. Earth Science* 38:1229–1262.

Jamieson, R.A., Unsworth, M.J., Harris, N.B.W., Rosenberg, C.L. and Schulmann, K. 2011. Crustal Melting and the Flow of Mountains. *Elements* 7 (4): 253–260.

Jamieson, J.W., Hannington, M.D., Tivey, M.K. Hansteen, T., Williamson, N.M.B., Stewart, M., Fietzke, J., Butterfield, D., Frische, M., Allen, L., Cousens, B., and Langer, J. 2016. Precipitation and growth of barite within hydrothermal vent deposits from the Endeavour Segment, Juan de Fuca Ridge, *Geochimica and Cosmochimica Acta* 173:64–85.

Janssen, D.P., Collins, A.S., and Fitzsimons, I.C.W. 2003. Structure and tectonics of the Leeuwin Complex and Darling Fault Zone, southern Pinjarra Orogen, Western Australia—a field guide, *Western Australia Geological Survey, Record* 2003/15.

Jell, P.A. ed. 2013. *Geology of Queensland*. Brisbane, Australia: Geological Survey of Queensland.

Jones, J.V., Daniel, C.G. and Doe, M.F. 2015. Tectonic and Sedimentary Linkages Between the Belt-Purcell Basin and Southwestern Laurentia During the Mesoproterozoic ca. 1.60–1.40 Ga. *Lithosphere* 7(4):465–472.

Karlstrom, K., Crossey, L., Mathis, A., and Bowman, C. 2021. Telling time at Grand Canyon National Park: 2020 update. *Natural Resource Report NPS/ GRCA/NRR—*2021/2246. National Park Service, Fort Collins, Colorado.

Keller, M. 2012. The Argentine Precordillera: a little American carbonate bank; in: Derby, J.R., Fritz, R.D., Longacre, W.P., and Sternbach, C.A. (Eds.), The Great American Carbonate Bank: The geology and economic resources of the Cambrian–Ordovician Sauk Megasequence of Laurentia, *AAPG Memoir 98*, pp. 985–1000.

Kennedy, J. 1990. *Analytical Chemistry: Practice*, Saunders College Publishing, New York.

Kimura, H. and Watanabe, Y. 2001. Oceanic anoxia at the Precambrian-Cambrian boundary, *Geology* 29(11):995–998.

King, P. B. 1976. Precambrian geology of the United States: An explanatory text to accompany the geologic map of the United States. *U.S. Geological Survey Professional Paper* 902.

Klein, C. 2005. Some Precambrian banded iron-formations (BIFs) from around the world: Their age, geologic setting, mineralogy, metamorphism, geochemistry, and origin, *American Mineralogist* 90:1473–1499.

Kleinhanns, I.C., Kramers, J.D. and Kamber, B.S. 2003. Importance of water for Archaean granitoid petrology: A comparative study of TTG and potassic granitoids from Barberton Mountain Land, South Africa. *Contributions to Mineralogy and Petrology* 145:377-389.

Knoll, A.H., and Walter, M.R. 1992. Latest Proterozoic Stratigraphy and Earth History. *Nature* 356 (6371): 673–78.

Kocsis, A.T. and Scotese, C.R. 2021. Mapping paleocoastlines and continental flooding during the Phanerozoic. *Earth-Science Reviews* 213(103463):1-15.

Krabbendam, M., Bonsor, H., Horstwood, M.S.A. and Rivers, T. 2017. Tracking the evolution of the Grenvillian Foreland Basin: Constraints from sedimentology and detrital zircon and rutile in the Sleat and Torridon Groups, Scotland. *Precambrian Research* 295:67–89.

Kroner, A. and Stern, R.J. 2004. Pan-African Orogeny, *Encyclopedia of Geology*, vol. 1, Elsevier, Amsterdam.

Lambert, M.B. 2011. Stromatolites of the late Archean Back River stratovolcano, Slave structural province, Northwest Territories, Canada. *Canadian Journal of Earth Sciences* 35, no. 3:290-301.

Large, R.R., Bull, S.W., McGoldrick, P.J., Walters, S., Derrick, G.M. and Carr, G.R. 2005. Stratiform and Strata-Bound Zn-Pb-Ag Deposits in Proterozoic Sedimentary Basins, Northern Australia. *Economic Geology* 100th Anniversary Volume: 931–64.

Lascelles, D.F. 2013. Plate tectonics caused the demise of banded iron formations, *Applied Earth Science* 122(4):230–241.

Lau, K.V., Macdonald, F.A., Maher, K., and Payne, J.L. 2017. Uranium isotope evidence for temporary ocean oxygenation in the aftermath of the Sturtian Snowball Earth, *Earth and Planetary Science Letters* 458:282–292.

Laurin, M. 2011. Terrestrial vertebrates—Stegocephalians: tetrapods and other digitbearing vertebrates, *The Tree of Life Web Project*, tolweb.org/Terrestrial%20 Vertebrates/14952.pdf, 21 April 2011.

Lee, C.-T., Yeung, L.Y., McKenzie, R., Yokoyama, Y., Ozaki, K. and Lenardic. L.A. 2016. Two-step rise of atmospheric oxygen linked to the growth of continents. *Nature Geoscience* 9:417-424.

Libby, W.G. and De Laeter, J.R. 1979. Biotite dates and cooling history at the western margin of the Yilgarn Block,

Geological Survey of Western Australia Annual Report for 1978, pp. 79–87.

Libby, W.G. and De Laeter, J.R.1998. Biotite Rb-Sr age evidence for early Palaeozoic tectonism along the cratonic margin in southwestern Australia, *Australian J. Earth Sciences* 45(4):623–632.

Lindsay, J.F. 1999. Heavitree Quartzite, a Neoproterozoic (Ca 800–760 Ma), high-energy, tidally influenced, ramp association, Amadeus Basin, central Australia, *Australian J. Earth Sciences* 46:127–139.

Loewenthal, D., Bruce, R.H., and Bruner, I. 1993. Are millions of years necessary for petroleum formation? *Israel Geological Society, Annual Meeting 1993*, p. 85.

Loiselle, M.C. and Wones, D.R. 1979. Characteristic and origin of anorogenic granites, *Geological Society of America*, Abstracts with Programs 11: 468.

London, D. 1992. The application of experimental petrology to the genesis and crystallization of granitic pegmatites. *Canadian Mineralogist* 30:499–540.

Lu, S. 2016. *The thermotectonic evolution of the southwest Yilgarn Craton, Western Australia*, PhD thesis, University of Melbourne.

Lu, S., Phillips, D., Kohn, B.P., Gleadow, A.J.W., and Matchan, E.L.2015. Thermotectonic evolution of the western margin of the Yilgarn Craton, Western Australia: new insights from ^{40}Ar/^{39}Ar analysis of muscovite and biotite, *Precambrian Research* 270: 139–154.

Lucas, S.B., and M.R. St-Onge. 1998. *Geology of the Precambrian Superior and Grenville Provinces and Precambrian fossils in North America.* C-1, Geology of North America series, Geological Society of America.

Luther III, G.W., Findlay, A.J., MacDonald, D.J., Owings, S.M., Hanson, T.E., Beinart, R.A., and Girguis, P.R. 2011. Thermodynamics and kinetics of sulfide oxidation by oxygen: a look at inorganically controlled reactions and biologically mediated processes in the environment, *Frontiers in Microbiology* 2:1–9.

Lydon, J.W. 2007. Geology and metallogeny of the Belt-Purcell Basin. In *Mineral Deposits of Canada: A Synthesis of Major Deposit Types, District Metallogeny, the Evolution of Geological Provinces, and Exploration Methods*, ed. W.D. Goodfellow, pp. 581-607. Geological Association of Canada, Mineral Deposits Division, Special Publication 5.

Lyons, T.W., Gellatly, A.M., McGoldrick, P.J. and Kah, I.C. 2006. Proterozoic sedimentary exhalative (SEDEX) deposits and links to evolving global ocean chemistry. In *Evolution of Early Earth's Atmosphere, Hydrosphere, and Biosphere – Constraints from Ore Deposits*, eds. S.F. Kesler and H. Ohmoto. Geological Society of America Memoir 198:169-184.

Lyons, T.W., Reinhard, C.T., Planavsky, N.J., 2014. The rise of oxygen in Earth's early ocean and atmosphere. Nature. 506, pp. 307–315.

Macdonald, F.A., Schmitz, M.D., Crowley, J.L., Roots, C.F., Jones, D.S., Maloof, A.C., Strauss, J.V. et al. 2010.

Calibrating the Cryogenian. *Science* 327 (5970): 1241–1243.

Macdonald, F.A., Schmitz, M.D., Strauss, J.V., Halverson, G.P., Gibson, T.M., Eyster, A., Cox, G., Mamrol, P. and Crowley, J.L. 2018. Cryogenian of Yukon. *Precambrian Research*, *319*, 114–143.

Macdonald, G.A. 1972. *Volcanoes*. Englewood Cliffs, New Jersey: Prentice-Hall.

Mackenzie, N.R., Hughes, N.C., Gill, B.C., and Myrow, P.M. 2014. Plate tectonic influences on Neoproterozoic-early Paleozoic climate and animal evolution, *Geology* 42(2):127–130.

Macouin, M., Roques, D., Rousse, S., Ganne, J., Denele, Y. and Trindade, R.I.F. 2015. Is the Neoproterozoic oxygen burst a supercontinent legacy? *Frontiers in Earth Science* 3, no. 44:1-10.

Martel, E., Turner, E.C., and Fischer, B.J. (Eds.), 2012. Geology of the central Mackenzie Mountains of the northern Canadian Cordillera, Sekwi Mountain (105P), Mount Eduni (106A), and northwestern Wrigley Lake (95M) map-areas, Northwest Territories, *NWT Special Volume 1*, NWT Geoscience Office.

Martin, J. W. 2007. *Concise Encyclopedia of the Structure of Materials*. Oxford, United Kingdom: Elsevier. Matthews, S. C., and J. W. Cowie. 1979. Early Cambrian Transgression. *Journal of Geological Society* 136 (2): 133–35.

Mapes, R.W., D.S. Coleman, D.S., Nogueira, A.C.R. and Housh, T.B. 2004. How Far Do Zircons Travel? Evaluating the Significance of Detrital Zircon Provenance Using the Modern Amazon River Fluvial System. *Geological Society of America*, Rocky Mountain (56th Annual) and Cordilleran (100th Annual) Joint Meeting (May 3–5, 2004). Abstracts with Programs 36: 78.

Matthews, S.C., and Cowie, J.W. 1979. Early Cambrian Transgression. *Journal of the Geological Society* 136 (2): 133–135.

McGee, K.A., Doukas, M.P., Kessler, R. and Gerlach, T.M. 1997. *Impacts of Volcanic Gases on Climate, the Environment, and People*. U.S. Geological Survey Open-File Report, 97- 262. Reston, Virginia: U.S. Geological Survey.

McKenzie, N.R., Hughes, N.C., Gill, B.C. and Myrow, P.M. 2014. Plate tectonic influences on Neoproterozoic-early Paleozoic climate and animal evolution, *Geology* 42(2):127–130.

McKeogh, M.A., Lentz, D.R., McFarlane, C.R.M. and Brown, J. 2013. Geology and evolution of pegmatite-hosted U-Th +- REE-Y-Nb mineralization, Kulyk, Eagle, and Karin Lakes region, Wollaston Domain, northern Saskatchewan, Canada: examples of the dual role of extreme fractionation and hybridization processes. *Journal of Geosciences* 58:321-346.

McLaurin, B.T., and Steel, R.J. 2007. Architecture and Origin of an Amalgamated Fluvial Sheet Sand, Lower

Castlegate Formation, Book Cliffs, Utah. *Sedimentary Geology* 197 (3–4): 291–311.

Miall, A.D., ed. 2008. *The Sedimentary Basins of the United States and Canada.* Elsevier.

Middleton, G.V. 1973. Johannes Walter's Law of the Correlation of Facies. *Geological Society of America Bulletin* 84 (3): 979–88.

Middleton, M.F., Wilde, S.A., Evans, B.J., Long, A., Dentith, M., and Morawa, M. 1995. Deep seismic reflection traverse over the Darling Fault Zone, Western Australia, *Australian J. Earth Sciences* 42: 83–93.

Meert, J.G., and Powell, C. McA. 2001. Assembly and break-up of Rodinia: Introduction to the special volume. *Precambrian Research* 110:1-8.

Mints, M.V. 2007. Paleoproterozoic supercontinent: Origin and evolution of accretionary and collisional orogens exemplified in northern cratons. *Geotectonics* 41(4):257-280.

Mints, M.V. 2015. [Appendix II-4] North American craton: Emergence and evolution of the Paleoproterozoic orogens. In *East European Craton: Early Precambrian History and 3D Models of Deep Crustal Structure*, eds. M.V. Mints, K.A. Dokukina, A.N. Konilov, I.B. Philippova, V.L. Zlobin, P.S. Babayants, E.A. Belousova, Y.I. Blokh, M.M. Bogina, W.A. Bush, P.A. Dokukin, T.V. Kaulina, L.M. Natapov, V.B. Piip, V.M. Stupak, A.K. Suleimanov, A.A. Trusov, K.V. Van, N.G. Zamozhniaya, pp. 397-402. Geological Society of America Special Paper 510.

Mints, M.V. 2018. A Neoarchean-Proterozoic supercontinent (~2.8-0.9 Ga): An alternative to the model of supercontinent cycles. *Doklady Earth Sciences* 480, no. 1:69-72.

Morgan, B. and Lahav, O. 2007. The effect of pH on the kinetics of spontaneous Fe(II) oxidation by O2 in aqueous solution—basic principles and a simple heuristic description, *Chemosphere* 68:2080–2084.

Morris, H.M. 1984. *The Biblical Basis for Modern Science.* Baker Book House, Grand Rapids, Michigan.

Mortenson, T. 2007. The Historical Development of the Old-Earth Geological Timescale. *Answers in Depth* 2:120-137.

Morton, G.R. 1984. Global, continental and regional sedimentation systems and their implications, *Creation Research Society Quarterly* 21:23–33.

Mulder, J.A., Karlstrom, K.E., Fletcher, K., Heizler, M.T., Timmons, J.M., Crossey, L.J., Gehrels, G.E. and M. Pecha. 2017. The Syn-Orogenic Sedimentary Record of the Grenville Orogeny in Southwest Laurentia. *Precambrian Research* 294: 33–52.

Myers, J.S. 1990a. Albany-Fraser Orogen; in: Geology and Mineral Resources of Western Australia, *Western Australia Geological Survey, Memoir 3*, pp. 255–263.

Myers, J.S. 1990b. Pinjarra Orogen; in: Geology and Mineral Resources of Western Australia, *Western Australia Geological Survey, Memoir 3*, pp. 265–274.

Narbonne, G.M., LaFlamme, M., Trusler, P.W., Dalrymple, R.W., and Greentree, C. 2014. Deep-water Ediacaran fossils from northwestern Canada: taphonomy, ecology, and evolution, *J. Paleontology* 88(2):207–223.

Nathan, Y., Bremner, M., Loewenthal, R.E. and Monteiro, P. 1993. Possible Active Role of Bacteria in Phosphorite Genesis. *Israel Geological Society Annual Meeting 1993*, 93.

Neoproterozoic, <en.wikipedia.org/wiki/Neoproterozoic>, 28 December 2005

Nelson, K.D., Baird, D.J., Walters, J.J., Huack, M., Brown, L.D., Oliver, J.E., Ahern, J.L., Hajnal, Z., Jones, A.G., and Sloss, L.L. 1993. Trans-Hudson orogeny and Williston Basin in Montana and North Dakota: New COCORP deep profiling results. *Geology* 21:447-450.

Nesbitt, H.W., and Young, G.M. 1982. Early Proterozoic climates and plate motions inferred from major element chemistry of lutites. *Nature* 299:715-717.

Nicholas, C. J. 1996. The Sr Isotope Evolution of the Oceans During the 'Cambrian Explosion'. *Journal of the Geological Society* 153 (2): 243–54.

Northolt, A.J.G., Sheldon, R.P., and Davidson, D.F. (Eds.), 1989. *Phosphate Deposits of the World, 2: Phosphate rock resources*, Cambridge University Press, Cambridge.

Nyquist, D.D., Bogard, D.D., Garrison, D.H., Bansal, B.M., Wiesmann, H. and Shih, C-Y. 1991. Thermal resetting of radiometric ages. II: Modeling and applications. *Abstracts of the Lunar and Planetary Conference* 22:987.

Oard, M. J. 1997. A Classic Tillite Reclassified as a Submarine Debris Flow. *Creation Ex Nihilo Technical Journal* 11 (1): 7.

Oard, M. 2008. *Flood by Design: Receding Water Shapes the Earth's Surface*, Master Books, Green Forest, AR.

Och, L.M., and Shields-Zhou, G.A. 2012. The Neoproterozoic oxygenation event: Environmental perturbations and biogeochemical cycling. *Earth Science Reviews* 110:26-57.

Okajangas, R.W. 1985. Review of Archean clastic sedimentation, Canadian Shield: major felsic volcanic contributions to turbidite and alluvial fan-fluvial facies associations. In *Evolution of Archean Supracrustal Sequences*, eds. L.D. Ayres, P.C. Thurston, K.D. Card, and W. Weber, pp. 23-42. Geological Association of Canada Special Paper 28.

O'Neill, C., Lenardic, A. and Condie, K.C. 2013. Earth's punctuated tectonic evolution: cause and effect. In *Continent Formation Through Time*, eds. N.M.W. Roberts, M. van Kranendonk, S. Parman, S. Shirey, S. and P.D. Clift, pp. 17-40. Geological Society, London, Special Publications 389.

Ootes, L., Gleeson, S.A., Turner, E., Rasmussen, K., Gordey, S., Falck, H., Martel, E., and Pierce, K. 2013. Metallogenic evolution of the Mackenzie and eastern Selwyn Mountains of Canada's Northern Cordillera, Northwest Territories: a compilation and review, *Geoscience Canada* 40:40–69.

Palfreyman, W.D. 1984. *Guide to the Geology of Australia. BMR Bulletin 181.* Canberra, Australia: Australian Government Publishing Service.

Palmer, S.E., Kyser, T.K. and Hiatt, E.E. 2004. Provenance of the Proterozoic Thelon Basin, Nunavut, Canada, from Detrital Zircon Geochronology and Detrital Quartz Oxygen Isotopes. *Precambrian Research* 129 (1–2): 115–140.

Pearson, D.G., Brenker, F.E., Nestola, F., McNeill, J., Nasdala, L., Hutchison, M.T., Matveev, S., Mather, K., Silversmit, G., Schmitz, S., Vekemans, B. and Vincze, L. 2014. Hydrous mantle transition zone indicated by ringwoodite included within diamond. *Nature* 507:221-224.

Percival, J.A. and western SNATMAP working group. 2004. Orogenic framework for the Superior Province: Dissection of the Kenoran Orogeny. In *The LITHOPROBE Celebratory Conference: From Parameters to Processes – Revealing the Evolution of a Continent.*

Percival, J.A. 2004. Orogenic Framework for the Superior Province: Dissection of the 'Kenoran Orogeny'. *The LITHOPROBE Celebratory Conference: From Parameters to Processes—Revealing the Evolution of a Continent.* Geological Survey of Canada.

Peters, S.E. 2006. Macrostratigraphy of North America, *J. Geology* 114:391–412.

Peters, S.E. and Gaines, R.R. 2012. Formation of the 'Great Unconformity' as a trigger for the Cambrian explosion. *Nature* 484(4):363-366.

Peters, S.E. and Husson, J.M. 2018. We need a global comprehensive stratigraphic database: here's a start. *The Sedimentary Record*. March 2018. 4-9.

Piper, J.D.A. 2009. Comment on "Assembly, configuration, and breakup history of Rodinia: A synthesis" by Li et al. 2008.[Precambrian Research 160:179-210]. *Precambrian Research* 174:200-207.

Piper, J.D.A. 2015. The Precambrian supercontinent Paleopangaea: Two billion years of quasi-integrity and an appraisal of geological evidence. *International Geology Review* 57(11-12):1389-1417.

Pirajno, F. 1992. *Hydrothermal Mineral Deposits: Principles and Fundamental Concepts for the Exploration Geologist*. Berlin, Germany: Springer-Verlag.

Pisarevsky, S.A., Murphy, J.B., Cawood, P.A. and Collins, A.S. 2008. Late Neoproterozoic and Early Cambrian Palaeogeography: Models and Problems. In *West Gondwana: Pre-Cenozoic Correlations Across the South Atlantic Region, Geological Society of London, Special Publication* 294. Edited by R.J. Pankhurst, R.A.J. Trouw, B.B. de Brito Neves, and M.J. de Wit, 9–31. Bath, United Kingdom: The Geological Society Publishing House.

Planavsky, N.J., Rouxel, O.J., Bekker, A., Lalonde, S.V., Konhauser, O., Reinhard, C.T., and Lyons, T.W. 2010. The evolution of the marine phosphate reservoir, *Nature* 467:1088–1090.

Porter Geoconsultancy Database. 2011. *Georgina Basin—Phosphate Hill, Duchess—Queensland, Australia.*

Pough, F.H., Heiser, J.B. and McFarland, W.N. 1989. *Vertebrate Life*. New York, New York: McMillan Publishing Company.

Powell, C.McA., Li, Z.X., McElhinny, M.W., Meert, J.G., and Park, J.K. 1993. Paleomagnetic constraints on timing of the Neoproterozoic breakup of Rodinia and the Cambrian formation of Gondwana, *Geology* 21:889–892.

Presnell, R.D. 2004. Metallogenic evolution of North America. In *Proceedings of Society of Economic Geologists 2004 Conference,* ed. D.I. Groves, pp. 257-259. Perth, Western Australia.

Purdom, G., and Snelling, A.A. 2013. Survey of microbial composition and mechanisms of living stromatolites of the Bahamas and Australia: Developing criteria to determine the biogenicity of fossil stromatolites. In *Proceedings of the Seventh International Conference of Creationism*, ed. M.F. Horstmeyer. Pittsburgh, Pennsylvania: Creation Science Fellowship.

Pyle, L.J. 2012. Cambrian and Lower Ordovician Sauk Megasequence of Northwestern Canada, Northern Rocky Mountains to the Beaufort Sea; in: Derby, J.R., Fritz, R.D., Longacre, S.A., Morgan, W.A., and Sternbach, C.A. (Eds.), The Great American Carbonate Bank: The geology and economic resources of the Cambrian –Ordovician Sauk Megasequence of Laurentia, *AAPG Memoir* 98, pp. 675–723.

Rainbird, R.H. 2008. Ancient pancontinental river systems revealed by detrital zircon geochronology of Proterozoic cratonic sheet sandstones. *American Geophysical Union, Fall Meeting 2008*, abstract #H51J-08.

Rainbird, R., Cawood, P.G. and Gehrels, G. 2012. The great Grenvillian sedimentation episode: Record of supercontinent Rodinia's assembly. In *Tectonics of Sedimentary Basins: Recent Advances*, eds. C. Busby, and A. Azor, pp. 583-601. John Wiley and Sons.

Rainbird, R.H., Jefferson, C.W. and G.M. Young, G.M. 1996. The Early Neoproterozoic Sedimentary Succession B of Northwestern Laurentia: Correlations and Paleogeographic Significance. *Geological Society of America Bulletin* 108 (4): 454–470.

Rainbird, R.H., McNicoll, V.J., Theriault, R.J., Heaman, L.M., Abbott, J.G., Long, D.F.G. and Thorkelson, D.J. 1997. Pan-continental river system draining Grenville Orogen recorded in U-Pb and Sm-Nd geochronology of Neoproterozoic quartzarenites and mudrocks, northwestern Canada. *Journal of Geology* 105(1):1-17.

Rainbird, R.H., Rayner, N.M., Hadlari, T., Heaman, L.M., A. Ielpi, A., Turner, E.C. and MacNaughton, R.B. 2017. Zircon Provenance Data Record the Lateral Extent of Pancontinental, Early Neoproterozoic Rivers and Erosional Unroofing History of the Grenville Orogen. *Geological Society of America Bulletin*. doi.org/10.1130/B31695.1.

Rainbird, R.H. and Young, G.M. 2009. Colossal rivers, massive mountains and Supercontinents. *Earth* 54(4): 52-61.

Raine, R.J. and Smith, M.P. 2012. Sequence stratigraphy of the Scottish Laurentian margin and recognition of the Sauk

Megasequence; in: Derby, J.R., Fritz, R.D., Longacre, S.A., Morgan, W.A., and Sternbach, C.A. (Eds.), The Great American Carbonate Bank: The geology and economic resources of the Cambrian – Ordovician Sauk Megasequence of Laurentia, *AAPG Memoir 98*, pp. 575–596.

Reddy, S.M., and Evans, D.A.D. 2009. Paleoproterozoic supercontinents and global evolution: correlations from core to atmosphere. In *Paleoproterozoic Supercontinents and Global Evolution,* eds. S.M. Reddy, R. Mazumder, D.A.D. Evans, and A.S. Collins, pp. 1-26. Geological Society, London, Special Publications. 323:1-26.

Rey, P.F., Coltice, N., Flament, N.E. and Thebaud, N. 2013, A geological model for the evolution of early continents. *American Geophysical Union*, Fall Meeting, abstract #T22A-05.

Rino, S., Kon, Y., Sato, W., Maruyama, S., Santosh, M. and Zhao, D. 2008. The Grenvillian and Pan-African Orogens: World's Largest Orogenies Through Geologic Time, and Their Implications On the Origin of Superplume. *Gondwana Research* 14 (1–2): 51–72.

Rivers, T. 2015. Tectonic Setting and Evolution of the Grenville Orogen: An Assessment of Progress Over the Last 40 Years. *Geoscience Canada* 42 (1): 77–124.

Roberts, N.W., and Spencer, C.J. 2015. The zircon archive of continent formation through time. In *Continent Formation Through Time*, eds. N. M.W. Roberts, M. van Kranendonk, S. Parman, S. Shirey, S. and P.D. Clift, pp.

197-225. Geological Society, London, Special Publications 389.

Roehl, P.O., and Choquette, P.W. eds. 1985. *Carbonate Petroleum Reservoirs*. Berlin, Germany: Springer-Verlag.

Ronov, A.B., Khain, V.E., Balukhovsky, A.N. and Seslavinsky, K.B. 1980. Quantitative analysis of Phanerozoic sedimentation, *Sedimentary Geology* 25:311–325.

Sahoo, S.K., Planavsky, N.J., Jiang, G., Kendall, B., Owens, J.D., Wang, X., Shi, X., Anbar, A.D., and Lyons, T.W. 2016. Oceanic oxygenation events in the anoxic Ediacaran ocean, *Geobiology* 14:457–468.

Salop, L.J. 1982. *Geological Evolution of the Earth During the Precambrian*. Springer-Verlag, 459 pp.

Santosh, M., Maruyama, S., Komiya, T. and Yamamoto, S. 2010. Orogens in the evolving Earth: From surface continents to 'lost continents' at the core–mantle boundary. In *The Evolving Continents: Understanding Processes of Continental Growth*, eds. T.M. Kusky, M-G Zhai, and W. Xiao, pp. 77-116. Geological Society, London, Special Publications, 338.

Sawaki, Y., Tahata, M., Ohno, T., Komiya, T., Hirata, T., Maruyama, S., Han, J., Shu, D. 2014. The anomalous Ca cycle in the Ediacaran ocean: Evidence from Ca isotopes preserved in carbonates in the Three Gorges area, South China. *Gondwana Research* 25:1070-1089.

Schermerhorn, L.J.G. 1974. Late Precambrian mixtites: Glacial and/or nonglacial? *American Journal of Science* 274(7):673–824.

Schmandt, B., Jacobsen, S.D, Becker, T.W., Liu, Z. and Dueker, K.G. 2014. Dehydration Melting at the Top of the Lower Mantle. *Science* 344 (6189): 1265–68.

Schmidt, R.G. 1980. The Marquette Range Supergroup in the Gobebic Iron District, Michigan and Wisconsin. *U.S. Geological Survey Bulletin* 1460.

Schopf, T.J.M. 1980. *Paleoceanography*. Cambridge, Massachusetts: Harvard University Press.

Schulz, H.N., and Schulz, H.D. 2005. Large Sulfur Bacteria and the Formation of Phosphorite. *Science* 307 (5708): 416–18.

Servais, T. and Harper, D.A.T. 2018. The Great Ordovician Biodiversification Event (GOBE): definition, concept and duration. *Lethaia* **51**:151–164.

Sharkov, E.V., and Bogatikov, O.A. 2010. Tectonomagmatic evolution of the earth and moon. *Geotectonics* 44, no. 2:85-101.

Shields, G.A. 2005. Neoproterozoic cap carbonates: A critical appraisal of existing models and the Plumeworld Hypothesis. *Terra Nova* 17, no.4:299–310.

Sigler, R., and Wingerden, V. 1998. Submarine flow and slide deposits in the Kingston Peak Formation, Kingston Range, Mojave Desert, California: Evidence for catastrophic initiation of Noah's Flood. In *Proceedings of the Fourth*

International Conference on Creationism, ed. R.E. Walsh, pp. 487–501. Pittsburgh, Pennsylvania: Creation Science Fellowship.

Sigurdsson, H., Houghton, B., McNutt, S.R., Rymer, H. and Stix, J. 2015. *The Encyclopedia of Volcanoes*. Philadelphia, Pennsylvania: Elsevier.

Slack, J.F., and Cannon, W.F. 2009. Extraterrestrial demise of banded iron formations 1.85 billion years ago. *Geology* 37, no. 11:1011-1014.

Sloss, L.L. 1964. Tectonic Cycles of the North American Craton. In *Symposium on Cyclic Sedimentation*. Edited by D. F. Merriam, 449–459. *Kansas Geological Survey, Bulletin* 169.

Snelling, A.A. 1984. The Recent, Rapid Formation of the Mount Isa Orebodies During Noah's Flood. *Ex Nihilo* 6 (3): 40–46.

Snelling, A.A. 2005. Isochron Discordances and the Role of Inheritance and Mixing of Radioisotopes in the Mantle and Crust; in: Vardiman, L., Snelling, A.A. and Chaffin, E.F. (Eds.), *Radioisotopes and the Age of the Earth: Results of a Young-Earth Creationist Research Initiative*, Institute for Creation Research, El Cajon, California and Creation Research Society, Chino Valley, Arizona, chapter 6, pp. 393–524.

Snelling, A.A. 2008. Catastrophic granite formation: Rapid melting of source rocks, and rapid magma intrusion and cooling. *Answers Research Journal* 1:11-25.

Snelling, A.A. 2009. *Earth's Catastrophic Past: Geology, Creation and the Flood*. Dallas, Texas: Institute for Creation Research.

Snelling, A.A. 2010. The geology of Israel within the Biblical Creation-Flood framework of history: 1—The pre-Flood rocks, *Answers Research J.* 3:165–190.

Snelling, A.A. 2015. Radioisotope dating of meteorites: V. Isochron ages of groups of meteorites. *Answers Research Journal* 8:449-478.

Snelling, A.A. and Purdom, G. 2013. Survey of microbial composition and mechanisms of living stromatolites in the Bahamas and Australia: developing criteria to determine the biogenicity of fossil stromatolites; in: Horstemeyer, M. (Ed.), *Proceedings of the Seventh International Conference on Creationism*, Creation Science Fellowship, Pittsburgh, PA.

Spencer, C.J., Cawood, P.A., Hawkesworth, C.J., Prave, A.R., Roberts, N.M.W., Horstwood, M.S.A. and M.J. Whitehouse, M.J. 2015. Generation and preservation of continental crust in the Grenville Orogeny. *Geoscience Frontiers* 6, no. 3:357-372.

Spencer, C.J., and Kirkland, C.L. 2016. Visualizing the Sedimentary Response Through the Orogenic Cycle: A Multidimensional Scaling Approach. *Lithosphere* 8 (1): 29–37.

Stanley, S.M. 1999. *Earth System History*, 134. New York: W. H. Freeman and Company.

Stern, R.J. 2002. Subduction zones. *Reviews of Geophysics* 40, no. 4: 1012–1049.

Stern, R.J. 2005, Evidence from ophiolites, blueschists, and ultrahigh-pressure metamorphic terranes that the modern episode of subduction tectonics began in Neoproterozoic time. *Geology* 33:557–560.

Stockwell, C.H. 1964. Fourth report on structural provinces, orogenies, and time-classification of rocks of the Canadian Precambrian Shield. *Geological Survey of Canada* Paper 64-17 (Part II).

Stockwell, C.H. 1982. Proposals for time classification and correlation of Precambrian rocks and events in Canada and adjacent areas of the Canadian Shield, part I: a time classification of Precambrian rocks and events, *Geological Survey of Canada, Paper* 80–19.

Stockwell, C.H., McGlynn, J.C., Emslie, R.F., Sanford, B.V., Norris, A.W., Donaldson, J.A., Fahrig, W.F. and Currie, K.L. 1970. IV Geology of the Canadian Shield. In *Geology and Economic Minerals of Canada*. Geological Survey of Canada. Economic Geology Report No. 1. Department of Energy, Mines and Resources Canada.

Strong, J. 2007. *Strong's Exhaustive Concordance of the Bible*. Peabody, Massachusetts: Hendrickson Publishers, Inc. Tarling, D. H. ed. 1981. *Economic Geology and Geotectonics*. Oxford, United Kingdom: Blackwell Scientific Publications.

Taner, M.F., and M. Chemam. 2015. Algoma-type banded iron formation (BIF), Abitibi Greenstone Belt, Quebec, Canada. *Ore Geology Reviews* 70:31-46.

Tarling, D.H. (Ed.). 1981. *Economic Geology and Geotectonics*, Blackwell Scientific Publications, 213 pp.

Taylor, S.R., and McLennan, S.M. 1995. The geochemical evolution of the continental crust. *Reviews in Geophysics* 33:241-265.

Ten Bruggencate, J. 2001. *Hawaii Land of Volcanoes.* Mutual Publishing: Honolulu, Hawaii.

The Mesoproterozoic, 1 October 2004, <www.palaeos.com/Proterozoic/Mesoproterozoic.html>, 20 October 2006.

Timmons, J.M., Karlstrom, M.K. and Dehler, C. 1999. Grand Canyon Supergroup six unconformities make one Great Unconformity a record of supercontinent assembly and disassembly. *Boatman's Quarterly Review.* 12, 1:29–32.

Timmons, J.M., Karlstrom, K.E., Dehler, C.M., Geissman, J.W. and Heizler, M.T. 2001. Proterozoic Multistage (ca. 1.1 and 0.8 Ga) Extension Recorded in the Grand Canyon Supergroup and Establishment of Northwest- and North-Trending Tectonic Grains in the Southwestern United States. *Geological Society of America Bulletin* 113 (2): 163–181.

Tree of Life Web Project. 2008. "Terrestrial Vertebrates." www.tolweb.org/Terrestrial Vertebrates/14952.pdf.

Trendall, A.F. 1990. Hamersley Basin; in: Geology and Mineral Resources of Western Australia, *Western Australia Geological Survey*, Memoir 3:163–189.

Tucker, M.E. 1992. The Precambrian-Cambrian boundary: seawater chemistry, ocean circulation and nutrient supply in metazoan evolution, extinction and biomineralization, *J. Geological Society* 149:655–668.

USGS 1997. Comparisons with other eruptions, pubs.usgs.gov/gip/msh/comparisons.html, 25 June 1997.

Vail, P.R., Mitchum, R.M., Todd, R.G., Widmier, J.M., Thompson, S., Songree, J.B., Bubb, J.N., and Hatfield, W.G. 1977. Seismic stratigraphy and global changes of sea level, *American Association of Petroleum Geologists Memoir* 26:49–212.

Van Gemeren, W.A. ed. 1997. *New International Dictionary of Old Testament Theology and Exegesis*. Grand Rapids, Michigan: Zondervan.

Van Kranendonk, M.J., and Kirkland, C.L. 2013. Orogenic climax of earth: The 1.2-1.1 Ga Grenvillian superevent. *Geology* 41(7):735-738.

Vardiman, L., S.A. Austin, S.A., Baumgardner, J.R., Chaffin, E.F., DeYoung, D.B., Humphreys, D.R. and Snelling, A.A. 2003. Radioisotopes and the Age of the Earth. In *Proceedings of the Fifth International Conference on Creationism*, ed. R.L. Ivey, Jr., pp. 337–348. Pittsburgh, Pennsylvania: Creation Science Fellowship

Veizer, J.D. Ala, D., Azmy, K., Bruckkshen, P., Buhl, D., Bruhn, F., Carden, G.A.F., Diener, A., Ebneth, S., Godderis,

Y., Jasper, T., Korte, C., Pawellek, F., Podlaha, O.G., and Strauss, H. 1999. $^{87}Sr/^{86}Sr$, δ13C and δ18O evolution of Phanerozoic seawater, *Chemical Geology* 161:59–88.

Veizer, J., and Compston, W. 1974. $^{87}Sr/^{86}Sr$ composition of seawater during the Phanerozoic, *Geochimica et Cosmochimica Acta* 38(9):1461–1484.

Veizer, J. and Mackenzie, F.T. 2014. Evolution of sedimentary rocks; in: Holland, H.D. and Turekian, K.K., *Environmental Geochemistry: Treatise on geochemistry*, vol. 9, 2nd edn, Elsevier, Oxford, pp. 399–435.

Voice, P.J., Kowalewski, M. and Eriksson, K.A. 2011. Quantifying the timing and rate of crustal evolution: Global compilation of radiometrically dated detrital zircon grains. *Journal of Geology* 119:109-126.

Von Strandmann, P.A.E.P., Stüeken, E.E., Elliott, T., Poulton, S.W., Dehler, C.M., Canfield, D.E., and Catling, D.C. 2015. Selenium isotope evidence for progressive oxidation of the Neoproterozoic biosphere, *Nature Communications* 6(10157.

Walker, L.J., Wilkinson, B.H. and Ivany, L.C. 2002. Continental drift and Phanerozoic carbonate accumulation in shallow-shelf and deep-marine settings, J. *Geology* 110:75–87.

Walker, T. 2015. The sedimentary Heavitree Quartzite, Central Australia, was deposited early in Noah's Flood, J. *Creation* 29(1):103–107.

Walker, T. 2017. Massive erosion on California's Oroville Dam, *creation.com/* oroville-dam-spillway-crisis-california, 23 March 2017.

Wallace, M.W., Hood, A., Shuster, A., Greig, A., Planavsky, N.J., and Reed, C.P. 2017. Oxygenation history of the Neoproterozoic to early Phanerozoic and the rise of land plants, *Earth and Planetary Science Letters* 466:12–19.

Walter, M.R., Veevers, J.J., Calver, C.R., Gorjan, P., and Hill, A.C. 2000. Dating the 840–544 Ma Neoproterozoic interval by isotopes of strontium, carbon, and sulfur in seawater, and some interpretative models, *Precambrian Research* 100:371–433.

Weigelt, J. 2009. *Recent Vertebrate Carcasses and Their Paleobiological Implications*. University of Chicago Press, Chicago, IL.

Whitmeyer, S.J., and Karlstrom, K.E. 2007. Tectonic model for the Proterozoic growth of North America. *Geosphere* 3(4):220-259.

Wilde, S.A.W. 1999. Evolution of the western margin of Australia during the Rodinian and Gondwanan supercontinent cycles, *Gondwana Research* 2(3): 481–499.

Williams, J.J., Mills, J.W., and Lenton, T.M. 2019. A tectonically driven Ediacaran oxygenation event, *Nature Communications* 10(2690):1–10.

Wingerden, V. 2003. Initial Flood deposits of the western Northern American Cordillera: California, Utah and Idaho; in: Ivey Jr, R.L. (Ed.), *Proceedings of the Fifth International*

Conference of Creationism, Creation Science Fellowship, Pittsburgh, PA, pp. 349–358.

Wise, K.P. 2003. The hydrothermal biome: A pre-Flood environment. In *Proceedings of the Fifth International Conference of Creationism*, ed. R.L. Ivey, Jr., 349–358. Pittsburgh, Pennsylvania: Creation Science Fellowship.

Wojtowicz, J.A. 2001. Factors affecting precipitation of calcium carbonate, J. *Swimming Pool and Spa Industry* 3(1):18–23.

Xu, L., Lehmann, B., Jingwen, M., Wenjun,Q. and Andao, D. 2011. Re-Os Age of Polymetallic Ni-Mo-PGE-Au Mineralization in Early Cambrian Black Shales of South China—A Reassessment. *Economic Geology* 106 (3): 511–22.

Yeo, G.M. 1981. The Late Proterozoic Rapitan glaciation in the northern Cordillera. In *Proterozoic Basins of Canada*, ed, F.H.A. Campbell, pp. 25-46. Geological Survey of Canada, Paper 81-10:25-46.

Yochelson, E.L. 2006. The Lipalian interval: a forgotten, novel concept in the geologic column, *Earth Science History*, 25:251–269.

Yonkee, W.A., Dehler, C.D., Link, P.K., Balgord, E.A., Keeley, J.A., Hayes, D.S., Wells, M.L., Fanning, C.M., and Johnston, S.M. 2014. Tectono-stratigraphic framework of Neoproterozoic to Cambrian strata, west-central US: protracted rifting, glaciation, and evolution of the North American Cordilleran margin, *Earth-Science Reviews* 136:59–95.

Young, G.M. 1978. Proterozoic (<1.7 b.y.) Stratigraphy, Paleocurrents and Orogeny in North America. *Egyptian Journal of Geology* 22: 45–64.

Young, G.M. 1995. Are Neoproterozoic Glacial Deposits Preserved on the Margins of Laurentia Related to the Fragmentation of Two Supercontinents? *Geology* 23 (2): 153–156.

Young, G.M. 2013. Precambrian supercontinents, glaciations, atmospheric oxygenation, metazoan evolution, and an impact that may have changed the second half of Earth history. *Geoscience Frontiers* 4:247-261.

Zhang, L. 2017. A review of recent developments in the study of regional lithospheric electrical structure of the Asian continent, *Surveys in Geophysics*, published online 15 September 2017.

Zhao, G., P.A. Cawood, P.A, Wilde, S.A. and Sun, M. 2002. Review of global 2.1-1.8 Ga orogens: Implications for a pre-Rodinia supercontinent. *Earth Science Reviews* 59:125-162.

Zhou, T., Pan, X., Sun, R., Deng,C., Shen, J., Kwon, S., Grasby, S., Xiao, J., Yin, R. 2021. Cryogenian interglacial greenhouse driven by enhanced volcanism: Evidence from mercury records. *Earth and Planetary Science Letters* 564:116902.

Zientek, M.L., and Orris, G.J. 2005. *Geology and Nonfuel Mineral Deposits of the United States.* U.S. Geological Survey Open-File Report 2005-1294A.

APPENDIX A:

A proposed stratigraphic chart

and Bible correlator

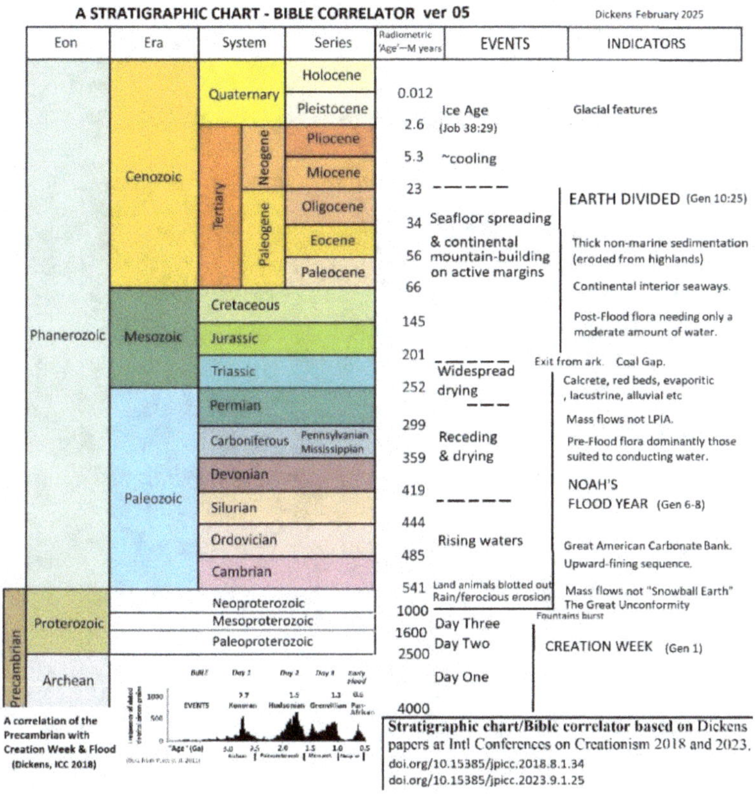

APPENDIX B:

GEOLOGY: PAST, PRESENT AND FUTURE FIERY DESTRUCTION

(2 Peter 3)

PRESENT DAY UNIFORMITARIANISM

... knowing this, first of all, that scoffers will come in the last

... and that by means of these the world that then existed was

==

REPENTANCE

Repentance is a change of heart and mind that brings us closer to God. It includes turning away from sin [wrong thought, deed or word] and turning to God for forgiveness.

It is motivated by love for God and a sincere desire to obey His commandments.

... for all have sinned and fall short of the glory of God,

CONFESS AND BE SAVED

... because, if you confess with your mouth that Jesus is Lord

YOU CAN SEEK A LOCAL CHURCH

Should you want to follow Jesus Christ, you are encouraged to prayerfully seek a local church that will help you grow as a new Christian by the clear teaching of the Bible.

YOU CAN ACCESS THE BIBLE

Read or listen to the Bible in many languages using apps, for example via

http://gideons.bible.is/

APPENDIX C:

Some other publications of interest by Dickens

The drying and related stages of Noah's Flood (Article)

Dickens, H. 2022. A Proposed Model For The Drying And Related Stages of Noah's Flood. *Origin Research Journal.* 2(1):38-64.
https://www.researchgate.net/publication/361332018_Proposed_model_stages_of_Noah's_Flood_including_its_end_and_its_aftermath

Receding Noah's Flood as trigger for seafloor spreading (Book)

Dickens, H. 2024. *Receding Noah's Flood as trigger for seafloor spreading. Receding Then Spreading (RTS) Flood Model.* Lambert Academic Publishing. ISBN: 978-620-6-15135-7.
https://www.researchgate.net/publication/378977985_RECEDING_NOAH'S_FLOOD_AS_TRIGGER_FOR_SEAFLOOR_SPREADING#fullTextFileContent

This item's Research Interest Score on ResearchGate is higher than 98% of research items published in 2024.

Hardcopy book available via Amazon.

Petroleum systems do not require millions of years (Article)

Dickens, H. 2023b. Petroleum systems do not require millions of years. *Journal of Creation* 37(3):12-15. https://www.researchgate.net/publication/375579297_Petroleum_systems_do_not_require_millions_of_years